September 2012

Dear Friends,

You're holding another of my "oldie but goodie" volumes, two stories originally published in the 1980s. Both *A Friend or Two* and *No Competition* are set in San Francisco, which is one of my all-time favorite places. It's a city with charm and character, and my wish is that you'll enjoy this vicarious visit.

It just so happens that 2012 is also the 50th anniversary of Tony Bennett's hit song "I Left My Heart in San Francisco." You'll recognize the reference in the title of this volume....

Wayne and I had the pleasure of seeing Tony in concert last summer, and at eighty years of age he's still impressive— maybe even more so. We learned quite a bit about him at the concert. Early in his singing career, he lost a national talent contest to another singer. The woman who walked away with the top prize was Rosemary Clooney. With typical humor, he called the show the first *American Idol.* He was born Antonio Dominick Benedetto, but Bob Hope apparently told him they didn't make marquees long enough to print his name. He was the one who suggested the stage name Tony Bennett.

If you've ever visited the City by the Bay, you know how enchanting it can be, and to me it's the perfect setting for romance. So it seems fitting to dedicate this volume to the memory of Darlene Layman, fellow writer of romance fiction. Darlene, who died in 2011, was a wonderful friend and encourager and is deeply missed, so this dedication is in remembrance of all the laughter we shared (and all the two-hour birthday lunches).

I always enjoy hearing from my readers. You can reach me in a variety of ways. Through my website at DebbieMacomber.com, on Facebook or through regular mail at P.O. Box 1458, Port Orchard, WA 98366.

Warmest regards,

Debbie Macomber

D0951754

DEBBIE MACOMBER

I Left My HEART

HARLEQUIN®
entertain, enrich, inspire™

ISBN-13: 978-0-7783-1357-1

I LEFT MY HEART

Recycling programs
for this product may
not exist in your area.

In memory of Darlene Layman
Encourager and dear friend

Also by Debbie Macomber

CONTENTS

A FRIEND OR TWO

Prologue

"Miss Elizabeth?" The elderly butler's eyes widened, but he composed himself quickly. "This is a surprise. Welcome home."

"Thank you, Bently. It's good to *be* home." Elizabeth Wainwright felt comforted by his formality and British accent. She looked around the huge entry hall, with its elegant crystal chandelier and imported oriental rugs and sighed inwardly. Home. Would it offer her what she hadn't been able to find in Europe? Immediately doubts filled her.

"Would you see to my luggage?" she asked in a low, distracted tone. "And ask Helene to draw my bath?"

"Right away."

She looked around with a renewed sense of appreciation for everything this house represented. Wealth. Tradition. Family pride. With all this at her fingertips, how could she possibly be dissatisfied?

"Bently, do you know where Father is?"

"In the library, miss," he responded crisply.

Her smile faded as she started across the huge hall. She loved Bently. Nothing could ruffle him. She could recall the time… Loud voices drifted past the partially opened door, and she paused. Her father rarely raised his voice.

"I'm afraid I've failed her, Mother. Elizabeth is restless and unhappy."

Stunned, Elizabeth stood just outside the library door, listening.

"Give the girl time, Charles. She's suffered a great loss." Her grandmother's raspy voice sounded troubled, despite her words.

"She has no drive, no ambition, no purpose. Dear heavens, have you seen these bills from Paris?"

The sound of his fist against the desk shocked her.

"Elizabeth goes through money as if there's no tomorrow. I've pampered and indulged her since Mary died, and now I'm left to deal with it."

"But she's such a dear child."

"Dear, but hopelessly unhappy, I fear. The thing is—" her father's voice lowered and took on a slightly husky quality "—I don't know how to help her."

A twinge of guilt caused Elizabeth to lower her head fractionally. She'd thought she had concealed her unhappiness. And she couldn't argue with her father's earlier statement. Her spending *had* been extravagant the last few months.

"What can we do?" Again, it was her grandmother.

"I don't know, Mother."

Elizabeth had never heard such resignation from her

father. "I'll talk to her, but I don't know what good it will do. Perhaps if Mary had lived…" he continued soberly.

Elizabeth refused to listen to any more. Her father rarely spoke of her mother. Mary Elizabeth Wainwright's unexpected death two years before still had the power to inflict a deep sense of loss on them both. Elizabeth's brother had adjusted well, but he was older and constitutionally more able to cope with his grief.

Thoughtfully, she climbed the long, winding staircase to her rooms. A confrontation with her father was the last thing she wanted. How could she explain this lackadaisical attitude that had taken over her usually cheerful existence? And as for the benefits of wealth, she was well aware of the privileges and even the power that came with having money. But money wasn't everything; it didn't bring happiness or fulfillment. The best time she'd had in her life had been the summer she bummed her way across France, when she'd barely had two euros to rub together. Not only was she intelligent, she was gifted. She spoke fluent French, and enough Italian and German to make her last visits to Rome and Berlin worry-free. But what good was any of that to her now?

Sitting on her plush canopy bed, she forced her spine to straighten. She was a Wainwright. She was supposed to maintain her pride and independence at all times.

A gnawing ache churned her stomach. She didn't want to talk to her father. She didn't want to explain the fiasco in Paris and her extravagant expenses. All she wanted was peace and quiet. The germ of an idea began to form in her mind. Her bags were still packed. She could swear Bently to silence and slip out just as quietly as she'd slipped in. San Francisco sounded appealing. Her mother had spent a carefree summer there when she was about Elizabeth's age. With a renewed sense of purpose, she headed out of her bedroom door and down the back stairs.

One

The ever-present odor of fresh fish and the tangy scent of saltwater followed Elizabeth as she sauntered down Fisherman's Wharf. The wharf wasn't far from where she was staying at the St. Francis, one of San Francisco's most prestigious hotels. A little breeze ruffled her golden-brown hair and added a shade of color to her otherwise pale features.

With the morning paper tucked under her arm, she strolled into a small French café. It had only taken three days for the restless boredom to make its way into her thoughts. How could she sit in one of the most beautiful cities in the world with the homey scent of freshly baked bread drifting from the restaurant kitchen and feel this listless?

A friendly waitress dressed in a crisp pink uniform with a starched white apron took her order for coffee and a croissant. She wasn't hungry, but she had noticed this morning that her clothes were beginning to hang on her and decided to make the effort to eat more.

Lackadaisically her eyes ran over the front page of the newspaper. Nothing had changed. The depressing stories of war and hate were the same on this day as they had been the week before and the month before that. Sighing, she folded the newspaper and waited for the waitress to bring her food.

"Are you looking for a job?" the young waitress asked eagerly as she delivered Elizabeth's order.

"I beg your pardon?"

"I saw you looking through the paper and thought you might be job-hunting. I wouldn't normally suggest something like this, but there's an opening here, if you'd like to apply. You could start right now."

Elizabeth's pale blue eyes widened incredulously. What was this girl talking about?

"I know it's not much, but a position here could tide you over until you find what you're really looking for. The other girl who normally works with me called in this morning and quit." She paused to forcefully release her breath. "Can you imagine? Without a minute's notice. Now I'm left to deal with the lunch crowd all by myself."

Elizabeth straightened in her chair. Why not? She didn't have anything better to do. "I don't know that I'd be much help. I've never been a waitress."

"It doesn't matter." The younger girl's relief was obvious. "I can guarantee that by the end of the day you'll discover everything you ever cared to know about waitressing and a few things you didn't." Her laugh was light and cheerful. "By the way, I'm Gilly. Short for Gillian."

"And I'm Elizabeth."

"Glad to meet you, Elizabeth. Boy, am I glad." The breezy laugh returned. "Come on back to the kitchen, and I'll introduce you to Evelyn. He's the owner and chef, and I'm *sure* he'll hire you." With determined, quick-paced steps, Gilly led the way across the room to the swinging double doors. She paused and turned around. "Don't be shocked if Evelyn kisses you or something. He's like that. I think it's because he's French."

"I won't be surprised," Elizabeth murmured and had trouble containing her smile. What would Gilly say if she knew that Elizabeth spoke the language fluently and had lived in Paris?

A variety of pleasant smells assaulted her as she entered the spotless kitchen. As a little girl, her favorite place in the huge, rambling house had been the kitchen. The old cook would often sneak her pieces of pie dough or a cookie. Her childhood had been happy and untroubled.

"Evelyn," Gilly said, attracting the attention of the chef who was garbed completely in white and working busily at the stove. "This is Elizabeth. She's going to take Deanne's place."

The ruddy-faced man with a thick mustache that was shaped like an open umbrella over a full mouth turned and stared blankly at Elizabeth.

Giving in to impulse, she took a step forward and extended her hand. In flawless French, she explained that she hadn't done any waitressing but would be pleased to help them out this afternoon.

Laughing, Evelyn broke into a wild speech in his native language while pumping her hand as if she were a long-lost relative.

Again in perfect French, she explained that no, she wasn't from France or Quebec, but she had spent several years studying in his country.

An expression of astonishment widened Gilly's eyes. "You should have said you were from France."

"I'm not. I studied French in school." Elizabeth didn't explain that the school had been in Paris.

"You know, that's one thing I'm sorry for," Gilly said, thoughtfully pinching her bottom lip. "I wish I'd studied French. A lot of good Spanish does me here. But then—" she paused and chuckled "—I could always end up working in a Mexican restaurant."

Elizabeth laughed. Gilly was delightful. Amiable and full of enthusiasm, the younger girl was just the antidote for the long day that lay ahead.

Luckily, the two were close enough in size that Elizabeth could wear one of Gilly's extra uniforms.

After a minimum of instruction, Elizabeth was given a pad and pencil, and asked to wait on her first customers, an elderly couple who asked for coffee and croissants. Without incident, Elizabeth delivered their order.

"This isn't so bad," she murmured under her breath to Gilly, who was busy writing out the luncheon specials on the chalkboard that would be displayed on the sidewalk.

"I took one look at you and knew you'd do great," Gilly stated cheerfully.

"You took one look at me and saw an easy mark." A smile revealed deep grooved dimples in each of Elizabeth's cheeks.

"Does everyone call you Elizabeth?" Briefly, Gilly returned her attention to the chalkboard. "You look more like a Beth to me."

Beth, Elizabeth mused thoughtfully. No one had called her that since her school days, and then only her best friends. After all, she was a Wainwright. "Elizabeth" was the dignified name her family preferred.

"Call me anything you like," she said in a teasing tone. "No, on second thought, you better stick with Beth."

A half-hour later Elizabeth was answering to a variety of names, among them "Miss" and "Waitress." Never had she imagined that such a simple job could be so demanding, or that there were so many things to remember. The easy acceptance given her by the customers was a pleasant surprise. Most of the café's luncheon crowd were regulars from office buildings close to the wharf. Several of them took the time to chat before ordering. A couple of men blatantly flirted with her, which did wonders for her sagging ego. A few asked about Deanne and weren't surprised when they learned that she'd quit.

The highlight of the afternoon came when she waited on a retired couple visiting from France. She spoke to them in their native language for so long that Gilly had to point out that there were several other customers who needed attention. Later Gilly was shocked to see that the couple had left a tip as large as the price of their meal.

"Tutor me in French, would you?" she joked, as she passed by carrying a glass coffeepot.

Elizabeth couldn't believe the time when she glanced at her gold wristwatch. Four o'clock. The day had sped past, and she felt exhilarated, better than she had in months. Tonight she wouldn't need a pill to help her sleep.

"You were terrific. Everyone was saying how great you were," Gilly said, laying on the praise. "A couple of regulars said they hope you'll stay. And even if it was your first time waitressing, you were as good as Deanne ever was."

After all the orders she had mixed up, Elizabeth was surprised Gilly thought so. Of course, she had eaten in some of the world's best restaurants and knew what kind of service to expect. But giving it was something else entirely.

"Would you consider staying on for a while?" Gilly's tone held a mixture of hope and doubt. "I'm sure this isn't the kind of job you want. But the pay isn't bad, and the tips are good."

Elizabeth hesitated. "I…I don't know."

"It would only be until we could find someone to replace you," Gilly added quickly. "That shouldn't be long. A week or two. Three months at the most."

"Three months?" Elizabeth gasped.

"Well, to be honest, Evelyn saw you with the French couple and told me that he'd really like to hire you permanently. I suppose it's too much to ask, with your qualifications."

What qualifications? Elizabeth mused. Oh, sure, she knew all the finer points of etiquette, but aside from her fluency in several languages, she'd never had any formal job training.

"Just think about it, okay?" Gilly urged.

Elizabeth agreed with a soft smile.

"You'll be back tomorrow?" The doelike eyes implored, making it impossible to refuse.

Exhaling slowly, Elizabeth nodded. "Sure. Why not?"

Why not indeed? she mused later as she unlocked the door to her suite at the St. Francis. Her feet hurt, and there was an ache in the small of her back, but otherwise she felt terrific.

The hot water filling the tub was steaming up the bathroom when she straightened, struck by a thought. There was no one she wanted to visit this summer, no place she wanted to go. There wasn't anything to stop her from working with Gilly. It would be fun. Well, maybe not fun, but…different, and she was definitely in the mood for different.

With the sound of the hot water still running behind her, she knotted the sash of her blue silk robe and eased her feet into matching slippers. Sitting atop the mattress, she reached for the phone. For the first time in months, she felt like talking to her father. He had a right to know where she was staying and what she was up to. Over the last year she'd given him enough to worry about.

Bently answered the phone. "Good evening, Miss Elizabeth," he said after she identified herself.

"Hello, Bently. Is my father home?"

"I'll get him for you."

Had she detected a note of worry in Bently's tone? He was always so formal that it was difficult to discern any emotion.

"Elizabeth, dear." Her father spoke crisply. "Just exactly where are you?" He didn't wait for her to answer. "Bently said that you were home, and then, before anyone knew what had happened, you were off again."

"I'm sorry, Dad," she said, though in fact she wasn't the least bit regretful. "I'm in San Francisco. I've got a job."

"A job," her father repeated in a low, shocked tone. "Doing what?"

She laughed, mentally picturing the perplexed look working its way across her father's face. With a liberal arts degree as vague and unimpressive as her grades, she knew he doubted that anyone would want to hire her. "I'm a waitress in a small French café called The Patisserie."

"A waitress!" Charles Wainwright exploded.

"Now don't go all indignant on me. I know this is a shock. But I'm enjoying it. Some of the customers speak French, and the chef is from Paris."

"Yes, but…" Elizabeth could feel her father's shock.

"But if you wanted to work," he went on, "there are a hundred positions more suited to you."

"Honestly, Dad, I'd think you'd be happy that I'm out of your hair for the summer. Wish me well and kiss Grandmother for me."

"Elizabeth…"

"My bath's running. I've got to go."

A resigned note she recognized all too well entered his voice. "Take care of yourself, my dear."

"This is working out great," Gilly commented at the end of Elizabeth's first week. "I don't know what it is, but there's something about you that the customers like."

"It's because I can pronounce the name of Evelyn's pastries," Elizabeth returned in a teasing voice.

"That's not it," Gilly contradicted with a slight quirk of her head. Her short, bouncy curls bobbed with the action. "Though having you speak French does add a certain class to the place."

"My French may be good, but my feet are killing me." She faked a small, pain-filled sigh and rubbed the bottom of one expensive loafer over the top of the other.

"Your feet wouldn't hurt if you were wearing the right shoes."

Elizabeth glanced at her Guccis and groaned. Heavens, she'd spent more on these leather loafers than she made in a week at this restaurant. How could they possibly be the wrong kind of shoe?

"If you like, we can go shopping after work and I'll show you what you should be wearing."

Gilly's offer was a pleasant surprise. "Yes, I'd like that."

"It'll give me an excuse not to go home." Discontent coated Gilly's normally happy voice.

"What's the matter with home?"

One petite shoulder rose in a halfhearted shrug. "Nothing, I guess. It's just that I turned twenty last month, and I hate living with my parents."

"So get an apartment." Elizabeth suggested the obvious, wondering why Gilly hadn't thought of that herself.

Gilly's returning smile was stiff. "So speaks the voice of inexperience. I don't suppose you've gone looking for apartments lately. Have you seen how high rent is these days?"

Elizabeth had continued to live at the St. Francis. The hotel was convenient, and what meals she didn't eat at the Patisserie were promptly delivered to her room after a simple phone call.

"It isn't that I haven't tried," Gilly continued. "I found a boarding house and stayed there until my mother found out about my neighbors."

"Your neighbors?"

"I admit they were a bit unusual," Gilly mumbled. "I never saw the girl in the room next to me, but every morning there were two empty yogurt cartons outside her door."

Elizabeth couldn't restrain her soft laugh. "Suspicious yogurt, huh?"

"That was nothing," Gilly continued, her own laugh blending with Elizabeth's. "The woman on the other side looked like a Russian weight lifter who had failed a hormone test. One look at her—or him, whichever the case may be—and my mother had me out of there so fast my head was spinning."

Elizabeth could sympathize with her friend. "I know what you mean. I moved away from home as soon as I could, too."

"And if I left, my younger sister could have her own room and..." Gilly paused, her hand gripping Elizabeth's forearm. "He's back."

"Who?" Elizabeth glanced up to see a tall, broad-shouldered man enter the café. The first thing that impressed her was his size. He was easily six foot four. Yet he carried himself with an unconscious grace that reminded her of a martial arts expert. He wasn't handsome. His jaw was too angular, too abrupt. His mouth was firm, and even from this distance she noticed that it was slightly compressed, as if something had displeased him.

"Him," Gilly whispered under her breath. "How long has it been since you've seen such an indisputable stud?"

"Obviously too long," Elizabeth responded, picking up a menu and water glass. "But then, isn't one stud just like another?" she asked blandly. Although not strikingly handsome, this man was compelling enough to attract women's attention.

"One stud is just like another?" Gilly repeated on a low, disbelieving breath. "Beth, this guy is Secretariat."

Elizabeth had difficulty hiding her smile as she moved across to the room to deliver the ice water and menu.

Secretariat turned and watched her approach. Dark sunglasses reflected her silvery image and disguised his eyes. The glasses rested on a nose that could kindly be described as aquiline. He removed the glasses and set them on the table.

Not until she was at his table did she realize how big he actually was. Massive shoulders suited his height. His muscular biceps strained against a short-sleeved shirt stretched taut across a broad chest. She imagined that someone of his build would have difficulty finding clothes that were anything except tight. It was unfortunate that apparently he couldn't afford to have his clothes custom-made.

"Good afternoon," she said as she handed him the menu and set the glass on the red-checked tablecloth. Her heart lodged near her throat as his fingers innocently brushed hers. There was something indefinable about him that was almost intimidating. Not that he frightened her; "intrigued" was more the word.

"Hello." His smile revealed even white teeth. He opened the menu and quickly scanned it. Without looking at her he said, "Don't worry, I don't bite."

"I didn't think you did," she returned, resenting his absolutely incorrect belief that she was easily intimidated.

"I'll have coffee. Nothing more." A scowl made its way across his face.

She wrote down his order, thinking that he didn't look like the type to indulge in delicate French pastries.

As she returned to the counter, she could feel his gaze leveled between her shoulder blades. She was accustomed to the admiring glances of men. She had what her grandmother referred to as the Wainwright coloring, a warm blend of colors that often generated curious stares. Her eyes were the palest blue and her hair a lush shade of golden brown, worn loose so that it curled in natural waves at her shoulders.

"Did you notice the muscles on him?" she muttered under her breath to Gilly as she laid a spoon to the saucer. "I bet this guy wrestles crocodiles for a living."

Gilly pretended to be wiping down the long counter, her hand rubbing furiously as she stifled a giggle. "I think he's kinda cute."

"Yes, but you're so sweet you'd think boa constrictors were cuddly."

"He's different. I bet he's a real pussycat. Give me five minutes alone with him and I'll prove it."

"No way. He looks dangerous, like he would eat you for breakfast."

"You're teasing, aren't you?"

Elizabeth didn't answer as she delivered the coffee. Before she walked away, she noticed that he drank it quietly, cupping the mug with his massive hands as he stared out the window. A few minutes later, he stood and left a handful of change on the table, then turned to wink at Gilly.

"Goodbye." Gilly waved to him. "Come in again."

"I'd say you've got yourself an admirer," Elizabeth said, glancing from her friend to the retreating male figure.

"Not me," Gilly denied instantly. "He was watching you like a hawk. You're the one who interests him, not me."

"Then I give Tarzan to you," Elizabeth spoke somberly. "Men like him are a bit much for me." She had heard about egotistical males with bodies like his. They spent hours every day building up their muscles so they could stand in front of a mirror and admire themselves.

Just before closing time, Gilly stuck her head around the door into the kitchen, where Elizabeth was finishing refilling the condiments.

"I bet he works on the docks."

"Who?"

"Don't be obtuse."

"Oh, Tarzan. I suppose," Elizabeth murmured, not overly interested. "I don't think he'll be back."

"He will," Gilly asserted confidently. "And sooner rather than later. There was a look in his eyes. He's attracted to you, Beth. Even I noticed." The implication was that Elizabeth should have recognized it, too.

Gilly was right. The next afternoon he arrived at the same time. Elizabeth was carrying a tray of dirty dishes to the counter when she brushed against his solid male figure.

"Excuse me." The low, almost gravelly tone left no doubt as to who was speaking.

"My fault," she muttered under her breath, disliking the uncomfortable warmth that emanated from the spot where their bodies had touched. Easily six inches taller than she was, Tarzan loomed above her. Most women would have been awed by his closeness. But the sensations she was feeling were more troubling for the way they intrigued her than frightening. He wasn't wearing his reflective glasses today. The color of his eyes, along with his guarded look, was a surprise. Their amber shade resembled burnished gold marked by darker flecks, and he was staring at her as intently as any jungle beast. Again she had the impression that this man could be dangerous. Gilly might view him as a gentle giant, but she herself wasn't nearly as confident.

"What did I tell you?" Gilly whispered in a know-it-all voice.

"I guess you know your ape-men," Elizabeth returned flippantly.

For a second Gilly looked stunned at Elizabeth's cynicism. "How can you look at someone as gorgeous as this guy and call him an ape?" Righteously, she tucked the menu under her arm. "I'm taking his order today," she announced, and she strolled across the floor.

Watching her friend's movements, Elizabeth had to stifle a small laugh. Gilly's walk couldn't be more obvious; she was interested in him, and before the afternoon was over, Tarzan would know it.

"His name's Andrew Breed," Gilly cheerfully informed her as she scooted past Elizabeth on her return. "But he says most everyone calls him Breed." She moved behind the counter before Elizabeth could respond.

Elizabeth was too busy with her own customers to notice much about either Gilly or Andrew Breed. Only once was she aware that he was studying her, his strong mouth quirked crookedly. His attention made her self-conscious. Once she thought he was going to ask her something, but if he was, the question went unasked. As he'd done the day before, he left the money for his coffee on the table and sauntered out of the café, this time before she was even aware he'd gone.

The remainder of the afternoon dragged miserably. The weather was uncharacteristically hot and humid, and she could feel tiny beads of perspiration on her upper lip. A long soak in the bath, a light meal and the TV were sounding more appealing by the minute. She had spent most of her evenings looking for an apartment. The more she learned about Gilly's plight living at home, the more she wanted to help her friend. She had promised that if she found a place, they could move in together and share the rent, though Gilly need never know the actual figure.

Unfortunately, Elizabeth was quickly learning that Gilly hadn't underestimated the difficulty of finding a reasonably priced apartment in the city. She couldn't very well rent one for 2,000 a month and tell Gilly her share was 500. Her friend, although flighty, was smart enough to figure that out.

Gilly and Elizabeth worked together to close down the café that evening. Elizabeth's thoughts were preoccupied as Gilly chattered away excitedly about one thing or another. The girl's boundless enthusiasm affected everyone she met. She was amazing.

In the small break room behind the kitchen, Elizabeth sat, kicked off her shoes and rubbed her aching feet. Gilly hobbled around, one shoe on and the other off as she opened her purse and dug around for something in the bottom of the large bag. "What's the big hurry?" Elizabeth inquired.

"What's the hurry?" Gilly stammered. "Breed'll be out front any minute. We're going to dinner."

"Breed?" Her heart did a tiny flip-flop. "You mean to say you're going out to dinner with someone you hardly know?"

"What do you think I was telling you?"

Elizabeth straightened and slipped her feet back into the new practical pumps she'd purchased with Gilly's approval. "I guess I wasn't paying any attention."

"I guess not!" Gilly shook her head and did a quick glance in the small mirror. "Oh dear, I'll never make it on time." Her delicate oval face creased with concern. "Beth, do me a favor. Go out front and tell him I'm running a little late. I'll be there in a few minutes."

"Sure." Her response was clipped and short. She didn't want to date Breed herself, but she wasn't sure how she felt about Gilly seeing him. The thought was so ridiculous that she pinched her mouth closed, irritated with herself.

"You don't mind, do you?" Gilly jerked her head around to study Elizabeth.

"Of course not. It's the least I can do to smooth the course of true love."

"Not about that," Gilly said.

Elizabeth tipped her head to one side in confusion.

"I mean about me going out with Breed."

"Me mind?" Elizabeth asked, giving an indifferent shrug. "Why should I care one way or the other?"

Gilly arched both nicely arched brows. "Because it's really you he's interested in."

"You keep saying that," Elizabeth said, shaking her head in denial. "Either you've got some sixth sense or I'm completely dense."

Without hesitation, Gilly threw back her head, her tight curls bouncing. "You're dense."

Resolutely squaring her shoulders, Elizabeth headed for the front of the café. Evelyn followed her out to lock the door after her, just as Gilly stuck her head around the kitchen door. "He's coming!" she cried. "I can see him across the street." Her round, panic-stricken eyes pleaded with Elizabeth. "Keep him occupied, will you?"

"Don't worry." She smiled at Evelyn on the other side of the glass door as he turned the lock. He looked at her and playfully rolled his eyes.

When Elizabeth turned around, she was only a few inches from Breed. This man had the strangest effect on her. She wasn't sure how she felt about him. His appeal blossomed with every encounter. It hadn't taken her long to realize that her first impression of him as a muscle-bound egomaniac was completely wrong. He seemed almost unaware of the effect he had on women.

"Gilly will be ready in a minute. She's changing clothes now."

The tight corners of Breed's mouth edged upward. "No problem. I'm early."

She folded her arms around her slim waist. "She's looking forward to tonight." Realizing her body language was revealing her state of mind, she quickly dropped her hands to her sides.

"I make you uncomfortable, don't I?"

Color rose from her neck, brightening her cheeks. "It's not that. I...I don't think I've ever known anyone quite like you."

"As big, you mean?"

"No, not that."

His strong, angular chin tilted downward fractionally. "And I don't think I've ever known anyone as beautiful as you." The words were soft, husky.

She sensed immediately that he wished he could withdraw them. He hadn't intended to say that. She was sure of it.

"My size *is* intimidating," he stated flatly, taking a step in retreat. There was a strong suggestion of impatience in the way he moved, something she hadn't noted in the past. And right now he was angry with himself.

Ignoring his strong, male profile, she turned and looked up at the cloudless blue sky.

They both spoke at once.

"The weather..."

"How long…"

"You first." Breed smiled, and a pleasant warmth invaded her limbs.

"I was going to say that I was enjoying the weather this summer. After all that talk about the California smog and San Francisco's famous fog, I wasn't sure what to expect."

"You're not from California?" He looked surprised.

She didn't know why he should be; her light Boston accent wasn't difficult to decipher. "No, my roots are on the East Coast. Boston."

He nodded.

"Do you work on the wharf?" Conversation was easy with him; something else she hadn't expected. "Gilly and I were trying to guess."

"I'm a longshoreman."

It was her turn to give a polite nod. "It must be hard work." What else would give him muscles like that?

Fresh as a dewy rosebud, Gilly floated out the door in a light-blue summer dress. "Sorry to keep you waiting, Breed."

His amber eyes crinkled at the corners with a warm smile. "It was worth it," he said as he moved to her side, taking her hand in his.

Wiping a bead of perspiration from her forehead, Elizabeth gave Breed and Gilly a feeble smile. "Have fun, you two."

"Would you like to join us?" Gilly said.

Elizabeth took a step backward. As crazy as it

sounded, she was half tempted. "I can't tonight. I'm going to look at another apartment."

"Beth, it's hopeless," Gilly said, her voice emphatic.

Breed's eyes surveyed her with open interest. "You're looking for an apartment?"

"Are we ever!" Gilly proclaimed enthusiastically.

"Let me know what happens. I might be able to find something for you. My brother-in-law manages a building, and he told me he has a vacancy coming."

Gilly almost threw herself into his arms. "Really? Can we see it soon? Oh, Beth, what do you think?"

Elizabeth's smile wasn't nearly as enthusiastic. If Breed's brother-in-law showed them the apartment, he was sure to mention the rent, and Elizabeth knew Gilly couldn't afford much.

"Let me check out this ad tonight, and we can talk about it later."

A half-hour later Elizabeth was soaking in a hot tub filled with light-scented bubble bath. With the back of her head resting against the polished enamel, she closed her eyes, regretting that she hadn't gone with Breed and Gilly.

Two

"Oh, Beth!" Gilly exclaimed as she hurriedly stepped from room to room of the two-bedroom apartment in the marina district. "I can hardly believe how lucky you were to find this place. It's perfect."

Elizabeth was rather proud of it herself. The building was an older brick structure that had recently been renovated. She'd been fortunate to find it, even more fortunate to have convinced Gilly and Gilly's parents that the rent was cheaper for the first six months because there was still construction going on in the building. The perfection of the apartment made her deception easier. She could afford to pay three-quarters of the rent without Gilly ever being the wiser.

Polished wooden floors in the entryway led to a large carpeted living room that made liberal use of skylights.

"I still can't believe it," Gilly said as she turned slowly, her head tilted back to view the boundless blue sky through the polished glass ceiling. "I never dreamed you'd find something like this. Did you see that kitchen?" She returned her attention to Elizabeth. "Even my mother doesn't have such new appliances." With a deep sense of awe, she stepped into the kitchen and ran her hand along the marble counter. "I can't believe how well everything is working out for us." Pausing to glance at her wristwatch, she shook her head. "I've got one last load to bring over. I shouldn't be more than an hour."

"Don't worry. I'll hold down the fort," Elizabeth returned absently.

There were several things she wanted to do herself, including grocery shopping. She could fill the cupboards and Gilly would have no way of knowing how much she'd spent. When they divided the bill, Gilly wouldn't realize that she was only paying a fraction of the total. Elizabeth was enjoying the small duplicity. With a growing sense of excitement, she changed her clothes and started to make out an errand list. The Wainwrights were known for their contributions to charity, but this wasn't charity. She felt as though she owed Gilly something. If it hadn't been for Gilly, she was convinced she would still be trapped in the sluggish indifference that had dominated her life these past months. Her mother would have liked Gilly. Elizabeth pulled herself up straight. She hadn't thought about her mother in weeks. Even so, the memory remained sharp, with the power to inflict deep emotional pain. Just then the doorbell chimed. She couldn't imagine who it could be. Her step quickened as she walked to the door and opened it.

"Hello, Breed." Her hand tightened on the glass doorknob.

He handed her a large bouquet of flowers. "Welcome to the neighborhood," he said with a boyish grin.

"You live around here?" Her voice caught in her throat as she accepted the flowers. "Come in, please. I'm not being much of a hostess." She stepped back to allow him to enter and closed the door with her foot. "Gilly isn't here, but you're welcome to come in and tour the place if you like."

A smile glinted from his eyes as he followed her into the kitchen. "I'd like."

Deftly, she arranged the flowers and set them in the middle of the round kitchen table before leading the way through the apartment, glossing over the details.

"You're renting this for how much?"

Her heart dropped to her stomach. Gilly had apparently said something to Breed about their rent. She gave a light, breezy laugh, or what she hoped sounded light and breezy, and repeated what she'd told Gilly.

"Funny, I didn't notice any construction." He stood at the picture window.

"Of course you didn't." She continued the deception while keeping her gaze lowered. "Even carpenters go home in the evening." She was rescued from any further explanation by Gilly, who breathlessly barged through the door carrying a large box.

"Let me help." Immediately Breed took it from her and helped her carry in the remaining boxes.

When they'd finished, Gilly strolled into the kitchen.

"Breed offered to take us out to dinner. You'll come, won't you?"

Elizabeth's gaze flittered past her friend to Breed. She was uncomfortably aware of the unspoken questions he was sending her way.

"Not this time."

Gilly exhaled a heavy breath and pushed the curls away from her face in an exasperated movement. "But you will soon, right?" She glanced from Breed to Elizabeth.

"Another time," Elizabeth agreed, going back to her list.

"Promise?" Gilly prompted.

"Promise," Elizabeth returned, unsure why she felt the way she did. There was something about Breed that troubled her. Not his size, although he was right: that in itself *was* intimidating. His eyes often held a mischievous glint, as if he knew something she didn't. Not that he was laughing at her—far from it. There was understanding, compassion, and sometimes she thought she caught a glimmer of something close to sympathy. He was a complicated man, and she was afraid that if she investigated further, she would like him a lot more than she had a right to.

She should have realized that neither of them would go on accepting her refusal to join them. The following Saturday Gilly was adamant that Elizabeth go with them to the beach.

"You're coming!" she insisted, stuffing an extra beach towel in her bag.

"Gilly..." Elizabeth moaned.

"It's a gorgeous day. How can you even think about sitting at home when you can be lazing on the beach, soaking up the sun?"

"But I don't want to intrude."

"Intrude? Are you nuts? We want you to come."

Gilly had gone out with Breed twice in the last week. They'd asked Elizabeth along both times.

Elizabeth liked Breed. The intensity of her feelings both surprised and alarmed her. Each time Gilly and Breed went out they returned early, and then the three of them sat in the living room and talked while drinking coffee. At every meeting, Elizabeth grew more aware of him. Gilly had reacted naturally to the magnetic appeal of the man, but it had taken Elizabeth longer to recognize his potency.

He was a wonderful conversationalist. His experiences were broad and seemingly unlimited. Several times she had to bite her tongue to keep from revealing too much of herself and her background in response. In some ways she felt there wasn't anything she couldn't share with him.

She didn't know what to make of Gilly's relationship with him. They seemed to enjoy one another's company and had formed an easy friendship. But Gilly was the world's friend. After she and Breed had spent an evening together, Elizabeth would study her roommate closely. Gilly didn't appear to be falling in love, and Elizabeth found that conclusion comforting. Not that she was such an expert on love. There had been several times when she had wondered whether she was in love, but then she'd decided that if she had to wonder, she wasn't.

"Put on your swimsuit!" Gilly shouted from the kitchen now. "And hurry. Breed'll be here in ten minutes."

"You're sure you want me along?" Elizabeth continued to waver.

Gilly turned around and rolled her eyes theatrically. "Yes! You really do have a problem with the obvious, don't you?"

Elizabeth changed into her silky turquoise bikini. On the beaches of the Riviera, the skimpy two-piece had been modest. Now, studying herself in the mirror, she felt naked and more than a little vulnerable.

Gilly gave a low wolf whistle. "Wow! That doesn't look like it came from Best Beach Bargains dot com."

"Is it okay? There's not much to it." Elizabeth's gaze was questioning.

"I know. It's gorgeous—*you're* gorgeous."

"I'm not sure I should wear it…. I've got a sundress that would serve just as well."

"Elizabeth," Gilly insisted, "wear the bikini." She bit into a carrot stick. "Honestly, sometimes I swear you're the most insecure person I've ever met." She took the carrot stick out of her mouth and held it in her fingers like a cigarette. "By the way, where *did* you get that suit? I've never seen anything like it."

Elizabeth hesitated, her mind whirling in a thousand directions. "A little place…I don't remember the name."

"Well, wherever it is you shop, they sure have beautiful clothes."

"Thank you," Elizabeth mumbled as she put on a white cover-up. Quickly she changed the subject. "You're looking great yourself."

Gilly lowered her gaze to her rose-colored one-piece with a deep-veed neckline and halter top. "This old rag?"

"You just got that last week."

"I know, but next to you, it might as well be a rag."

"Gilly, that's not true, and you know it."

"Yes, but look at you. You're perfect. There isn't anything I wouldn't sacrifice for long legs and a figure like yours."

Elizabeth was still laughing when Breed arrived. He paused and gave Gilly an appreciative glance. "I should have suggested the beach sooner. You look fantastic."

She positively sparkled under his appraisal. "Wait until you see Elizabeth's suit. She's the one with the glorious body."

Breed didn't comment, but he exchanged a meaningful glance with Elizabeth that said more than words.

Admittedly, she wanted to impress him. Deep within herself she yearned for his eyes to reveal the approval he had given Gilly. To divert her mind from its disconcerting course, she tightened the sash of her cover-up and added suntan lotion to her beach bag.

"I'm ready if you are," she said to no one in particular. She continued to feel a little uneasy infringing on Gilly's time with Breed, but she was pleased to be spending the day in the sun. In past summers she had prided herself on a luxurious tan. Already it was the third week of June, and she looked as pale as eggwhite.

An hour later they had spread a blanket on a crowded beach at Santa Cruz, sharing the sand with a thousand other sun-worshippers. Breed sat with his knees bent as Gilly smoothed lotion into his broad shoulders.

Mesmerized, Elizabeth couldn't tear her eyes away. Gilly's fingers blended the tanning lotion with the thin sheen of perspiration that slicked his muscular back. She rubbed him with slow, firm strokes until Elizabeth's mouth went dry. The bronze skin rippled with the massaging movements, his flesh supple under Gilly's manipulations. Lean and hard, Breed was excitingly, sensuously, all male.

Elizabeth's breath caught in her throat as Breed turned his head and she felt his gaze. His eyes roamed her face, pausing on the fullness of her lips. They were filled with silent messages meant only for her. They were messages she couldn't decipher, afraid of their meaning. Her cheeks suffused with hot color, and she dragged her eyes from his.

"You probably should put on some lotion, too, Elizabeth," he commented. The slight huskiness of his voice was the only evidence that he was as affected as she by their brief exchange.

"He's right," Gilly agreed. "When I've finished here, I'll do you."

Elizabeth was amused at the look of disappointment

he cast her. He'd planned to do it himself, and Gilly had easily thwarted him.

After Gilly's quick application of lotion to her back, Elizabeth slathered her face, arms and stomach, and lay down on her big beach blanket. A forearm over her eyes blocked out the piercing rays of the afternoon sun. Pretending to be asleep, she was only half listening as Breed and Gilly chatted about one thing or another.

"Hey, look!" Gilly cried excitedly. "They've started a game of volleyball. You two want to play?"

"Not me," Elizabeth mumbled.

"You go ahead," Breed insisted.

A spray of sand hit Elizabeth's side as Gilly took off running. Judging by her enthusiasm, no doubt she was good at the game.

"Mind if I share the blanket with you?" Breed asked softly.

"Of course not." Despite her words, her mind was screaming for him to join Gilly at volleyball.

He stretched out beside her, so close their thighs touched. She tensed, her long nails biting into her palms. Her nerves had fired to life at the merest brush of his skin against hers. She attempted to scoot away, but granules of sand dug into her shoulder blade, and she realized she couldn't go any farther.

Never had she been more acutely aware of a man. Every sense was dominated by him. He smelled of spicy musk and fragrant tobacco. Did he smoke? She couldn't remember seeing him smoke. Either way, nothing had ever smelled more tantalizing.

Salty beads of perspiration dotted her upper lip, and she forced her mouth into a tight line. If he were to kiss her she would taste the salty flavor of his... She sat up abruptly, unable to endure any more of these twisted games her mind was playing.

"I think I'll take a swim," she announced breathlessly.

"Running away?" His gaze mocked her.

"Running?" she echoed innocently. "No way. I want to cool down."

"Good idea. I could use a cold water break myself." With an agility she was sure was unusual in a man his size, he got quickly to his feet.

As he brushed the sand from the backs of his legs, she ran toward the ocean. With her long hair flying behind her, she laughed as she heard him shout for her to wait. The water was only a few feet away, and they hit the pounding surf together.

The spray of cold water that splashed against her thighs took Elizabeth's breath away, and she stopped abruptly. Shouldn't the ocean off the California coast be warmer than this?

Breed dived into an oncoming wave and surfaced several feet away. He turned and waited for her to join him.

Following his lead, she swam to him, keeping her head above water as her smooth, even strokes cut into the swelling ocean.

"What's the matter?" he called. "Afraid to get your hair wet?"

"I don't want to look like Jack Sparrow."

He laughed, and she couldn't remember hearing a more exciting sound.

"You should laugh more often."

"Me?" A frown darkened his eyes. "You're the one who needs a few lessons on having fun." He placed a hand at her waist. "Let's take this wave together."

Without being given an option, she was thrust into the oncoming wall of water. As they went under the giant surge, she panicked, frantically lashing out with her arms and legs.

Breed pulled her to the surface. "Are you all right?"

"No," she managed to say, coughing and choking on her words. Saltwater stung her eyes. Her hair fell in wet tendrils over her face. "You did that on purpose," she accused him angrily.

"Of course I did," he countered. "It's supposed to be fun."

"Fun?" she spat. "Marie Antoinette's walk to the guillotine was more fun than that."

Breed sobered. "Come on. I'll take you back to the blanket."

"I don't want to go back." Another wave hit her, and her body rolled with it, her face going below the surface just as it crested. Again she came up coughing.

He joined her and helped her find her footing. "This is too much for you."

"It isn't," she sputtered. "If this is supposed to be fun, then I'll do it." With both hands she pushed the wet, stringy hair from her face. The feel of his body touching hers was doing crazy things to her equilibrium. The whole world began to sway. It might have been the effect of the ocean, but she doubted it.

"Will you teach me, Breed?" she requested in a husky whisper. She felt his body tense as the movement of the Pacific tide brought him close.

"Hold on," he commanded, just as another wave engulfed them.

She slipped her arms around his neck and held her breath. His arms surrounded her protectively, pressing her into the shelter of his body. Their feet kicked in unison, and they broke the surface together.

"How was that?" he asked.

Her eyes still closed, she nodded. "Better." Why was she kidding herself? This was heaven. Being held by Breed was the most perfect experience she could remember. That took her by surprise. She'd been held more intimately by others.

Slowly she opened her eyes. He pushed the hair from her face. "You're slippery," he murmured, pulling her more tightly into his embrace. His massive hands found their place at the small of her back.

"So are you. It must be the suntan lotion." Her breasts brushed his torso, and shivers of tingling desire raced through her. Such a complete physical response was as pleasant as it was unexpected.

"Watch out!" he called as they took the next wave. With their bodies intertwined, they rode the swell together.

A crooked smile was slanting Breed's mouth as they

surfaced. Again his fingers brushed the long strands of wet hair from her face. He tucked them behind her ear, exposing her neck.

Elizabeth could feel the pulse near her throat flutter wildly. He pressed his fingertips to it and raised his eyes to her. In their golden depths she read desire, regret, surprise. He seemed to be as unprepared for this physical attraction as she was.

His mouth gently explored the pounding pulse in her neck. Moaning softly, she rolled her head to one side. His lips teased her skin, sending unanticipated shivers of delight washing over her. When he stopped, his eyes again sought hers.

"You taste salty."

Words refused to form. It was all she could do to nod.

He had come with Gilly. She had no right to be in the ocean with him, wanting him to kiss her so badly that she could feel it in every pore of her body.

"We should go back." She heard the husky throb in her voice.

"Yes," he agreed.

But they didn't move.

His crooked grin returned. "Did you have fun?"

She nodded.

"I'm sorry about your hair."

"Are you trying to tell me I look like Jack Sparrow?"

"No. If you want the truth, I've never seen you look more beautiful."

Her skin chilled, then flushed with warmth. She

couldn't believe that his words had the power to affect her body temperature.

"You're being too kind," she murmured, the soft catch in her voice revealing the effect of his words.

They lingered in the water as if they both wanted to delay the return to reality for as long as possible. Then, together, they walked out of the surf, hand in hand.

When they reached their blanket, he retrieved their towels. "Here." He handed her the thickest one and buried his face in his own.

Sitting on the blanket, Elizabeth dug through her beach bag and came up with a comb. She was running it through her hair when Gilly came rushing up, a tall, blond man beside her.

"Breed and Elizabeth, this is Peter."

"Hi, Peter." Breed rose to his feet, standing several inches taller than the other man. The two of them shook hands. For a second Breed looked from Gilly to Peter, then back again. His brows pulled into a thick frown.

"Peter invited me to stay and play volleyball, then grab some dinner," Gilly explained enthusiastically. "He said he'd take me home later. You two don't mind, do you?"

Elizabeth's eyes widened with shock. Did Gilly honestly believe she should come to the beach with one man and leave with another?

"We don't mind," Breed answered for them both.

"You're sure?" Gilly seemed to want Elizabeth's approval.

"Go ahead," Elizabeth murmured, but her eyes refused to meet Gilly's.

"You guys looked like you were having fun in the water."

A gust of wind whipped Elizabeth's wet hair across her face. She pushed it aside. The action gave her vital moments to compose herself. Obviously Gilly had been watching her. Worse, it could be the reason her roommate had decided to stay there with Peter. She couldn't allow that to happen.

"We had a wonderful time." Breed answered for them both again.

"I'll see you tonight, then," Gilly said, walking backward as she spoke.

Frustrated, Elizabeth called out for Gilly to wait, but her friend ignored her, turned, and took off running. "We can't let her do that," she told Breed.

"What?" A speculative light entered his eyes.

"What's the matter with the two of you? Gilly's going off with a complete stranger. It isn't safe." She tugged the comb through her hair angrily. "Heaven knows what she's walking into. You didn't have to be so willing to agree to her crazy schemes. I'm not going to leave this beach without her." She knew she should say something about her fear that her own behavior with him had led to Gilly's decision, but her courage failed her.

"She's twenty and old enough to take care of herself." Despite his words, his low voice contained a note of vague concern.

"She's too trusting."

Ignoring her, he opened the cooler he'd brought and took out a bucket of chicken. "Want a piece?" he questioned, biting into a leg.

"Breed..." Elizabeth was quickly losing her patience. They were an hour from San Francisco, and he was literally handing Gilly over to a stranger.

"All right." He expelled his breath forcefully and closed the lid on the food. "Gilly knows Peter. I introduced them last week."

"What?" she gasped. None of this was making sense.

"The last time I went out with Gilly, we were really meeting Peter."

"I don't believe this."

"I didn't exactly need an expert to see that it was going to take weeks of coming to the Patisserie before you'd agree to go out with me."

"What's that got to do with anything?"

"Plenty." He didn't sound thrilled to be revealing his motivations. "I don't blame you. I know I can be a little intimidating at first."

She wanted to explain that it wasn't his size that intimidated her, but she didn't know how to account for her reticence. She couldn't very well explain that it was the way his eyes looked in a certain light or something equally vague. "So you dated Gilly instead?"

He nodded. "She knew that first night it was you I was interested in. We planned this today." The tone of his voice relayed his unwillingness to play the game.

No wonder Gilly had been so anxious for her to join them every time she'd gone out with Breed.

"But you looked surprised when Gilly brought Peter over." She recalled the partially concealed question his eyes had shot at Gilly and Peter.

"Those two should be nominated for the Academy Award. They were supposed to have been long-lost friends." His jaw tightened as he turned away from her to look out over the ocean. His profile was strong and masculine.

"You didn't have to tell me." His honesty was a measure of how much he cared.

"No, I didn't. But I felt you had the right to know." His arms circled his bent knees. "I hope Gilly realizes what a good friend you are."

Lightly, she traced her fingers over the corded muscles of his back. A smile danced at the edges of her mouth as she stretched out on the blanket. "No, I think you've got the facts wrong. It's me who needs to thank Gilly."

He turned just enough so that he could see her lying there, looking up at him.

"How could I have been so stupid?" She whispered the question, staring into the powerful face of this man whose heart was just as big as the rest of him.

He lay on his stomach beside her.

"Have you always been big?"

"Have you always had freckles on your nose?" he asked, turning the tables on her. His index finger brushed the tip of her nose.

Her hand flew to her face. "They're ugly. I've hated them all my life."

"You disguise them rather well."

"Of course I do. What woman wants orange dots glowing from her nose?"

"They're perfect."

"Breed," she said, raising herself up so that she rested her weight on her elbows, "how can you say that?"

"Maybe it's because I find you to be surprisingly delightful. You're refreshingly honest, hard-working, and breathtakingly beautiful."

She recalled all the flattery she'd received from men who had something to gain by paying attention to her. A large inheritance was coming to her someday. That was enough incentive to make her overwhelmingly attractive to any man.

But here she was on a crowded California beach with someone who didn't know her from Eve. And he sincerely found her beautiful. She cast her gaze downward, suddenly finding her deception distasteful. A lone tear found its way to the corner of her eye.

"Elizabeth, what's wrong?"

She didn't know how she could explain. "Nothing," she returned softly. "The wind must have blown sand in my eye." By tilting her chin upward toward the brilliant blue sky, she was able to quell any further emotion.

She lay down again, resuming her sun-soaking position. Breed rolled over, positioning himself so close she felt his skin brush hers.

"Comfortable?" he asked.

"Yes."

His large hand reached for hers, and they just lay

there together, fingers entwined. They didn't speak, but the communication between them was stronger than words.

Finally she dozed.

"Elizabeth." A hand at her shoulder shook her lightly. "If you don't put something on, you'll get burned."

Struggling to a sitting position, she discovered Breed kneeling above her, holding out her cover-up. "You'd better wear this."

She put it on. "Is there any of that chicken left?"

"Are you hungry?"

"Starved. I was in such a rush this morning, I didn't eat breakfast."

Opening the cooler, Breed fixed her a plate of food that was enough to feed her for three meals.

She didn't say so, though. She just took a big bite of the chicken. Fabulous. But she couldn't decide if it was the meal or the man.

The sun had sunk into a pink sky when Breed pulled up to the curb outside her apartment.

"You'll come in for coffee, won't you?" Elizabeth spoke the words even though they both knew that coffee had nothing to do with why he was coming inside.

She continued with the pretense, filling the coffeemaker with water and turning it on. She turned to discover his smoldering amber eyes burning into her. Her heart skipped a beat, then accelerated wildly at the promise she read there.

Wordlessly, she walked into his arms. This was the

first time he'd held her outside the water, and she was amazed at how perfectly their bodies fitted together. The top of her head was tucked neatly under his chin.

Her smile was provocative as she slipped her arms around his neck and tilted her head back to look up at him.

His eyes were smiling back at her.

"What's so amusing?"

"The glow from your freckles is blinding me."

"If I wasn't so eager for you to kiss me, I'd make you pay for that remark."

Breed lowered his mouth to an inch above hers. "I have a feeling I'm going to pay anyway," he murmured as he tightly wrapped his arms around her.

Being so close to this vibrant man was enough to disturb her senses. She tried to ignore the myriad sensations his touch aroused in her. As silly and crazy as it seemed, she felt like Sleeping Beauty waiting for the kiss that would awaken her after a hundred years.

Tenderly his mouth brushed over her eyelid, causing her lashes to flutter shut. Next he kissed her nose. "I love those freckles," he whispered.

Lastly he kissed her mouth with a masterful possession that was everything she had dreamed a kiss could be. It was a kiss worth waiting a hundred years for. He was gentle yet possessive. Pliant yet hard. Responsive yet restrained.

"Oh, Breed," she whispered achingly.

"I know." He breathed against her temple. "I wasn't expecting this, either."

She closed her eyes and breathed in the mingled scent of spicy musk and saltwater. With her head pressed close to his heart, she could hear the uneven beat and knew he was as overwhelmed as she was at how right everything felt between them.

"I should go," he mumbled into her hair. He didn't need to add that he meant he should leave while he still had the power to pull himself out of her arms. "Can I see you tomorrow?"

Eagerly, she nodded.

He pulled away. "Walk me to the door."

She did as he requested. He kissed her again, but not with the intensity of the first time. Then, lightly, he ran one finger over her cheek. "Tomorrow," he whispered.

"Tomorrow," she repeated, closing the door after him.

Three

Elizabeth adjusted the strap of her pink linen summer dress as Gilly strolled down the hall and leaned against the doorjamb, studying her. "Hey, you look fantastic."

"Thanks." Elizabeth's smile was uneasy. Breed had been on her mind all day, dominating her thoughts, filling her consciousness. Yesterday at the beach could have been a fluke, the result of too much sun and the attention of an attractive man. Yet she couldn't remember a day she had enjoyed more. Certainly not in the last two years. Breed made her feel alive again. This morning she'd been cooking her breakfast and humming. She couldn't remember the last time she'd felt so content. When she was with him, she wanted to laugh and throw caution to the wind.

Continuing to date him was doing exactly that. She couldn't see herself staying in San Francisco past the summer. When it came time to return to Boston, her heart could be so entangled with Breed that leaving would be intolerable. No, she decided, she had to protect herself…*and* him. He didn't know who she was, and she could end up hurting him. She couldn't allow herself to fall in love with him. She had to guard herself against whatever potential there was to this relationship. She couldn't allow this attraction to develop into anything more than a light flirtation.

"I sure wish I knew where you got your clothes," Gilly continued to chatter. "They're fantastic."

Elizabeth ignored the comment. "Do you think I'll need the jacket?" The matching pink top was casually draped over her index finger as her gaze sought Gilly's.

Gilly gave a careless shrug, crossing her arms and legs as she gave Elizabeth a thorough inspection. "I think I'd probably take it. You can never be certain what the weather's going to do. Besides, Breed may keep you out into the early-morning hours."

"Not when I have to work tomorrow, he won't," Elizabeth returned confidently.

The doorbell chimed just as she finished rolling the lip gloss across the fullness of her bottom lip.

"I'll get it," Gilly called from the kitchen.

Placing her hands against the dresser to steady herself, Elizabeth inhaled, deeply and soothingly, and commanded her pounding heart to be still. The way she reacted to Breed, someone would think she was a sixteen-year-old who had just been asked out by the captain of the football team.

"It's Breed," Gilly said, sauntering into the room.

Elizabeth gave herself one final inspection in the dresser mirror. "I thought it must be." Folding her jacket over her forearm, she walked into the living room, where he was waiting.

"Hi," she said as casually as possible. He looked good. So good. His earthy sensuality was even more evident now than in the dreams her mind had conjured up the previous night. Suddenly she felt tongue-tied and frightened. She could so easily come to love this man.

"Beth didn't say where the two of you were going," Gilly said before biting into a crisp apple.

"I thought we'd take in the outdoor concert at the Sigmund Stern Grove. A cabaret sextet I'm familiar with is scheduled for this afternoon. That is—" he hesitated and caught Elizabeth's eye "—unless you have any objection."

"That sounds great." By some miracle she found her voice. The corded muscles of Breed's massive shoulders relaxed. If she hadn't known better she would have guessed that he was as nervous about this date as she was. He glanced at his watch. "If we plan to get a seat in the stands, then I suggest we leave now."

Gilly followed them to the door. "I won't wait up for you," she whispered, just loud enough for Elizabeth to hear.

"I won't be late," Elizabeth countered with a saccharine-sweet smile, discounting her friend's assumption that she wouldn't be home until the wee hours of the morning.

Breed opened the door to a late-model, mud-splattered, army-green military-style Jeep and glanced up at her quizzically. "I had to bring Hilda today. Do you mind?"

A Jeep! The urge to laugh was so strong that she had to hold her breath. She'd never ridden in one in her life. "Sure, it looks like fun."

His hand supported the underside of her elbow as she climbed inside the vehicle. A vague disturbance fluttered along her nerve-endings at his touch, as impersonal as it was. He'd placed a blanket over the seat to protect her dress. His thoughtfulness touched her heart. The problem was, almost everything about this man touched her heart.

Once she was seated inside the open Jeep, her eyes were level with his. She turned and smiled as some of the nervous tension flowed from her.

When his warm, possessive mouth claimed her lips, Elizabeth's senses were overwhelmed with a rush of pleasure. The kiss, although brief, was ardent, and left her weak and shaking. Abruptly, Breed stepped back, as though he had surprised himself as much as he did her.

Dazed, she blinked at him. "What was that for?" she asked breathlessly.

He walked around to the other side of the Jeep and climbed inside without effort. He gripped the steering wheel as he turned and grinned at her. "For being such a good sport. To be honest, I thought you'd object to Hilda."

"To a fine lady like Hilda?" she teased. A trace of color returned to her bloodless cheeks. "Never. Why do you call her Hilda?"

"I don't know." He lifted one shoulder in a half-shrug. "Her personality's a lot like a woman's. It seems when I least expect trouble, that's when she decides to break down." The mocking glint of laughter touched his amber eyes. "She's as temperamental as they come."

"Proud, too," Elizabeth commented, but her words were drowned out by the roar of the engine. Hilda coughed, sputtered, and then came to life with a vengeance.

"See what I mean?" he said as he shifted gears and pulled onto the street.

By the time they'd reached the park, her carefully styled hair was a mess. The wind had whipped it from its loose chignon and carelessly tossed it about her neck and face.

"You all right?" he asked with a mischievous look in his eye.

She opened her purse and took out a brush. "Just give me a minute to comb my hair and scrape the bugs from my teeth and I'll be fine."

The pleasant sound of his laughter caused the sensitive muscles of her flat stomach to tighten. "I think Hilda must like you," he said as he climbed out and slammed the door. "I know I do." The words were issued under his breath, as if he hadn't meant for her to hear them.

The park was crowded, the free concerts obviously a popular program of the Parks and Recreation Department. Already the stands looked full, and it didn't seem as if they would find seats together. Other couples had spread blankets on the lush green grass.

With a guiding hand at her elbow, he led her toward the far end of the stands. "I think we might find a seat for you over here."

"Breed." She stopped him and turned slightly. "Couldn't we take the blanket from Hilda and sit on the lawn?"

"You'd want to do that?" He looked shocked.

"Why not?"

His eyes surveyed her dress, lingering momentarily on the jutting swell of her breasts. "But you might ruin your dress."

A flush of heat warmed her face at the bold look he was giving her. "Let me worry about that," she murmured, her voice only slightly affected.

"If you're sure." His eyes sought hers.

"Get the blanket, and I'll find us a place to sit."

A few minutes later they settled onto the grass and waited silently for the music to start. She had sat in the great musical halls of Europe and throughout the United States, but rarely had she anticipated a concert more. When the first melodious strains of a violin echoed through the air, she relaxed and closed her eyes.

The sextet proved to be as versatile as they were talented. The opening selection was a medley of classical numbers that she recognized and loved. Enthusiastic applause showed the audience's approval. Then the leader came to the front and introduced the next numbers, a variety of musical scores from classic films.

She shifted position, the hard ground causing her to fold her legs one way and then another.

"Here," Breed whispered, situating himself so that he was directly behind her, his legs to one side. "Use me for support." His hands ran down her bare arms as he eased her body against his. After a while she didn't know which score was louder, the one the musicians were playing or the one in her heart.

After the hour-long concert, Breed took her to a restaurant that he claimed served the best Mexican food this side of the Rio Grande.

"What did you think?" he asked as they sat across from one another in the open-air restaurant, eating cheese enchiladas and refried beans.

A gentle breeze ruffled her sandy hair about her shoulders as she set her fork aside. "How do I feel about the concert or the food?"

"The concert." He pushed his plate aside, already finished, while she was only half done.

"It was great. The whole afternoon's been wonderful." She cupped a tall glass of iced tea. Breed would be taking her home soon, and already she was dreading it. This day had been more enjoyable than all of the last six months put together, and she didn't want it to end. Every minute they were together was better than the one before. It sounded silly, but she didn't know how else to describe her feelings. Deliberately she took a long sip of her drink and set her fork aside.

"Are you finished already?"

Her gaze skimmed her half-full plate, and she nodded, her appetite gone.

"I suppose we should think about getting you back to the apartment."

Her heart sang at the reluctance in his voice. For one perfect moment their gazes met and locked. She didn't want to go home, and he didn't want to take her.

"How about a walk along the beach?" he suggested with a hint of reluctance.

She wondered why he was wary. Afraid of what she made him feel? No matter. She herself demonstrated no such hesitation. "Yes, I'd like that."

Hilda delivered them safely to an ocean beach about fifteen minutes outside the city. Others apparently had the same idea; several couples were strolling the sand, their arms wrapped around one another's waists.

"Do you need to scrape the bugs from your teeth this time?" Breed asked as he shifted into Park and turned off the engine. A smile was lurking at the edges of his sensuous mouth.

"No," she replied softly. "I've discovered that the secret of riding in Hilda is simply to keep my mouth closed."

His answering smile only served to remind her of the strength and raw virility that were so much a part of him. Her gaze rested admiringly on the smoothly hewn angles of his face as he climbed out of the Jeep and came around to her side. She must have been crazy to ever have thought of him as an ape-man. The thought produced a grimace of anger at herself.

"Is something wrong?" He even seemed sensitive to her thoughts.

"It's nothing," she said, dismissing the question without meeting his gaze.

Again his touch was impersonal as he guided her down a semi-steep embankment. A small, swiftly flowing creek separated them from the main part of the beach.

She hesitated as she searched for the best place to cross.

"What's the matter?" he teased with a vaguely challenging lilt to his voice. "Are you afraid of getting your feet wet?"

"Of course not," she denied instantly. "Well, maybe a little," she amended with a sheepish smile. It wasn't the water as much as the uncertainty of how deep it was.

"Allow me," he said as he swept her into his arms. One arm supported her back and the other her knees. Her hands flew automatically to his neck.

"Breed," she said under her breath, "what are you doing?"

"What any gallant gentleman would do for a lady in distress. I'm escorting you to safety." His amber eyes were dancing with mischief. He took a few steps and teetered, causing her grip on his neck to tighten.

"Breed!" she cried. "I'm too heavy. Put me down."

His chiseled mouth quirked teasingly as he took a few more hurried steps and delivered her safely to the other side. When he set her down, she noticed that his pants legs were soaking wet.

"You *are* a gallant knight, aren't you." Her inflection made the question a statement of fact.

Something so brief that she thought she'd imagined it flickered in his expression. It came and went so quickly she couldn't decipher its meaning, if there was one.

The dry sand immediately filled her sandals, and after only a few steps she paused to take them off. He did the same, removing his shoes and socks, and setting them beside a large rock. She tossed hers to join his.

They didn't say anything for a long time as they strolled, their hands linked. He positioned himself so that he took the brunt of the strong breeze that came off the water.

Elizabeth had no idea how far they'd gone. The sky was a glorious shade of pink. The blinding rays of the sinking sun cast their golden shine over them as they continued to stroll. The sight of the lowering sun brought a breathless sigh of wonder from her lips as they paused to watch it sink beneath the horizon.

Watching the sun set had seemed like such a little thing, and not until this moment, with this man at her side, had she realized how gloriously wondrous it was.

"Would you like to rest for a while before we head back?" he suggested. She agreed with a nod, and he cleared her a space in the dry sand.

With her arms cradling her knees, she looked into a sky that wasn't yet dark. "How long will it be before the stars come out?"

"Not long," Breed answered in a low whisper, as if he were afraid words would diminish the wonder of the evening. Leaning back, he rested his weight on the palms of his hands as he looked toward the pounding waves of the ocean. "What made you decide to come to San Francisco?" he asked unexpectedly.

Elizabeth felt her long hair dance against the back of her neck in the breeze. "My mother. She spent time here the summer before she married my father, and she loved it." Her sideward glance encountered deep, questioning eyes. "Is something wrong?"

He was still. "Are you planning on getting married?"

She wasn't sure she was comfortable with this line of questioning. "Yes," she answered honestly.

He sat up, and she noticed that his mouth had twisted wryly. "I wish you'd said something before now." The steel edge of his voice couldn't be disguised.

"Well, doesn't everyone?"

"Doesn't everyone what?" His fragile control of his temper was clearly stretched taut.

Scooting closer to his side, she pressed her head against his shoulder. "Doesn't everyone think about getting married someday?"

"So is there a Mr. Boston Baked Bean sitting at home waiting for you?"

"Mr. Boston Baked Bean?" She broke into delighted peals of laughter. "Honestly, Breed, there's no one."

"Good." He groaned as he turned and pressed her back against the sand. Her startled cry of protest was smothered by his plundering mouth. Immediately her arms circled his neck as his lips rocked over hers in an exchange of kisses that stirred her to the core of her soul.

Restlessly his hands roamed her spine as he half lifted her from the soft cushion of the sandy beach. She arched against him as he sensually attacked her lower lip, teasing her with biting kisses that promised ecstasy but didn't relieve the building need she felt for him.

"Breed," she moaned as her hands cupped his face, directing his hungry mouth to hers. Anything to satisfy this ache inside her. A deep groan slipped from his throat as she outlined his lips with the tip of her tongue.

Breed tightened his hold, and his mouth feasted on hers. He couldn't seem to give enough or take enough as he relaxed his grip and pressed her into the sand. Desire ran through her bloodstream, spreading a demanding fire as he explored the sensitive cord of her neck and paused at the scented hollow of her throat.

Her nails dug into his back as she shuddered with longing.

She felt the roughness of his calloused hand as he brushed the hair from her face. "I shouldn't have done that," he whispered. His voice was filled with regret. With a heavy sigh, he eased his weight from her. "Did I hurt you?" He helped her into a sitting position, but his hand remained on the curve of her shoulder, as if he couldn't let go.

"You wouldn't hurt me," she answered in a voice so weak she felt she had to repeat the point. "I'm not the least bit hurt." Lovingly, her finger traced the tight line of his jaw. "What's wrong? You look like you're sorry."

He nestled her into his embrace, holding her as he had at the concert, his arms wrapped around her from behind. His chin brushed against the crown of her head.

"Are you sorry?" She made it a question this time.

"No," he answered after a long time, his voice a whisper, and she wondered if he was telling the truth.

Without either of them being aware of it, darkness had descended around them. "The stars are out," she commented, disliking the finely strung tension their silence produced. "When I was younger I used to lean out my bedroom window and try to count the stars."

"I suppose that was a good excuse to stay up late," he said, his voice thick, rubbing his chin against her hair.

She smiled to herself but didn't comment.

His embrace slackened. "Do you want to go?"

"No." Her response was immediate. "Not yet," she added, her voice losing some of its intensity. She shifted position so that she lay back, her head supported by his lap as she gazed into the brilliant heavens. "It really is a gorgeous night."

"Gorgeous," he repeated, but she noted he was looking down on her when he spoke. "You certainly have a way of going to my head, woman."

"Do I?" She sprang to a sitting position. "Oh, Breed, do I really?"

He took her hand and placed it over his pounding heart. "That should answer you."

She let her hands slide over his chest and around his neck. Twisting, she turned and playfully kissed him.

"But the question remains, do I do the same thing to you?" he asked, his voice only slightly husky.

Elizabeth paused and shifted until she was kneeling at his side. Their eyes met in the gilded glow of the moon. "What does this tell you?" she said, more serious than she had been in her life. Taking his hand, she pressed it against her heart, holding it there as he inhaled a quivering breath.

"It tells me—" he hesitated as if gathering his resolve "—that it's time to go." He surged to his feet, then offered her a hand to help her up.

With a smile, she slipped her fingers into his.

The walk back to the Jeep seemed to take forever. Surely they hadn't gone this far.

"Isn't that Hilda?" she asked, pointing to the highway up ahead.

"Couldn't be." He squinted against the dark. "We haven't gone far enough yet."

"Far enough?" she repeated incredulously. "We couldn't possibly have wandered much farther than this." Their portion of the beach was deserted now, although she noted a few small fires in the distance, proof that there were others around. "Isn't that the rock where we left our shoes?" She pointed at the large boulder directly ahead of them.

"No." He was adamant. "We have at least another half mile to go."

Another half mile? Elizabeth's mind shouted. Already a chill had rushed over her bare arms, and the sand squishing between her toes was decidedly wet.

The surf was coming in, driving them farther and farther up the beach.

"I'm sure you're wrong," she told him with more confidence than she was feeling. "That's got to be the rock." She was unable to banish the slight quiver from her voice.

Angrily, he stripped off his shirt and placed it around her bare shoulders. "You're freezing." He made it sound like an accusation. "For heaven's sake, why didn't you say something?"

"Because I knew you'd do something silly like take off your shirt and give it to me," she shot back testily. "That's the rock, I'm sure of it," she reiterated, hurrying ahead. The only light was from the half moon above, and when she knelt down and discovered a sock, she leapt triumphantly to her feet. "Ah, ha!" She dangled it in front of his nose. "What did I tell you!"

"That's not mine," he returned impatiently. "Good grief, Elizabeth, look at the size. That belongs to a child."

"This is the rock," she insisted. "It's got to be."

"Fine." His voice was decidedly amused. "If this is the rock, then our shoes would be here. Right?" He crossed his arms and stared at her with amused tolerance.

Boldly, she met his glare. "Someone could have taken them," she stated evenly, feeling suddenly righteous.

"Elizabeth." He paused and inhaled a calming breath. "Trust me. The rock and Hilda are about a half-mile up the beach. If you'll quit arguing with me and walk a little way, you'll see that I know what I'm talking about."

"No." She knotted her fists at her sides in angry resolve. "I'm tired and I'm cold, and I think you've entirely lost your sense of direction. If you feel this isn't the rock, then go ahead and go. I'll be waiting for you here."

"You're not staying alone."

"I'm not going with you."

His eyes became hard points of steel, then softened. "Come on, it's not far."

"No." She stamped her foot, and splashed grit and sand against her bare leg from an incoming wave.

"You're not staying."

"Breed, listen to reason," she pleaded.

A wave crashed against his leg and he shook his head grimly.

"All right," she suggested. "Let's make a wager. Are you game?"

"Why shouldn't I be? You're wrong." The mood lightened immediately. "What do you want to bet?"

"I'll march the unnecessary half-mile up the beach with you. But once you realize you're wrong, you have to carry me piggyback on the return trip. Agreed?"

"Just a minute here." A smile twitched at the corners of his mouth. "What do I get if I'm right?"

"A personal apology?" she suggested, confident she wouldn't need to make one.

His look was thoughtful. "Not good enough."

She slowly moistened her lips and gently swayed her hips. "Ten slow kisses in the moonlight."

He shook his head. "That's *too* good."

She laughed. "Are you always so hard to please?"

"No," he grumbled. "Come on, we can figure it out as we walk." He draped his arm over her shoulders, pulling her close. She wasn't sure if it was because he was as cold as she was now or if he simply wanted her near his side. She tucked her arm around his waist, enjoying the cool feel of his skin against her.

"It's a good thing you've got those freckles," he said seriously about five minutes later. "Without those lighting the way, we'd be lost for sure."

In spite of herself, she laughed. Breed had the ability to do that to her. If someone else had made a similar comment she would have been angry and hurt. But not when it was Breed.

Ten minutes later they spied another large boulder in the distance.

"What did I tell you?" He oozed confidence.

"Don't be so sure of yourself," she returned, only slightly unnerved.

"If my eyes serve me right, someone was kind enough to place our shoes on top so they wouldn't be swept out with the waves."

Her confidence cracked.

"Listen, Sacajawea. If you ever get lost, promise me you'll stay in one place."

"I get the message," she grumbled.

"Promise me," he said more forcefully. "I swear, you'd argue with Saint Peter."

"Well, you're no saint," she shot back.

His grip tightened as his eyes looked into hers. "Don't remind me," he murmured just before claiming her lips in a hungry kiss that left her weak and breathless. "I think we'll go with those ten kisses after all," he mumbled against her hair. "You still owe me nine."

By the time they made it up to the highway and Hilda, then found an all-night restaurant and had coffee, it was well after one. And it was close to two when Elizabeth peeled back the covers to her bed.

When the alarm went off a few hours later, she was sure the time was wrong. Her eyes burned, and she felt as if she'd hardly slept.

Gilly was up and dressed by the time Elizabeth staggered into the kitchen and poured herself a cup of strong coffee.

"What time did you get in?" Gilly asked cheerfully.

"Two," Elizabeth mumbled almost inaudibly.

"I thought you were the one who insisted it was going to be an early night," Gilly said in a teasing, know-it-all voice.

"Do you have to be so happy in the morning?" Elizabeth grumbled, taking her first sip of coffee, nearly scalding her mouth.

"When are you seeing Breed again?"

He hadn't said anything the night before about another date. But they *would* be seeing one another again; Elizabeth had never been more sure of anything. A smile flitted across her face at the memory of their heated discussion about the rock. She could feel Gilly's gaze skimming over her.

"Obviously you're seeing him soon," the younger woman announced, heading toward her bedroom.

Breed came into the café later that afternoon at what she'd come to think of as his usual time.

He gave Elizabeth a warm smile and yawned. Almost immediately she yawned back and delivered a cup of coffee to his table.

"How do you feel?" he asked, his hand deliberately brushing hers.

"Tired. How about you?"

"Exhausted. I'm not used to these late nights and early mornings." He continued to hold her hand, his thumb stroking the inside of her wrist.

"And you think *I* am?" she teased.

His eyes widened for an instant. "Can I see you tonight?"

The idea of refusing never even occured to her. "Depends." No need to let him feel overconfident. "What do you have in mind?" She batted her eyelashes at him wickedly.

"Collecting on what's due me. Eight, I believe, is the correct number."

Four

The moon silently smiled down from the starlit heavens, casting its glow over the sandy beach. Breed and Peter had gathered driftwood, and blue tongues of fire flickered out from between the small, dry logs.

Elizabeth sat in the sand beside the fire and leaned against Breed, reveling in his quiet strength. His arms were wrapped around her from behind, enclosing her in his embrace. His breathing was even and undisturbed in the peace of the night. Communicating with words wasn't necessary. They'd been talking all week, often into the early hours of the morning. Now, words seemed unnecessary.

"I love this beach," she murmured, thinking how easy it would be to close her eyes and fall asleep in Breed's arms. "Ever since the first night you brought me here, I've come to think of this beach as ours."

His hold tightened measurably as he rubbed his jaw over the top of her head, mussing her wind-tossed hair all the more. Gently he lowered his head and kissed the side of her neck. "I'd say we're being generous sharing it with the world, wouldn't you?"

She snuggled deeper into his arms. "More than generous," she agreed.

The sound of Gilly's laughter came drifting down the beach. She and Peter had taken off running, playing some kind of teasing game. Elizabeth enjoyed it when the four of them did things together, but she was grateful for this time alone with Breed by the fire.

"Where do they get their energy?" she asked, having difficulty restraining a wide yawn. "I don't know about you, but I can't take another week like this."

"I always mean to get you home earlier," he murmured, his voice faintly tinged with guilt.

They'd gone out every night, and she hadn't once gotten home before midnight. Each time they promised one another they would make it an early night, but they hadn't met that goal once. The earliest she had crawled into bed had been twelve-thirty. Even then, she'd often lain awake and stared at the ceiling, thinking how dangerously close she was to falling in love with Breed.

"I wish I knew more about the constellations," she whispered, disliking the meandering trail of her thoughts. Love confused her. She had never been sure what elusive qualities distinguished love from infatuation. And if she did convince herself she was in love with Breed, would she ever be certain that it wasn't gratitude for the renewed lease on life he had so unwittingly given her? Tonight, in his arms, she could lie back and stare at the stars blazing in the black velvet sky. Only weeks ago she would have stumbled in the dark, unable to look toward the light. He had fixed that for her.

A hundred times she had flirted with the idea of telling him who she was. Each time, she realized that the knowledge would ruin their relationship. As it was, she would be faced with leaving him, Gilly and San Francisco soon enough.

She recognized that it was selfish to steal this brief happiness at the expense of others, but she couldn't help herself. It had been so long since she'd felt this good. Without even knowing it, Breed and Gilly had given her back the most precious gift of all: the ability to laugh and see beyond her grief. Being with them had lifted her from the mire of regret and self-pity. For that she would always be grateful.

"What's wrong?" Breed asked, tenderly brushing the hair from her temple.

His sensitivity to her moods astonished her. "What makes you ask?"

"You went tense on me for a moment."

She twisted so that she could lean back and study his ruggedly powerful face. His eyes were shadowed and unreadable, but she recognized the unrest in his look. Something was troubling him. She could sense it as strongly as she could feel the moisture of the ocean mist on her face. She'd recognized it in his eyes several times this past week. At first she'd thought it was her imagination. A yearning to understand him overcame her. "Things aren't always what they appear," she found herself saying. She hoped that he would trust her enough to tell her what was troubling him. But she wouldn't force his confidence.

Everything seemed to go still. Even the sound of the waves pounding against the beach faded. "What makes you say that?"

She resumed her former position, disappointed and a little hurt. Still, if Breed had secrets, so did she, and she certainly wasn't about to blurt out hers, so in all fairness, she shouldn't expect him to.

"Nothing." Her low voice was filled with resignation.

Slowly, tantalizingly, he ran his hands down her arms. "I have to go out of town next week."

"Oh." The word trembled on her lips with undisguised disappointment.

"I'll be flying out Monday, but I should be back sometime Tuesday," he explained.

"I'll miss you."

He drew her back against the unrestrained strength of his torso. "I wouldn't go if it wasn't necessary. You're right, you know." He spoke so low that she had to strain to hear him. "Things aren't always what they appear."

Later, when Breed had dropped her off at the apartment and she had settled in bed, his enigmatic words echoed in her mind. She couldn't imagine what was troubling him. But whatever it was, she sensed he was planning to settle it while he was out of town. He'd been quiet tonight. At first she had attributed his lack of conversation to how tired they both were. But it was more than that. She didn't know why she was so sure of it, but she was.

When she had first met Breed, she'd seen him only as muscular and handsome, two qualities she had attributed to shallow and self-centered men. But he had proved her wrong. This man was deep and intense. So intense that she often wondered what accounted for the powerful attraction that had brought them together.

A shadowy figure appeared in the doorway. "Are you asleep?" Gilly whispered.

Elizabeth sat up, bunching the pillows behind her back. "Not yet." She gestured toward the end of her bed, inviting her roommate to join her.

Gilly took a long swallow from a glass of milk and walked into the moonlit room, then sat on the edge of the bed. "I don't know what's wrong. I couldn't sleep, either."

"Did you have a good time tonight?" Elizabeth felt compelled to whisper, although there was no one there to disturb.

"I enjoy being with Peter," Gilly confessed with an exaggerated sigh, "but only as a friend."

"Is that a problem?"

Gilly's laugh was light and airy. "Not really, since I'm sure he feels the same way. It makes me wonder if I'll ever fall in love."

Elizabeth bit into her lip to keep from laughing out loud. "Do you realize how funny you sound? First you're happy because you and Peter are happy being just friends. Then you're disappointed because you aren't in love."

Gilly's smile was highlighted by the filtered light of the moon passing through the open window. "Yes, I suppose it does sound a little outrageous. I guess what I'd really like is to have the kind of relationship you and Breed share."

"He's a special man." Elizabeth spoke wistfully. Breed had taught her valuable lessons this past week. Without her long walk in the valley she might not have recognized the thrill of the mountaintop. Breed and Gilly had taught her to laugh and love life again. Life was beautiful in San Francisco. No wonder her mother had loved this city.

"I've seen the way he looks at you," Gilly continued, "and my heart melts. I want a man to feel that way about me."

"But not Peter."

"At this point I'm not choosy. I want to know what it's like to be in love. Really in love, like you and Breed."

"In love? Me and Breed?" Elizabeth tossed back the words in astonished disbelief.

"Yes, you and Breed," Gilly returned indignantly.

"You've got it all wrong." Elizabeth's thoughts were waging a fierce battle with one another. Gilly had to be mistaken. Breed couldn't be in love with her. She could only end up hurting him. The minute he learned about her wealth and position, he would feel betrayed and angry. She couldn't allow that to happen. "We're attracted, but we're not in love," she returned adamantly, nodding once for emphasis.

The sound of Gilly's bemused laugh filled the room. "Honestly, how can anyone be so blind?"

"But Breed and I hardly know one another," Elizabeth argued. "What we feel at this point is infatuation, maybe, but no one falls in love in two weeks."

"Haven't you read *Romeo and Juliet?*" Gilly asked her accusingly. "People don't need a long courtship to know they're in love."

"Breed's a wonderful man, and I'd consider myself fortunate if he loved me." A thickening lump tightened her throat, making it impossible to talk for a moment. "But it's too soon for either of us to know what we really feel. Much too soon," Elizabeth reiterated.

Gilly was uncharacteristically quiet for a long moment. "Maybe I'm way off," she murmured thoughtfully. "But I don't think so. I have the feeling that once you admit what's going on inside your heart and your head, you won't be able to deny it."

"Perhaps not," Elizabeth murmured, troubled by Gilly's words.

"Are you seeing him tomorrow?"

"Not until the afternoon. He decided that after all the sleep I lost this week, I should sleep late tomorrow."

"But you're awake because you're lying here thinking about him. Right?" Gilly asked softly.

"No." Elizabeth yawned loudly, raising her arms high above her head. She hoped her friend would take the not-so-subtle message.

"And not being able to sleep doesn't tell you anything?" Gilly pressed.

"It tells me that I'd have a much easier time if a certain know-it-all wasn't sitting on the end of my bed, bugging the heck out of me." As much as she wanted to deny her friend's assessment, Elizabeth had been impressed more than once with Gilly's insight into people and situations. At twenty, she was wise beyond her years.

"I can take a hint, unlike certain people I know," Gilly said, bounding to her feet. "You wait, Elizabeth Wainwright. When you realize you're in love with Breed, your head's going to spin for a week."

Turning onto her side, Elizabeth scooted down and pulled the covers up to her chin. "Don't count on it," she mumbled into the pillow, forcing her eyes closed.

Standing beside the foot of the bed, Gilly finished the rest of her milk. "I'll see you in the morning," she said as she headed toward the door.

"Gilly." Elizabeth stopped her. "Breed's not really in love with me, is he?"

Staring pointedly at the ceiling, Gilly slowly shook her head in undisguised disgust. "I swear the girl's blind," she said to the light fixture, then turned back to Elizabeth. "Yes, Breed's head over heels in love with you. Only a fool wouldn't have guessed. Good night, fool."

"Good night," Elizabeth murmured with a sinking feeling. She'd been naive to believe that she could nurture this relationship and not pay an emotional price. She had to do something soon, before it was too late. If it wasn't already.

"All right," Breed said, breathing heavily. He tightened his grip on Hilda's steering wheel. "Out with it."

Elizabeth's face paled as she glanced out the side of the Jeep. The afternoon had been a disaster from the start, and all because of her and her ridiculous mood. She had hoped to speak honestly with Breed. She wanted to tell him that she was frightened by what was happening between them. At first she'd thought to suggest that he start seeing someone else, but the thought of him holding another woman had made her stomach tighten painfully. The crazy part was that she'd never thought of herself as the jealous type.

"Are you pouting because I'm going away? Is that the reason for the silent treatment?"

"No," she denied in a choked whisper. "That's not it." She kept her face averted, letting the wind whip her honey curls in every direction. She was so close to tears it was ludicrous.

When he pulled over to the curb and parked so he could face her, her heart sank to her knees. His gentle hand on her shoulder was nearly her undoing. She didn't want him to be gentle and concerned. If he were angry, it would be so much easier to explain her confused thoughts.

"Beth, what is it?"

Like Gilly, Breed had started calling her Beth. But it wasn't what he called her, it was the way he said it, the tender, almost loving way he let it roll from his lips. No name had ever sounded so beautiful.

Miserable, she placed her hand over his and turned around so that she could see his face. Of their own volition, her fingers rose to trace the angular lines of his proud jaw.

He emitted a low groan and took hold of her shoulders, putting some distance between them. "I have enough trouble keeping my hands off you without you doing that."

She dropped her hands, color rushing to her cheeks. "That's what's wrong," she said in a low voice she hardly recognized as her own. "I'm frightened, Breed."

"Of what?"

She swallowed back the uneasiness that filled her. "I'm worried that we're becoming too intense."

He dropped his hands and turned so that he was staring straight ahead. As if he needed something to do with his fingers, he gripped the steering wheel. She could tell that he was angry by the way his knuckles whitened. His look proved he didn't understand what she was saying.

"Things are getting too hot and heavy for you. Is that it?"

It wasn't, but she didn't know how else to explain her feelings. "Yes…yes they are."

"Then what you're saying is that you'd prefer it if we didn't see each other anymore?"

"No!" That thought was intolerable.

"The trouble with you is that you don't know what

you want." The icy edge to his tone wrapped its way around her throat, choking off a reply.

He didn't appear to need one. Without hesitating, he turned the ignition key, and Hilda's engine roared to life. Jerking the gearshift, he pulled back onto the street.

"I feel we both need time to think." She practically had to shout to be heard above the noise of the traffic. Breed didn't answer. Before she could think of another way to explain herself, he had pulled up in front of her brick apartment building. He left the engine running.

"I agree," he said, his voice emotionless. "We've been seeing too much of one another."

"You've misunderstood everything I've said," she murmured miserably, wishing she had explained herself better.

"I don't think so," he replied, his jaw tightening. "I'll call you Tuesday, after I get back to town. That is, if you want to hear from me again."

"Of course I do." Frustration rocked her. "I'm sorry I said anything. I don't want you to go away angry."

He hesitated, and although he didn't say anything for several moments, she could feel the resentment fade. The air between them became less oppressive, lighter. "The thing is, you're right," he admitted tightly. "Both of us needed to be reminded of that. Take care of yourself while I'm away."

"I will," she whispered.

"I'll phone you Tuesday."

"Tuesday," she agreed, climbing out of the car. She

stood on the sidewalk as he pulled away and merged with the flowing traffic.

A flick of her wrist turned the key that allowed her into the apartment. Gilly was sitting on the sofa, reading a romance novel and munching on a carrot. "How did everything go?" she asked.

"Fine," Elizabeth responded noncommittally. But she felt miserable. Her talk with Breed hadn't settled anything. Instead of clearing the air, it had only raised more questions. Now she was left with three days to sort through her thoughts and decide how she could continue to see him and not complicate their relationship by falling in love.

"If everything's so wonderful, why do you look like you're going to burst into tears?"

Elizabeth tried to smile, but the effort failed miserably. "Because I am."

"I take it you don't want to talk."

It was all Elizabeth could manage to shake her head.

Later that evening, as the sun was sinking low into a lavender sky, Gilly dressed for an evening out. Her cousin was getting married, and her parents expected her to attend the wedding although she never had cared for this particular cousin.

"Are you sure you won't come?" Gilly asked Elizabeth for the sixth time.

"I'm sure," Elizabeth responded from the kitchen table, making an exaggerated stroke along the side of her nail with a file. Fiddling with her fingernails had given the appearance she was busy and untroubled. But she doubted that her smoke screen had fooled Gilly. "I thought you'd conned Peter into going with you?"

"I regret that," Gilly said with frank honesty.

"Why?" Elizabeth glanced down at her collection of nail polish.

"Knowing my dad, he's probably going to make a big deal about my bringing Peter. This whole thing's going to end up embarrassing us both. I hate being forced to attend something just because it's family."

Elizabeth cast her a sympathetic look. She'd suffered through enough family obligations to empathize with her friend's feelings.

Gilly and Peter left soon afterward, and she finished her nails, wondering if Breed would notice when she saw him next. She watched television for a while, keeping her mind off him. But not for long.

She picked up the paperback Gilly had been reading, and quickly read the first couple of chapters, surprised at how much she was enjoying the book. The next thing she knew, Gilly was shaking her awake and telling her to climb into bed or she would get a crick in her neck.

It was the middle of the morning when she woke again. Feeling out of sorts and cranky, she read the morning paper and did the weekly grocery shopping. When Gilly suggested a drive, she declined. Not until later did she realize that she'd been waiting for Breed to phone, even though he'd said he wouldn't, and was keenly disappointed when he didn't.

Monday evening, when her cell did ring she all but

flew across the room in her eagerness to grab it from her purse. She desperately wanted it to be Breed. But it wasn't. Instead, she found herself talking to her disgruntled father.

"I haven't heard from you in a while. Are you okay?"

"Of course I am." Although disappointment coated her voice, she had to admit she was pleased to hear from her father. She was even more grateful that Gilly was taking a shower and wasn't likely to overhear the conversation. "I'm happy, Dad, for the first time since Mom died."

"I was thinking about this job of yours. Are you still working as a…waitress?" He said the word as though he found it distasteful.

"Yes, and I'm enjoying it."

"I've been talking to some friends of mine," he said in a tone that told her he was anxious about her. "If you feel you need to work, then we could get you on at the embassy. Your French is excellent."

"Dad," she interrupted, "I like it at the Patisserie. Don't worry about me."

"But as a common waitress?" The contemptuous disbelief was back in his voice again. "I want so much more for you, Princess." Her father hadn't called her that since she was thirteen. "When are you coming home? I think it might be a good idea if you were here."

"Dad," she said impatiently, "for the first time in months I'm sleeping every night. I'm eager for each new morning. I'm happy, really happy. Don't ruin that."

She could hear her father's uncertainty, feel his in-decision. "Have you met someone special?" he said.

The question was a loaded one, and she wasn't sure how to respond, especially in light of her discussion with Breed. "Yes and no."

"Meaning…?" he pressed.

"I've made some friends. Good friends. What makes you ask?"

"No reason. I just don't want you to do something you'll regret later."

"Like what?" Indignation caused her voice to rise perceptibly.

"I don't know." He paused and exhaled forcefully. "Siggy's phoned for you several times."

Elizabeth released an inward groan. Siegfried Winston Chamberlain III was the most boring stuffed shirt she'd ever known. More than that, she had openly dis-liked him from the day a small, helpless bird had flown into a freshly washed window and broken its neck. The look in Siggy's eyes revealed that he'd enjoyed witness-ing its death. From that time on she'd avoided him. But he had pursued her relentlessly from their teenage years, though she was certain he wasn't in love with her. She wasn't even sure he liked her. What she did recognize was the fact that a union between their two families would be financially expedient to the Chamberlains.

"Tell Siggy the same thing you told him when I was in Paris."

"Siggy loves you."

"Dad…" Elizabeth didn't want to lose her temper,

not on the phone, when it would be difficult to settle their differences. "I honestly don't think Siggy knows what love is. I've got to go. I'll phone you next week. Now, don't worry about me. Promise?"

"You'll phone next week? Promise?"

She successfully repressed a sharp reply. Her father had never shown such concern for her welfare. He was acting as though she was working undercover for the CIA.

Honestly, she mused irritably. Would she ever understand her father?

"You miss him, don't you?" Gilly asked her later that evening.

Elizabeth didn't even try to pretend. She knew Gilly was referring to Breed. She had confided in her friend, and was again grateful for Gilly's insight and understanding. He had been on her mind all weekend. Monday had dragged, and she was counting the hours until she heard from him again. "I do," she admitted readily. "I wish I'd never said anything."

Gilly nodded sympathetically.

But it was more than missing Breed, Elizabeth thought to herself. Much more. For three days it had been as though a vital part of her was missing. The realization frightened her. He had come to mean more to her in a few weeks than anyone she'd known. Gilly, too. As she'd explained to her father, she was making friends. Maybe the first real friends of her life. But

Breed was more than a friend, and it had taken this separation to prove it.

Tuesday Elizabeth kept taking out her cell to see if she had missed his call.

"From the look of you, someone might think you're waiting to hear from someone," Gilly teased.

"Am I that obvious?"

"Is the sun bright? Do bees buzz?" Gilly sat on the chair opposite Elizabeth. "Why not call him? Women do that these days, you know."

Elizabeth hesitated long enough to consider the idea. "I don't know."

"Well, it isn't going to hurt anything. His pride's been bruised. Besides, anything's better than having you mope around the apartment another night."

"I do not mope."

Gilly tried unsuccessfully to disguise a smile. "If you say so."

Elizabeth waited until nine for Breed to phone. She could call him, but seeing him in person would be so much better. Maybe Gilly was right and, despite what he'd said about calling her, he was waiting for her to contact him. She wouldn't sleep tonight unless she made the effort to see him. It wouldn't do any good to try to fool herself otherwise.

"I think I'll go for a walk," she announced brightly, knowing she wasn't fooling her friend.

"Tonight's perfect for a stroll," Gilly murmured, not taking her attention from the television, but Elizabeth noticed the way the corners of her eyes crinkled as she struggled not to reveal her amusement. "I don't suppose you want me to wait up for you."

With a bemused smile, Elizabeth closed the door, not bothering to answer.

There were plenty of reasons that could explain why Breed hadn't called. Maybe his trip had been extended. He might not even be home. But as Gilly had pointedly stated, the evening *was* perfect for a stroll. The sun had set below a cloudless horizon and darkness had blanketed the city. The streets were alive with a variety of people. Elizabeth didn't notice much of what was going on around her. Her quick, purpose-filled strides took her the three blocks to Breed's apartment in a matter of a few short minutes. She had never been there, yet the address was burned into her memory.

For all her resolve, when she saw the light under his door, her heart sank. Breed was home and hadn't contacted her.

Her first light knock went unnoticed, so she pressed the buzzer long and hard.

"Beth!" Breed sounded shocked when he opened the door.

"So you made it back safely after all," she said, aware of the faintly accusatory note in her voice. He must have realized that she would be waiting for his call. "What time did you get back?" The minute the question slipped from her lips, she regretted having asked. Her coming was obvious enough.

"About six." He stepped back, silently and grudgingly issuing the invitation for her to come inside.

She was surprised at how bare the apartment looked. The living area displayed nothing that stamped the apartment with his personality. There were no pictures on the walls, or books and magazines lying around. The place seemed sterile, it was so clean. It looked as if he'd just moved in.

"I thought you said you would phone."

"I wasn't sure you wanted to hear from me."

Without waiting for an invitation, she sat on the sofa and crossed her long legs, hoping to give a casual impression.

He took a chair on the other side of the room and leaned forward, his elbows resting on his knees. There was a coiled alertness about him that he was attempting to disguise. But Elizabeth knew him too well. In the same way that he was sensitive to her, she was aware of him. He seemed to be waiting for her to speak.

"I missed you," she said softly, hoping her words would release the tension in the room. "More than I ever thought I would."

He straightened and looked uncomfortable. "Yes. Well, that's only natural. We've been seeing a lot of each other the last couple of weeks."

Her fingers were laced together so tightly that they began to ache. She unwound them and flexed her hands before standing and moving to the window on the far side of the room. "It's more than that," she announced with her back to him. Deliberately she turned, then leaned back with her hands resting on the windowsill. "Nothing seemed right without you...."

Breed vaulted to his feet. "Beth, listen to me. We're tired. It's been a long day. I think we should both sleep on this." His look was an odd mixture of tenderness and impatience. "Come on, I'll drive you home."

"No." She knew a brush-off when she heard one. He didn't want her here; that much was obvious. He hadn't been himself from the moment she set foot in the door. "I walked here, I'll walk back."

"All right, I'll come with you." The tone of his voice told her he would brook no argument.

She lifted one shoulder in a half-shrug. "It's a free country."

He relaxed the minute he locked the door. There was something inside the apartment he hadn't wanted her to see, she realized. Not a woman hiding in his bedroom; she was sure of that. Amusement drifted across her face and awoke a slow smile.

"What's so funny?" he wanted to know.

"Nothing."

His hand gripped hers. "Come on, and I'll introduce you to BART."

She paused midstride, making him falter slightly. With her hands positioned challengingly on her hips, she glared defiantly at him. "Oh, no, you don't, Andrew Breed. If you don't want to see me again, then fine. But I won't have you introducing me to other men. I can find my own dates, thank you."

A crooked smile slashed his face as he turned toward her, his eyes hooded. "Bay Area Rapid Transit. BART is the subway."

"Oh." She felt ridiculous. The natural color of her cheeks was heightened with embarrassment.

"So you missed me," he said casually as they strolled along the busy sidewalk. "That's nice to know."

She greeted his words with silence. First he had shunned her, and now he was making fun of her. Other than a polite "good night" when they arrived at her building, she didn't have anything to say to him. The whole idea of going to him had been idiotic. Well, she'd learned her lesson.

"The thing is, I discovered I missed you, too."

Again she didn't respond.

"But missing someone is a strange thing," he continued. "There are varying degrees. Like after your mother died, I imagine…"

Elizabeth felt a chill rush over her skin that had nothing to do with the light breeze. "I never told you my mother was dead," she said stiffly.

Five

"You don't mind, do you?" Gilly asked contritely. "I wouldn't have mentioned your mother to Breed if I'd known you objected."

"No, don't worry about it," Elizabeth said gently, shaking her head.

"Even though Breed and I went out several times before you started dating him, I knew from the beginning that he was really only interested in you. From the first date you were all he talked about."

Breed had explained to Elizabeth yesterday that Gilly had told him about her mother. Yet she'd doubted him. Everything about last night remained clouded in her mind. From the moment she'd entered his apartment, she had felt like an unwelcome intruder. None of his actions made sense, and her suspicions had begun to cross the line into outright paranoia.

"Peter and I are going to dinner and a movie," Gilly said, changing the subject.

"I have some shopping I want to do," Elizabeth returned absently.

Not until later that evening, when she was facing the store detective, did she remember that she couldn't phone Gilly, whose cell would be off in the theater, and have her come. A heaviness pressed against her heart, and she struggled to maintain her composure as the balding man led her toward the department store office.

She walked past the small crowd that had gathered near her and saw a tall, familiar figure on the far side of the floor in the men's department.

"Breed!" she called, thanking heaven that he had chosen this day to shop.

He turned at the sound of her voice, his brows lowering. "Beth, what is it?"

She bit into her bottom lip, more embarrassed than she could ever remember being. "Someone stole my purse. I haven't got any way to get home or a key to the apartment."

Elizabeth's face was buried in her hands when Breed delivered a steaming cup of coffee to the kitchen table where she sat. The manager had let her into the apartment, but she still had so much to deal with to straighten everything out that the feeling was overwhelming.

"Tell me again what happened," Breed said as he straddled a chair beside her.

She shook her head. Everything important was inside her purse. Her money, credit cards, cell phone, identification. Everything. Gone in a matter of seconds. As crazy as it sounded, she felt as if she had been personally violated. She was both stunned and angry.

"I don't want to talk about it," she replied stiffly. What she wanted was for Breed to leave so she could be alone.

"Beth." He said her name so gently that she closed her eyes to the emotion he aroused in her. "Honey, I can't help unless I know what happened."

One tear broke past the thick dam of her lashes and flowed unrestrained down her pale face. Resolutely, she wiped it aside.

"I decided to do a little shopping after work. Peter had picked up Gilly, and they were going out, and I didn't want to go home to an empty house." Breed hadn't mentioned anything last night about getting together, and she didn't want to sit around in an empty apartment missing him.

"Go on," he encouraged. He continued to hold her hand, his thumb stroking the inside of her wrist in a soothing action that at any other time would have been sensuous and provocative.

"I'd only bought a couple of things and decided to stop in the rest room before taking BART home. I set my purse and the packages on the counter while I washed. I turned to dry my hands. When I turned back, my purse, the packages…everything was gone. I was so stunned, I didn't know what to do."

"You must have seen something."

"That's what Detective Beaman thought. But I didn't. I didn't even hear anything." She paused, reliving the short seconds. She could tell them nothing.

Even now, an hour later, sitting in her kitchen, a feeling of disbelief filled her. This couldn't really be happening. This was a bad dream, and when she woke, everything would be fine again. At least that was what she desperately wanted to believe.

"What did they take?"

"Breed, don't. Please. I can't talk about it anymore. I just want to take a bath and pretend this never happened." Later she would have to contact her father. It didn't take much of an imagination to know what his response was going to be. He would insist she leave San Francisco, and then they would argue. She let the unpleasant thoughts fade. She didn't want to think about it.

Breed released her wrist and stood. His hands were positioned on his lean hips, his expression grim and unyielding. "Beth," he insisted in a low, coaxing tone. "Think. There's something you're not remembering. Something small. Close your eyes and go over every minute of the time you were shopping."

She clenched her teeth to keep from yelling. "Don't you think I haven't already?" she said with marked impatience. "Every detail of every minute has been playing back repeatedly in my mind."

He exhaled sharply, letting her know his patience was as limited as her own.

She stared pointedly at the bare surface of the table,

which blurred as the welling tears collected in her eyes. She managed to restrain their fall, but she couldn't keep her chin from trembling. Tears were a sign of weakness, and the Wainwrights frowned on signs of weakness.

Breed sighed as he eliminated the distance between them and stood behind her. Gently he comforted her by massaging her shoulders and neck. The demanding pressure of his fingers half lifted her from the chair, forcing her to stand.

She held herself stiffly, angry. "This is your fault," she whispered in a faintly hysterical tone.

"Mine?" He turned her around. His amber eyes narrowed into thin slits.

She didn't need him to tell her how unreasonable she was being, but she couldn't help herself. Her tears blurred his expression as she lashed out at him bitterly. "Why were you so unwelcoming last night? Why didn't you want me at your apartment? Not to mention that you said you'd call and then you didn't." She inhaled shakily. "Don't bother to deny it. I'm not stupid. I know when I'm not wanted. And why…why didn't you come into the café today?" Her accusations were fired as quick as machine gun bullets.

He groaned as his hands cupped her face. Anger flashed across his features, then vanished. "There wasn't a single minute that you weren't on my mind." Self-derisive anger darkened his eyes.

"Then why…?" Her heart fluttered uncertainly, excited and yet afraid.

Motionless, he held her, revealing none of his

thoughts. "Because," he admitted as the smoldering light of desire burned in his eyes. His hand slid slowly along the back of her waist, bringing her infinitesimally closer.

When he fitted his mouth to hers, a small, happy sound escaped from her throat. His thick arms around her waist lifted her from the kitchen floor. Her softness was molded to his male length as he kissed her until her lips were swollen and trembling.

"I missed you so much," she admitted, wrapping her arms around his neck. "I was so afraid you didn't want to see me again."

"Not want to see you?" he repeated. His husky tone betrayed his frustration. "You confuse me. I don't know what kind of game you're playing."

Anxiously, she brushed the hair from his face and kissed him, her lips exploring the planes and contours of his angular features with short, teasing kisses. "I'm not playing any game," she whispered.

He loosened his grip so that her feet touched the floor once again. "No games?" Amusement was carved in the lines of his face. "I don't believe that."

Deliberately she directed his mouth to hers and kissed him long and slow, her lips moving sensuously over his.

He broke the contact and held her at arm's length as he took several deep breaths.

"What's wrong?" she whispered. She didn't want him to pull away from her. A chill seeped through her bloodstream as she tried to decipher his attitude. The messages he sent her were confused. He wanted to be with her, but he didn't. He liked coming to her apartment but didn't want her at his. His kisses affected her as much as they affected him, yet he pulled away whenever things became too intense.

The phone rang, and he dropped his hands and stared at it as if it were an intruder. "Do you want me to answer it?" he questioned.

She shook her head and answered it herself. "Hello." She couldn't disguise the soft tremble in her voice. "Yes, yes, this is Elizabeth Wainwright."

Breed brushed his fingers through his hair as he paced the room.

"Yes, yes," she repeated breathlessly. "I did lose my purse." Not until the conversation was half over did the words sink into her consciousness.

"Breed!" she cried excitedly as she replaced the receiver. "They've found my purse!"

"Who did?" He turned her in his arms, his tense features relaxing.

"The store. That was them on the phone. Apparently whoever took it was only after the cash. Someone turned it in to the office only a few minutes ago after finding it in the stairway."

"Your credit cards and identification?"

"There. All they took was the cash."

He hauled her into his arms and released a heavy sigh that revealed his relief. Her own happy sigh joined his. "They said I should come and pick it up. Let's go right away," she said, laughing. "I feel naked without my purse." Giddy with relief, she waltzed around the room until he captured her and swung her in the air as if she weighed no more than a doll.

"Feel better?"

"Oh, yes!" she exclaimed, kissing him lightly. "Can we go now?"

"I think we should." He laced his fingers through hers, then lifted their joined hands to his lips and kissed the back of her hand.

He locked the apartment with the spare key the manager had given her and tucked it into his pocket. Hand in hand, they walked outside.

She patted Hilda's seat cushion as she got in. "You know what I thought last night?" she asked as Breed revved the engine.

He turned and smiled warmly at her. "I can't imagine." His finger lingered longer than necessary as it removed a long strand of silken hair that the wind had blown across her happy face.

"For one fleeting instant I was convinced you were hiding a woman in your bedroom." At the shocked look he gave her, she broke into delighted giggles.

"Beth." Thick lines marred his smooth brow. "Whatever made you suspect something like that?"

Pressing her head against his shoulder, she released a contented sigh. "I don't know." She *did* know, but she wanted to relish this moment. Yesterday's ghosts were buried. Today's happiness shone brightly before her. Her joy was complete. "Forward, Hilda. Take me to my purse."

Breed merged with the heavy flow of traffic. "I suppose you're going to insist on celebrating."

"Absolutely."

"Dinner?"

She sat up and placed her hand on his where it rested on the gearshift. She had to keep touching him to believe that all this was real. "Yes, I'm starved. I don't think I've eaten all day."

"Why not?" He gave her a questioning glance.

She poked his stomach. "You know why."

He reclaimed her hand, and again he kissed her fingers. She had the sensation he felt exactly as she did and couldn't keep his hands off her.

"What did Beaman say?"

"It wasn't Beaman. He said his name, but I can't remember it now."

"What did he say?" Breed glanced briefly in her direction.

"Just that I should come right away."

"That you should come right away." He drawled the words slowly. Then he dropped her hand and tightened his hold on the steering wheel as he glanced in the rearview mirror. The tires screeched as he made a U-turn in the middle of the street. The unexpected action caused Hilda to teeter for an instant.

"Breed!" Elizabeth screamed, holding on to the padded bar on the dash. "What is it? What's wrong?"

He didn't answer her as he weaved in and out of the traffic, blaring his horn impatiently. When they pulled up in front of her apartment again, he looked around and tensed.

She had no idea what had gotten into him. "Breed?" She tried a second time to talk to him. He sat alert and stiff. The look in his eyes was frightening. She had never seen anything more menacing.

"Call the police," he told her as he jumped from the Jeep.

"But, Breed—"

"Now. Hurry."

Confused, she jumped out, too. "What am I supposed to tell them?" she asked as she followed him onto the sidewalk and reached for his hand.

He pushed her arm away. "That wasn't the store that called," he explained impatiently. "It was whoever took your purse, and they're about to rob you blind."

"How do you know?" Nothing made sense anymore. Breed was like a dangerous stranger. Rage contorted his features until she hardly recognized him.

He grabbed her shoulders, his fingers biting mercilessly into her flesh. "Look." He jerked his head toward a moving van parked in front of the building. "Do as I say and call 9-1-1," he ordered in a threatening voice. "And don't come into the apartment until after the police arrive. Now go."

"Breed…" Panic filled her as he walked toward the door. "Don't go in there!" she shouted frantically, running after him. He was so intent that he didn't hear her. His glance of surprise when she grabbed his arm was quickly replaced with an angry scowl. "Get out of here."

With fear dictating her actions, she ran across the street to the safety of a beauty salon. She was sure the women thought she was crazy when she pulled out her cell, dialed the emergency police number, and reported a robbery in progress, all the while staring out through the large front window.

Like a caged animal, she paced the sidewalk outside her apartment, waiting for the patrol car. She held both hands over her mouth as she looked up and down the street. Everything was taking so long. Each second was an hour, every minute a lifetime. Not until the first police vehicle pulled up did she realize how badly she was trembling.

"In there," she said, and gave them her apartment number. "My boyfriend went up to stop them."

Another police car arrived, and while one officer went into the building on the heels of the first two, the other stayed outside and questioned her. At first she stared at him blankly, her mind refusing to concentrate on her own responses. Her answers were clipped, one-word replies.

Fifteen minutes later, two men and a woman were led out of the building by the police. Breed followed, talking to an officer. He paused long enough to search out Elizabeth in the growing crowd and smile reassuringly.

Her answering smile was shaky, but she felt her heart regain its normal rhythm. Her eyes followed him as he spoke to one officer and then another. When he joined her a few minutes later, he slipped an arm around her waist with familiar ease. Her fears evaporated at his touch.

"Do you recognize any of them?" he asked her.

Lamely, she nodded. "The woman was in the elevator with me, but she didn't go into the rest room."

"But she got off on the same floor?"

She wasn't sure. "I don't remember, but she must have."

"It doesn't matter if you remember or not. There's enough evidence here to lock them up." His arm remained on her waist as he directed her inside.

"How'd you know?" Dazed and almost tongue-tied, she stared up at him. "What clued you in to what was going on?"

"To be honest, I don't know," he admitted. "Something didn't ring true. First, it wasn't Beaman who phoned, and then there was something about the way you were instructed to come right away. They were probably waiting within sight of the building and watched us leave."

"But how'd they know my address and phone number?" All her identification listed her Boson address. Even her driver's license was from Massachusetts. There hadn't been any reason to obtain a California license, since she didn't have a car and was only planning on staying for the summer.

"Your name, address, and telephone number are printed on your checks."

She groaned. "Of course."

"We need to go to the police station and fill out a few forms. Are you up to that?"

"I'm fine. But I want to know about you. What happened in there?"

"Nothing much." It didn't sound like he wanted to talk about it. "I counted on the element of surprise."

"Yes, but there were three of them." She wasn't about to let the subject drop. "How did you defend yourself?"

His wide shoulders tensed as he hesitated before answering. "I've studied the martial arts."

"Breed!" she exclaimed. "Really? You should have said something." The longer she was with him, the more she realized how little she actually knew about him. She had actually avoided asking too many questions, afraid of revealing too much about herself. But she wouldn't shy away from them anymore.

Gilly and Peter returned to the apartment chatting happily.

Elizabeth glanced up and sighed. "Where were you when I needed you?" she teased her roommate.

"When did you need me?"

"Today. Someone took my purse."

"They did more than that," Breed repeated with a trace of anger.

"What happened?" Peter looked incredulous. "I think you better start at the beginning."

Slowly, shaking her head, Elizabeth sighed. "Let me explain."

An hour later Breed glanced pointedly at his wristwatch and held out his hand to Elizabeth. "Walk me to the door." The quiet firmness of his request and the tender look in his eyes sent her pulse racing.

"Sure," she said, eagerly moving around the sofa to his side.

He waited until they reached the entryway to turn her into his arms. Her back was supported by the panels of the door. His hands were on each side of her head as his gaze roamed slowly over her upturned face. For one heart-stopping second his eyes rested on her parted lips; his look was as potent as a physical touch.

"I want to see you tomorrow."

She released a heavy sigh. "Oh, thank goodness," she said, offering him a brilliant smile. "I was afraid I was going to be forced to ask *you* out."

His look grew dark and serious. "You'd do that?"

"Yes." She didn't trust herself to add an explanation.

He pulled his gaze from hers. "Would you like to go fishing?"

"You mean with poles and hooks and worms?"

"I've got a sailboat. We could leave tomorrow afternoon, once you're off work."

"Can I bring anything?"

"The worms," Breed teased.

"Try again, buddy. How about some sandwiches?" She could have Evelyn make some up for her before she left the Patisserie tomorrow.

"Fine."

Breed's kiss was disappointingly short but immeasurably sweet. Long after he left, she felt his presence linger. Twice she turned and started to say something to him before realizing he'd left for the evening.

Elizabeth felt Gilly's curious stare as she came out of the bedroom the following afternoon.

"Where's Breed taking you, for heaven's sake? You look like you just finished plowing the back forty."

Self-consciously, Elizabeth looked down at her tennis shoes and the faded jeans that were rolled midway up her calf. The shirttails of her red-checkered blouse were tied loosely at her midriff.

"Fishing. I'm not overdressed, am I? I have my swimsuit on underneath."

"You look…" One side of Gilly's mouth quirked upward as she paused, her face furrowed in concentration. "Different," she concluded.

"I'll admit I don't usually dress like this, but—"

"It's not the clothes," Gilly interrupted. "There's a certain aura about you. A look in your eye."

Turning, Elizabeth found a mirror and examined herself closely. "You're crazy. I'm no different than I was last week—or last night, for that matter."

Gilly ignored her and paid excessive attention to the crossword puzzle she was doing.

"No quick reply?" Elizabeth asked teasingly. She was used to doing verbal battle with her roommate.

Gilly bit into the eraser at the end of the pencil. "Not me. I learned a long time ago that it's better not to argue with you." But she rolled her eyes when she thought Elizabeth wasn't looking.

Breed arrived just then, and Elizabeth didn't have the opportunity to banter further with Gilly. If there was something different about her, as her friend believed, then it was because she was happier, more complete.

Outside the building, Elizabeth scanned the curb for Hilda, but the Jeep wasn't parked within sight.

"Here." Breed held open the door to a silver sedan, the same car he'd driven before introducing her to Hilda.

"Where's Hilda?"

"Home." Breed's reply was abrupt.

"Good grief, how many cars have you got?"

The smile that lifted the corners of his mouth looked forced. "One too many," he answered cryptically.

She wanted to question him further, but he closed her door and walked around to the driver's side. He paused and glanced warily at the street before climbing inside the car.

"Are you planning on kidnapping me?" she teased.

For an instant his sword-sharp gaze pinned her against the seat. "What makes you ask something as crazy as that?" Impatience sounded in his crisp voice.

She had meant it as a joke, so she was surprised that he had taken her seriously. She arched one delicately shaped brow at his defensive tone and cocked her head. "What's gotten into you?"

"Nothing."

Releasing her breath slowly, she gazed out the side window, watching as the scenery whipped past. From the minute he had asked her on this outing, she had been looking forward to their time together. She didn't want anything to ruin it.

At the marina, his heavy steps sounded ominously as he led her along the long wooden dock toward his sailboat. But his mood altered once they were slicing through the water, the multicolored spinnaker bloated with wind. Content, she dragged her fingers in the dark- ish green waters of San Francisco Bay, delighting in the cool feel against her hand, while Breed sat behind her at the tiller.

"This is wonderful!" she shouted. But he couldn't hear her, because a gust of wind carried her voice for- ward. Laughing, she scooted closer, rose to her knees and spoke directly into his ear, smiling.

His returning smile revealed his own enjoyment. He relaxed against the gunnel, his long legs stretched out and crossed at the ankles. With one hand he managed the tiller as he motioned with the other for Elizabeth to sit at his side.

She did so willingly.

When he reached a spot that apparently met his spec- ifications, he lowered the sails and dropped anchor.

Giving her nothing more than the basic instructions, he baited her hook and handed her a fishing pole.

"Now what?" She sat straight-backed and unsure as he readied his own pole and lowered the line into the deep waters on the opposite side of the boat.

"We wait for a hungry fish to come along and take a nibble."

"What if they're not hungry?"

"Are you always this much trouble?" he asked her, chuckling at her indignant look. "Your freckles are flashing at me again."

Involuntarily she brushed at her nose, as though her fingers could rub the tan flecks away. She was about to make a feisty retort when she felt a slight tug on her line.

"Breed," she whispered frantically. "I…I think I've got one." The pole dipped dramatically, nearly catching her off guard. "What do I do?" she cried, looking back to him, her eyes unsure.

"Reel it in."

"I can't," she said, silently pleading with him to take the pole from her. She should have known better.

"Sure you can," he assured her calmly. To offer her moral support, he reeled in his own line and went over to her, encouraging her as she struggled to bring in the fish.

She couldn't believe how much of a battle one small fish could wage. "What have I caught?" she shouted in her excitement. "A whale?" Perspiration broke out across her forehead as she pulled back on the pole and reeled in the fish inch by inch.

When the line snapped and she staggered backward, Breed caught her at the shoulders. "You all right?"

"No, darn it, I wanted that fish. What happened?"

He looked unconcerned and shrugged. "Any number of things. Want to try again?"

"Of course," she replied indignantly. He seemed to think she was a quitter, and she would like nothing better than to prove him wrong.

With her line back in the bay, Elizabeth leaned against the side, lazily enjoying the sun and wind. "Have you ever stopped to think that after all the times we've gone out, we still hardly know anything about each other?" she asked.

Her statement was met with silence. "What's there to know?"

She was treading on dangerous ground, and she knew it. Her relationship with Breed had progressed to the point where she felt he had a right to know who she was. But fear and indecision prevented her from broaching the subject boldly. "There's lots I'd like to know about you."

"Like what?" There was the slightest pause before his mouth thinned. He didn't seem overly eager to reveal more of himself.

"Well, for one thing…your family." If she led into the subject, then maybe he would ask her about hers, and she could explain bits and pieces of her background until things added up in his mind, since telling him outright was bound to be fatal to their promising relationship.

"Not much to tell you there. I'm the oldest of four boys. My great-grandfather came to California from Germany in search of lumber. He died here and left the land to his son." He paused and glanced at her. "What about you?"

She pressed her lips tightly together. For all her desire for honesty and despite her earlier resolution, when it came time to reveal the truth about her family, she found she couldn't. The bright, healthy color the wind and the sun had given her cheeks was washed swiftly away, leaving her unnaturally pale.

"I've got one older brother, Charlie." She swallowed tightly. "I don't think you'd like him."

"Why not?"

She lifted one petite shoulder. "He's…well, he's something of a stuffed shirt."

"Lawyer type."

She nodded, wanting to change the subject. "How much longer before I lure another fish to my bait?"

"Patience," Breed said, his back to her.

Her eyes fluttered closed. Her heart was pounding so hard she was sure he would notice. Unwittingly, he had given good advice. She had to be patient. Someday soon, when the time was right, she would tell him everything.

Six

The stars were twinkling like diamond chips in an ebony sky. The water lapped lightly against the side of Breed's boat, which, sails lowered, rocked gently in the murky water of San Francisco Bay. Four pairs of eager eyes gazed into the night sky, anticipating the next rocket burst to explode into a thousand shooting stars and briefly light up the heavens.

"I love the Fourth of July," Elizabeth murmured. Breed sat beside her, his arm draped casually over her shoulder. Gilly and Peter sat on the other side of the boat, holding hands. They might not be in love, but as Gilly had explained, they were certainly good friends.

One burst after another brightened the sky. Breed had said something earlier that week about going to Candlestick Park to watch the fireworks, but once the four of them had piled into Breed's sedan, they discovered that the traffic heading for the park was horrendous. He'd suggested that they take his sailboat into the bay and observe the fireworks from there, instead, an idea that had been met with enthusiasm by the others.

For nearly a week Breed had taken Elizabeth out on his boat every night after work. Sometimes they fished, depending on how much time they had and what their plans were afterward. He had led her forward a couple of times to raise and lower the sails. She loved to sail as much as he did, and the time they shared on the water had become the high point of her day. They talked openly, argued over politics, discussed books. He challenged her ideas on conservation and pollution, forcing her to stop and think about things she had previously accepted because of what she'd been told by others. Gently, but firmly, he made her form her own opinions. And she loved him for it.

She hadn't told him that she loved him, of course. The emotion was new to her and frightened her a little. The love she'd experienced in the past for her family and friends had been a mixture of respect and admiration. The only person with whom she had ever shared such a close relationship had been her mother. Of course, she would have grieved if her father had been the one who had suffered the stroke and died. But her mother had been her soulmate.

The love she felt for Breed went beyond friendship. Her love was fiery and intense, and the physical desire was sometimes overwhelming. Yet the joy she felt in his arms exceeded desire. Yes, she wanted him. More than that, she wanted to give herself to him. He must have known that, but he never allowed their lovemaking to go beyond a certain point. She didn't know why he was holding himself back. Not that she minded; that aspect of their relationship was only a small part of her feelings. When they could speak openly and honestly about their feelings and their commitment to one another, then they could deal with the physical aspect of their relationship. Her love went so much deeper. In analyzing her feelings, she thought that they also met on a higher plane, a spiritual one. Perhaps because of that, he felt it was too soon to talk about certain things. In some ways, they didn't need to.

She often wanted to talk to Gilly about her feelings, but she wasn't sure her friend, who was so much younger, would understand. If her mother had been alive, Elizabeth could have spoken to her. But she wasn't, and Elizabeth was forced to keep the inexplicable intensity of this relationship buried deep within her heart.

The only thing that marred her happiness was the sensation that something was troubling Breed. She'd tried to question him once and run up against a granite wall. Lately he'd been brooding and thoughtful. Although he hadn't said anything, she was fairly certain he'd lost his job. His hours had been flexible in the past, but lately he'd been coming into the Patisserie at all hours. Some days he even came in the morning and then again in the afternoon. Another thing she'd noticed was that they rarely ate in restaurants anymore. All the things they did together were inexpensive. Every Sunday they returned to Sigmund Stern Grove for the free concert. They took long walks on the beach and sailed almost daily. His apparent financial problems created others, effectively killing her desire to tell him about her background. How could she talk about her family's money without sounding insensitive? She had no doubt that the information could ruin what they shared.

When she glanced up from her musings she noted that Peter's arm was around Gilly, who had her head pressed against his shoulder. The look in Gilly's eyes seemed troubled, although Elizabeth realized she could have misread it in the reflected moonlight.

"Gilly, are you feeling okay?" she felt obliged to ask.

Gilly straightened. "Of course. Why shouldn't I be?"

"You're so quiet."

"I think we should enjoy the novelty," Peter interjected. "Once ol' motor-mouth gets going, it's hard to shut her up."

"Motor-mouth?" Gilly returned indignantly, poking Peter in his ribs. Peter laughed and the joking resumed, but not before Elizabeth witnessed the pain in her friend's expression.

An hour later, she helped Breed stow the sails after docking. Gilly and Peter carried the picnic basket and blankets to the car.

"Something's bothering Gilly," Elizabeth murmured to Breed the minute their friends were out of hearing distance.

"I noticed that, too," he whispered conspiratorially. "I think she's falling in love with Peter."

"No." She shook her head decisively. "They're just good friends."

"It may have started out like that, but it's not that way anymore." He sounded completely confident. He hardly paused as he moved forward to store the sails.

Elizabeth followed him. "What makes you so sure Gilly's in love?"

A weary look stole across his features. "She has that look about her." From his tone, she could tell he didn't want to discuss the subject further.

"Apparently you've seen that look in a lot of women's eyes," she stated teasingly, though with a serious undertone.

"A few," he responded noncommittally.

The thought of him loving another woman produced a curious ache in her heart. She paused and straightened. *So this is jealousy*, she mused. This churning sensation in the pit of her stomach, this inexplicable pain in her chest. As crazy as it seemed, she was jealous of some nameless other woman.

Breed's hand at her elbow brought her back to the present. He took her hand as he stepped onto the dock. "Peter and Gilly are waiting."

The silence coming from the backseat of the car where Gilly and Peter were sitting was heavy and unnatural. A storm cloud seemed to have settled in the sedan, the air heavy with electricity. Breed captured Elizabeth's gaze and arched his brows in question.

She motioned weakly with her hand, telling him she had no more idea of what had happened between their friends than he did. Twice she attempted to start a conversation, but her words were met with uninterested grunts.

Breed pulled up and parked in front of the apartment she and Gilly shared. As he was helping Elizabeth, Gilly practically jumped from the car.

"Night, everyone," she said in a voice that was high-pitched and wobbly.

"Gilly, wait up. I want to talk to you." Peter bolted after her, his eyes filled with frustration. He cast Breed and Elizabeth an apologetic look on his way past.

Breed glanced at Elizabeth and shrugged. "I'd say those two need some time alone."

"I agree."

"Do you want to go for a drive?" he suggested, tucking her hand under his folded arm as he led her back to the sedan.

"How about a walk instead? After sailing all evening, I could use some exercise."

He turned her in his arms. "We could. But I'd rather drive up to Coit Tower and show you the city lights. The view is fabulous."

Spending time alone with Breed was far more appealing than watching the city lights. "I'd like that," she admitted, getting back inside the car.

A long, winding drive through a dense neighborhood led to the observation tower situated high above the city. He parked, and as she stared out the windshield she realized that he hadn't exaggerated the view. She had seen some of the most beautiful landscapes in the world, but sitting with Breed overlooking San Francisco, she couldn't recall one more beautiful. Words couldn't describe the wonder of what lay before her.

"It's late," he murmured against her hair.

She acknowledged his words with a short nod, but she didn't want to leave and didn't suggest it.

"You have to work tomorrow." His voice was rough and soft, more of an aching whisper.

A smile touched her eyes. Breed couldn't decide if they should stay or go. Alone in the dark with nothing to distract them, the temptations were too great.

She tipped her head back. "Let me worry about tomorrow. I'll survive," she assured him. The night shaded his eyes, but she could feel the tension in him. His breathing was faintly irregular. "Why do you want to leave so much?" she asked in a throbbing whisper.

Her question went unanswered. A long moment of silence followed as he gazed down on her. Gently, he brushed the wispy strands of hair from her cheek, then curled his fingers into her hair. Elizabeth was shocked to realize he was trembling.

Slowly his head moved downward and paused an inch above her lips. "You know why we should leave," he growled.

All day she had yearned for him. Not for the first time, she noticed that he had been physically distant today, his touch casual, as though he was struggling to hold himself back. His restraint made her want him all the more.

"Beth." He whispered her name, and something

snapped within him. His mouth plundered hers, and all her senses came to life. She rose slightly from the seat to press closer to him.

A tiny moan slipped from her as his lips found her neck and shot wave after wave of sensual delight through her. Her hands roamed his back, then moved forward and unfastened his shirt. Eagerly she let them glide down the smooth flat muscles of his broad chest.

He groaned and straightened, then buried his face in her neck and held her to him. "Beth…" he moaned. She could feel and see the conflict in his eyes.

He rubbed one hand across his face and eyes, but he continued to hold her tightly to him with the other, as though he couldn't bear to release her yet.

His control was almost frightening. The marvel of it silenced her for several seconds.

With her arms linked behind his head, she pressed her forehead to his.

The tension eased from his muscles, and she could hear the uneven thud of his heart slowly return to normal. When his breathing was less ragged, she lightly pressed her lips to his.

"Don't do that," he said harshly, abruptly releasing her. The tension in him was barely suppressed.

She turned away and leaned her head against the back of the seat, staring straight ahead. When tears of anger and frustration filled her eyes, she blinked hurriedly to forestall their flow.

"There's only so much of this a man can take." He, too, stared straight ahead as he savagely rubbed his hand along the back of his neck. "You know as well as I do what's happening between us."

"I can't help it, Breed," she whispered achingly.

"Yes, you can," he returned grimly.

The aching desire to reach across the close confines of the car and touch him was unbearable. But she didn't dare. She couldn't look at him. "Is…is there something wrong with me?" she asked in a tortured whisper. "I mean, do my freckles turn you off…or something?" Out of the corner of her eye, she saw a muscle twitch in his lean jaw.

"That question isn't worthy of an answer." His eyes hardened as he turned the ignition key and revved the engine.

"Maybe we should stop seeing so much of each other." Her pride was hurt, but the ache extended deep into her heart.

"Maybe we should," he said at last.

Elizabeth closed her eyes against the onrush of emotional pain. One tear escaped and made a wet track down her pale face, followed by another and another.

When he pulled up in front of her apartment building, she didn't turn to him to say good-night. She didn't want him to see her tears. That would only humiliate her further.

"Thanks for a lovely day," she whispered, barely able to find her voice; then she hurriedly opened the door and raced into the apartment foyer.

Breed didn't follow her, but he didn't leave either. His car was still parked outside when Elizabeth reached her apartment and, from deep within the living-room shadows, glanced out the window to watch him. The streetlight silhouetted a dejected figure of a man leaning over the steering wheel.

After a moment she realized that soft, whimpering cries were coming from the bedroom. Trapped in her own problems, she had forgotten Gilly's.

Wiping the moisture from her cheeks, she turned and headed down the hall to knock against her friend's open bedroom door.

"Gilly," she whispered, "what's wrong?"

Gilly sat up on her bed and blew noisily into a tissue. "Beth, I am so stupid."

"If you want to talk, I have all the time in the world to listen." She entered the darkened room and sat on the end of the bed. With all the problems she was having, she chastised herself for not recognizing what had been happening to her friend.

Gilly took another tissue and wiped her eyes dry. "Do you remember how I told you that Peter and I are just friends?"

"I remember."

"Well…" Gilly sniffled noisily, "something changed. I don't know when or why, but sometime last week I looked at Peter and I knew I loved him."

Elizabeth patted Gilly's hand. "That's no reason to cry. I'd think you'd be happy."

"I was, for two glorious days. I wanted to tell someone, but I didn't think it was fair to confide in you. I thought Peter should be the first one to know."

Her roommate *had* appeared exceptionally happy lately, Elizabeth recalled. Gilly had been particularly enthusiastic about the four of them spending the holiday together. She hadn't really thought much about it, though, because Gilly was always happy.

"Then I made the mistake of telling him," she continued. "You were helping Breed put the sails away, and Peter and I were carrying things to the car." She inhaled a quivering breath.

"What happened?" Elizabeth encouraged her roommate softly.

"I guess I should have waited for a more appropriate moment, but I was eager to talk to him. Everything about the day had been perfect, and we were alone for the first time. So, like an idiot, I turned to him and said, 'Peter, I don't know what's happened, but I love you.'"

"And?"

"First he looked shocked. Then embarrassed. He stuttered something about this being a surprise and looked like he wanted to run away, but then you and Breed returned and we all piled into the car."

"What happened when Breed dropped the two of you off here?"

"Nothing. I wouldn't talk to him."

"Gilly!"

"You wouldn't have wanted to talk, either," she insisted, defending her actions. "I was humiliated enough without Peter apologizing to me because he didn't share my feelings."

"I'm sure he's going to want to talk to you." Elizabeth appealed to the more reasonable part of her friend's nature.

"He can forget it. How could I have been so stupid? If I was going to fall in love, why couldn't it be with someone like Breed?"

Elizabeth lowered her gaze to her hands. "There's only one Breed, and he's mine."

"Oh, before I forget..." Gilly sat up and looked around her, finally handing Elizabeth a piece of paper with a phone number written across the top. "Your brother phoned."

"My brother? From Boston?"

"No, he's here in San Francisco. He's staying at the Saint Francis. I told him I didn't know what time you'd be back, so he said to tell you that he'd expect you tomorrow night for dinner at seven-thirty at his hotel."

Ordering instead of asking. That sounded just like her brother.

"Did he say anything else?" It would be just like Charlie to say something to embarrass her.

Gilly shook her head. "Not really, except..."

"Yes?" Elizabeth stiffened.

"Well, your brother's not like you, is he?"

"How do you mean?" Elizabeth asked.

"I don't know, exactly. But after I hung up, I wondered if I should have curtsied or something."

After a single telephone conversation, the astute Gilly had her brother pegged. "He's like that," Elizabeth admitted.

"Well, anyway, I gave you the message."

"And I'll show up at the hotel and hope I use the right spoon or my dear brother will be outraged."

For the first time that evening, Gilly smiled.

The café hadn't been open for more than five minutes when Breed strolled in and sat at his regular table. Elizabeth caught sight of his broad shoulders the moment he entered. Even after all these weeks her heart stirred at the sight of him, and now it throbbed painfully. One part of her wanted to rush to him, but she resisted.

Carrying the coffeepot, she approached his table slowly. He turned over the ceramic mug for her.

"Morning," she said as unemotionally as possible.

"Morning," he echoed.

Her eyes refused to meet his, but she could feel his gaze concentrating on her. "Would you like a menu?"

"No, just coffee."

She filled his cup.

"We need to talk," he announced casually as his hands folded around the cup.

She blinked uncertainly. "I can't now," she replied nervously. "Mornings are our busiest time."

"I didn't mean now." The words were enunciated slowly, as if his control over his patience had been stretched to the limit. "Tonight would be better, when we're able to discuss things freely, don't you think?"

She shifted her weight from one foot to the other. "I can't," she murmured apologetically. "My brother's in town, and I'm meeting him for dinner."

His level gaze darted to her, his eyes disbelieving.

"It's true," she declared righteously. "We're meeting at the Saint Francis."

"I believe you."

Frustrated, she watched as a hard mask stole over his face. "Go have dinner with your brother, then."

"I wasn't waiting for your approval," Elizabeth remarked angrily.

His amber eyes blazed for a furious second. "I didn't think you were."

Indecision made her hesitate. She wanted to turn and give him a clear view of her back, yet at the same time she wanted to set things right between them. The harmony they'd shared so often over these past weeks was slowly disintegrating before her eyes.

"Would you care to join us?" The question slipped from her naturally, although her mind was screaming for him to refuse.

"Me?" He looked aghast. "You don't mean that."

"I wouldn't have asked you otherwise." What, she wondered, had she been thinking? The entire evening would be a disaster. She could just imagine Charlie's reaction to someone like Breed.

Breed appeared to give her invitation some consideration. "No," he said at last, and she couldn't prevent the low but controlled breath of relief. "Maybe another time."

"Do you want to meet later?" she asked, and her voice thinned to a quavering note. "Dinner shouldn't take long," she said, glancing down at her practical white shoes. "I want to talk to you, too."

"Not tonight." The lines bracketing his mouth deepened with his growing impatience. Although she'd asked him to join her and Charlie, she realized that he knew she didn't want him there. "I'll give you a call later in the week." He stood, and with determined strides left the café.

She watched him go and had the irrational urge to throw his untouched coffee after him. That arrogant male pride of his only fueled her anger.

That night Elizabeth dressed carefully in a raspberry-colored dress with a delicate white miniprint. A dress that would meet with Charlie's approval, she mused as she examined herself in the mirror. Not until it was time to go did she stop to consider why he was in town. The family had no business holdings on the West Coast. At least none that she knew about. She hoped he hadn't come to persuade her to return to Boston. She'd just about made up her mind to make San Francisco her permanent home. The city was lovely, and the thought of leaving Breed was intolerable. She wouldn't—couldn't—leave the man she loved.

The taxi delivered her to the entrance of the prestigious hotel at precisely seven-twenty. The extra minutes gave her the necessary time to compose herself. She was determined to make this a pleasant evening. A confrontation with her brother was the last thing she wanted.

"Lizzy."

She groaned inwardly. Only one person in the world called her that.

"Hello, Siggy." She forced herself to smile and extended her hand for him to shake. To her acute embarrassment, he pulled her into his arms and kissed her soundly. Her mouth was opened in surprise, and Siggy seemed to assume she was eager for his attention and deepened the kiss.

Without making a scene, Elizabeth was left to endure his despicable touch.

The sound of someone clearing his throat appeared to bring Siggy back to his senses. He broke the contact, and it was all Elizabeth could do not to rub the feel of his mouth from hers with the back of her hand. His touch made her skin crawl, and she glared angrily from him to her brother.

"There are better places for such an intimate greeting," Charlie said, slapping Siggy on the back. "I told you she'd be happy to see you."

Siggy ignored Charlie and said, "It's good to see you, Lizzy."

She was unable to restrain her involuntary grimace. "Don't call me Lizzy," she said between clenched teeth.

Charlie glanced at his slim gold watch. "Our table should be ready. Names are something I'll leave for you two to discuss later."

Later. She cringed at the thought. There wasn't going to be a later with Siggy, though at least now she understood why Charlie had come to San Francisco. He wanted to foist Siggy on her. She hadn't thought about it at the time, but Charlie had mentioned Siggy at every opportunity lately. That was the reason she'd found herself avoiding her brother, who stood to benefit from any marriage between the two families. His selfishness made her want to cry.

By some miracle she was able to endure the meal. She spoke only when a question was directed to her and smiled politely at appropriate intervals. The knot in her throat extended all the way to her abdomen and felt like a rock in the pit of her stomach. The two men discussed her at length, commenting several times on how good she looked. Charlie insisted that she would make a radiant bride and declared that their father would be proud of her, knowing she had chosen so well. He made marriage between her and Siggy sound like a foregone conclusion. Questions buzzed around her head like irritating bees. In the past she'd had her differences with her father, but he wouldn't do this to her. She had to believe that. Yet her father *had* mentioned Siggy during their last few telephone conversations.

Resignedly, she accompanied her brother and Siggy to Charlie's suite for an after-dinner drink.

The small glass of liqueur helped chase the chill from her slender frame. Siggy sat on the plush sofa beside her and draped his arm possessively around her shoulders. She found his touch suffocating and pointedly removed his arm, then scooted to the other end of the sofa. Undaunted, he followed.

"I can see that you two have a lot to discuss," Charlie said, exchanging knowing smiles with the younger man. Without another word, he excused himself and left Elizabeth alone to deal with Siggy. The moment the door clicked closed, Siggy was on her like a starving man after food.

Pinned against the corner of the couch, she jerked her head left and right in an effort to avoid his punishing kiss.

"Siggy!" she gasped, pushing him off her. "Stop it!"

Composing himself, Siggy sat upright and made a pretense of straightening his tie. "I'm sorry, Lizzy. It's just that I love you so much. I've wanted you for years, and now I know you feel the same way."

"What?" she exploded.

Siggy brushed a stray hair from her flushed cheek. "Charlie told me how you've had a crush on me for years. Why didn't you say something? You must have known how I feel about you. I've never made any secret of that."

A lump of outrage and shocked disbelief grew in her. Charlie had selfishly and maliciously lied to Siggy. Her own brother had sold her for thirty pieces of silver. She was nothing more to Charlie than the means of securing a financial coup that would link two wealthy families.

"Where is my brother?" Elizabeth managed finally. "I'd like to talk to him."

"He'll be back," Siggy said, as he stood, crossed the room and helped himself to another glass of brandy. "He wanted to give us some time alone. Want some, darling?" He held up the brandy and eyed her solicitously.

"No." Irritated, she shook her head. "So what would happen to the two companies if our families were linked?"

Smug and secure, Siggy silently toasted her. "A merger. It will be the financial feat of the year, Charlie says. My family will give him the exclusive distribution contract for our stores. Already we're planning to expand within a three-state area."

Momentarily shocked, Elizabeth felt tears form in her eyes. It was little wonder that Charlie was doing this. A lucrative—and exclusive—contract with Siggy's family's chain of department stores was something the Wainwrights had sought for years. But the price was far too high. Her happiness was not a bargaining chip.

Charlie returned a few minutes later, looking pleased and excited.

"If you'll excuse us a minute, Siggy," Elizabeth said bluntly, "I'd like to talk to my brother. Alone."

"Sure." Siggy glanced from brother to sister before setting his drink aside. "I'll be in the lounge when you're finished."

The second the door clicked closed, Elizabeth whirled on her brother. "How could you?" she demanded.

Charlie knotted his fists at his sides. "Listen, little sister, you're not going to ruin this for me. Not this time."

"Charlie, I'm your only sister. How could you ask me to marry a man I don't love? A man I don't even respect..."

His mouth tightened grimly. "For once in your life, stop thinking of yourself."

"Me?"

"Yes, you." He paced the floor in short, angry strides. "All right, I admit I went about this poorly, but marrying Siggy is what Mother would have wanted for you."

"That's not true." Her mother knew her feelings about Siggy and would never have pressured her into something like this.

"What do you know?" He hurled the words at her furiously. "You only thought of yourself. You never knew what Mother was really thinking. It was your selfishness that killed her."

The blood drained from Elizabeth's face. She and her mother had spent the afternoon shopping, and when they got back her mother, who wasn't feeling well, had gone to lie down before dinner. Within an hour she was dead, the victim of a massive stroke. In the back of her mind, she had always carried the guilt that something she had done that day had caused her death.

"Charlie, please," she whispered frantically. "Don't say that. Please don't say that."

"But it's true!" he shouted. "I was with father when the doctor said that having you drag her from store to store was simply too much. It killed her. *You* killed her."

"Oh, dear God." She felt her knees buckle as she slumped onto the sofa.

"There's only one thing you can do now to make up for that, Elizabeth. Do what Mother would have wanted. Marry Siggy. It would have made her happy."

He was lying. In her soul, she knew he was lying. But her own flesh and blood, her only brother, whom she had loved and adored in her youth, had used the cruellest weapon in his arsenal against her. With hot tears scalding her cheeks, she stood, clenched her purse to her breast and walked out the door.

She didn't stop walking until she found a taxi. Between breathless but controlled sobs, she gave the cabbie her address. Not until he pulled away from the curb did she realize how badly she was shaking.

"Are you all right, lady?" The cabbie looked at her anxiously in the rearview mirror.

She couldn't manage anything more than a nod.

When they arrived in front of her apartment, she handed him a twenty-dollar bill and didn't wait for the change. Though she had calmed down slightly on the ride home, she didn't want Gilly to see her, so she hurried in the door and headed for her bedroom.

"You're back soon." The sound of the television drifted from the living room.

"Yes," Elizabeth mumbled, keeping her head lowered, not wanting her friend to see her tears. She continued walking. "I think I'll take a bath and go to bed."

Gilly must have looked up for the first time. The sound of her surprised gasp was like an assault, and Elizabeth flinched. "Elizabeth! Good grief, what's wrong?"

"Nothing." Elizabeth looked at the wall. "I'm fine. I just need to be alone." She went into the bedroom and closed the door, leaning against it. Reaction set in, and she started to shake uncontrollably again. Fresh tears followed. Tears of anger. Tears of hate. Tears of pain and pride.

Softly Gilly knocked on the closed bedroom door, but Elizabeth ignored her. She didn't want to explain. She couldn't, not when she was crying like this. She fell into bed and curled up in a tight ball in an attempt to control the freezing cold that made her shake so violently.

When she inhaled between sobs, she heard Gilly talking to someone. Her friend's voice was slightly high-pitched and worried. She felt guilty that she was worrying Gilly like this, but she couldn't help it. Later she would make up some excuse. But she couldn't now.

Five minutes later there was another knock on her door. Elizabeth ignored it.

"Beth," a male voice said softly. "Open up. It's me."

"Breed," she sobbed, throwing back the covers. "Oh, Breed." She opened the door and fell into his arms, weeping uncontrollably. Every part of her clung to him as he lifted her into his arms and carried her into the living room.

With an infinite gentleness he set her on the couch and brushed the hair from her face.

One look at her and he stiffened. "Who did this to you?"

Seven

Elizabeth was crying so hard that she couldn't answer. Nor did she know how to explain. She didn't want to tell Breed and Gilly that the brother she loved had betrayed her in the worst possible way.

Breed said something to Gilly, but Elizabeth didn't hear. "Beth," he whispered, leading her to the couch and half lifting her onto his lap. "Tell me what's upset you."

Forcefully, she shook her head and inhaled deep breaths that became quivering sobs as she tried to regain control of herself. Crying like this was only making matters worse.

She knew the terrible, crippling pain of Charlie's betrayal was there in her eyes, and she couldn't do anything to conceal it. A nerve twitched in Breed's hard, lean jaw, his features tense, and pain showed clearly in his eyes. *Her* pain. She was suffering, and that caused him to hurt as well. She couldn't have loved anyone more than she loved him right at that moment. She didn't know what he thought had happened, and she couldn't utter a word to assure him.

"I'm fine. No one hurt me…not physically," she finally said in a trembling voice she barely recognized as her own. "Just hold me." She had trouble trying to control her breathing. Her body continued to shake with every inhalation.

"I'll never let you go," he promised as his lips moved against her hair. She felt some of the tension leave him, felt his relief that things weren't as bad as he'd thought.

Warm blankets were wrapped around her, so warm they must have recently been taken from the dryer. That must be what Breed had asked Gilly to do, Elizabeth realized.

He continued to talk to her in a low, soothing tone until her eyes drifted closed. Caught between sleep and reality, she could feel him gently free himself from her embrace and lay her on the sofa. A pillow cushioned her head, and warm blankets surrounded her. She didn't know how long he knelt beside her, smoothing her hair from her face, his touch so tender she felt secure and protected. Gradually a calmness filled her, and she knew she was on the brink of falling asleep. Breed left her side but she sensed that he hadn't gone far. He had told her he wouldn't leave, and she was comforted just by knowing he was in the same room.

"All I know," Elizabeth heard Gilly whisper, "was that she was meeting her brother for dinner. What could he have done to cause this?"

"You can bet I'm going to find out," Breed stated in a dry, hard voice that was frightening in its intensity.

"No." Elizabeth struggled to a sitting position. "Just drop the whole thing. It's my own affair."

Breed's eyes narrowed.

"Elizabeth," Gilly murmured, her eyes wide and worried, "I've never seen you like this."

"I'm fine, really." She brushed back her tear-dampened hair. "I'm just upset. I apologize for making a scene."

"You didn't make a scene," Gilly returned soothingly.

Breed brought her a damp cloth and, kneeling at her side, gently brushed it over her cheeks. It felt cool and soothing over her hot skin. His jaw was clenched and pale, as if he couldn't stand to have her hurt in any way, physically or emotionally.

Elizabeth stroked the side of his face, then pulled him to her, wrapping her arms around his neck. "Thank you."

"For what? I should have been there for you."

"You couldn't have known." It wasn't right that he should shoulder any blame for what had happened.

He took her hands and gently raised them to his mouth, then kissed her knuckles. "Beth…" His eyes implored hers. "I want you to trust me enough to tell me what happened tonight."

She lowered her gaze and shook her head. "It's done. I don't want to go over it."

The pressure on her fingers was punishing for a

quick second. "I'll kill anyone who hurts you like this again."

"That's exactly why I won't talk about it."

The tension between them was so palpable that she could taste it. Their eyes clashed in a test of wills. Unnerved, she lowered hers first. "I need you here," she whispered in a soft plea. "It's over now. I want to forget it ever happened."

Gilly hovered close. "Do you feel like you could drink something? Tea? Coffee? Soda?"

The effort to smile was painful. "All I want is a hot bath and bed." Her muscles ached, and she discovered that when she stood, her legs wobbled unsteadily, so she leaned against Breed for a moment.

Gilly hurried ahead and filled the bathtub with steaming, scented water. Next she brought in fluffy, fresh towels.

"You want me to stay in the bathroom while you soak?" Breed asked, and a crooked smile slanted his mouth, because of course he knew the answer. The humor didn't quite touch his eyes, but Elizabeth appreciated the effort.

"No. If I need anyone, Gilly can help."

"Pity," he grumbled.

The hot water helped relieve the aching tension in her muscles. Even now her body was coiled and alert. The throbbing in her temples diminished, and the pain in her heart began to recede. As she rested against the back of the tub, she kept running over the details of the evening, but she forced the painful images to the back of her mind. She didn't feel strong enough emotionally to deal with things now. Maybe tomorrow.

Gilly stayed with her, more on Breed's insistence than because she felt Elizabeth needed her. Together they emerged from the steam-filled bathroom, Elizabeth wrapped in her thick terry robe. Breed led Elizabeth into her room. The sheets on her bed had been folded back, and her weak smile silently thanked him.

"You won't leave me?" Her eyes pleaded with him as he tucked her under the covers.

"No," he whispered. "I said I wouldn't." His kiss was so tender that fresh tears misted her eyes. "Go to sleep," he whispered encouragingly.

"You'll be here when I wake up?" She needed that reassurance.

"I'll be here."

The dark void was already pulling her into its welcoming arms. As she drifted into sleep, she could hear Breed's low voice quizzing Gilly.

The sound of someone obviously trying to be quiet and not succeeding woke Elizabeth. The room was dark, and she glanced at her clock radio to note that it was just after three. She sat up in bed and blinked. The memory of the events of the evening pressed heavily against her heart. Although she was confident Charlie would never have abandoned her to Siggy if her brother had known what Siggy was capable of doing, the sense of betrayal remained. To try to push her off on Siggy was deplorable enough. Slipping from between the sheets, she put on her silk housecoat and moved into the living room.

"Hello there," she whispered to Breed, keeping quiet so she wouldn't disrupt Gilly's sleep.

"Did I wake you?" He sat up and wiped a hand across his weary face. The sight of him trying to sleep on the couch was ludicrous. His feet dangled far over the end, and he looked all elbows and arms.

"You wake me? Never. I thought an elephant had escaped and was raging through the living room."

His smile was evident in the moonlight. "I got up to use the bathroom and walked into the lamp," he explained with a chagrined look.

"It was selfish of me to ask you to stay," she said, sitting down beside him.

"I would have stayed whether you asked me to or not." He reached for her hand and squeezed it gently. "How do you feel?"

She shrugged and lowered her gaze to her knees. "Like a fool. I don't usually overreact that way."

"I know," he murmured. "That's what concerned me most." He put his arm around her, and she rested her head against his shoulder. "Sometimes the emotional pain can be twice as bad as anything physical." She gave a long, drawn-out yawn. "When you love and trust someone and they hurt you, then the pain goes beyond anything physical." She began explaining the situation to Breed, though carefully tiptoeing around any discussion of her family's wealth. He'd asked her to trust him, and she did, at least with her feelings. It was important that he realize that.

He didn't comment, but she felt him stiffen slightly. When she leaned against his solid support, he pulled her close, holding her to his chest.

Soon the comfort of his arms lured her back to sleep. When she woke again, she discovered that they had both fallen asleep while sitting upright. His arm was still draped around her, and he rested his head against the back of the sofa. His breathing was deep and undisturbed.

Even from a sitting position, waking up in Breed's arms felt right. She pressed her face against the side of his neck and kissed him, enjoying the light taste of salt and musk.

"Are you pretending to be Sleeping Beauty kissing the handsome prince to wake him?" he asked, opening one eye to study her.

She barely allowed his sideways glance to touch her before straightening. "You've got that tale confused. It was the prince who kissed Sleeping Beauty awake."

"Would it hurt you if I did?" The teasing left his voice as he brought her closer within the protective circle of his arms.

Her eyes sought his. "You could never hurt me," she said in a whisper that sounded as solemn as a vow.

"I don't ever want to," he murmured as his lips claimed hers. The kiss was gentle and sweet. His mouth barely touched hers, enhancing the sensuality of the contact. His hands framed her face, and he treated her as if he were handling a rare and exotic orchid.

"You're looking much more chipper this morning," Gilly said, standing in the doorway of her bedroom. She raised her hands high above her head and yawned.

"I feel a whole lot better."

"I'm happy to hear that. I don't mind telling you that you had me worried."

"You?" Breed inhaled harshly. "I don't think I've ever come closer to wanting to kill a man. It's a good thing you didn't tell who did this last night, Beth. I wouldn't have been responsible for my actions."

Elizabeth lowered her gaze to the hands folded primly in her lap. "I think I already knew that."

"Take the day off," Gilly insisted as she sauntered into the kitchen and started the coffee.

"I can't do that," Elizabeth objected strenuously. "You need me."

"I'll make do," Gilly returned confidently. She opened the refrigerator, took out a pitcher of orange juice and poured herself a small glass. "But only for today."

Elizabeth returned to her bedroom to change clothes. When she studied herself in the mirror she saw no outward mark of what she'd been through, but the mirror couldn't reveal the inner agony of what Charlie had tried to do.

"I don't believe it," she grumbled as she walked into the living room. "Last night I wanted to die, and today

I feel like the luckiest woman alive to have you two as my friends."

"We're the lucky ones," Gilly said sincerely.

"But I acted like such a fool. I can't imagine what you thought."

"You were shocked, upset," Breed insisted with a note of confidence. "Shock often exaggerates the messages transmitted to the brain."

"Such a know-it-all," Gilly complained, running a brush through her short, bouncy curls. She looked at Elizabeth with a mischievous gleam. "Why do you put up with him?"

Elizabeth shrugged and shook her head. "I don't know. But he's kinda cute."

"I amuse you, is that it?" Breed joined in the teasing banter.

"You're amusing, but not always correct," Elizabeth remarked jokingly. "My brain wasn't confused by shock. But I'll admit, you had me going there for a minute."

He had the grace to look faintly embarrassed. "Well, it sounded good at the time."

Gilly paused on her way out the door. "Have a good day, you two. Call if you need anything. And—" she hesitated and lowered her gaze "—don't hold up dinner for me."

"Working late?" Elizabeth quizzed, experiencing a twinge of guilt that her friend would be stuck at the café alone.

Gilly shook her head. "Peter said he'd be coming by, and I don't want to be here when he does."

"Honestly, Gilly, you're acting like a child."

"Maybe." Gilly admitted. "But at least I've got my pride."

Breed murmured something about pride doing little to keep her warm at night, but luckily Gilly was too far away to hear him.

The door clicked, indicating Gilly had left for work.

"Are you hungry?" Breed asked as he walked across the living room, his hands buried deep inside his pants pockets.

She hadn't eaten much of her dinner the previous night, but even so, she discovered she didn't have much of an appetite. "Not really."

"What you need is something scintillating to tempt you."

Wickedly batting her eyelashes, she glanced at him and softly said, "My dear Mr. Breed, what exactly do you have in mind?"

He chose to ignore the comment.

"I think I'll go over to my place to shower and change. When I come back, I'll bring us breakfast."

Her mouth dropped in mute surprise. She couldn't believe he hadn't risen to her bait, and, selfishly, she didn't want him to leave her alone. Not now. "I'll come with you," she suggested eagerly. "And while you're in the shower, I'll cook us breakfast."

His expression revealed his lack of enthusiasm for her suggestion. "Not this time."

She bristled. "Why not?" The memory of her last visit to his apartment remained vivid. She hadn't been imagining things. He really didn't want her there. And yet she couldn't imagine why.

"You need to stay here and rest."

Her eyes widened in bewildered protest.

"I was thinking that while I'm gone you can get an extra hour's sleep."

Sleep? She was dressed and had downed a cup of strong coffee. He didn't honestly expect her to go back to bed, did he?

"I won't be long," he told her, and without a backward glance he hurried out the door.

"Don't worry about breakfast. I'll have something ready when you come back," she called after him. She didn't like this situation, but there wasn't much she could do. The impulse to speak her mind died on her lips. Now wasn't the time to confront Breed with petty suspicions about her cool welcome at his apartment.

With a cookbook resting on the kitchen counter, she skimmed over the recipe for blueberry muffins. For the moment, keeping busy was paramount. When she stopped to think, too many dark images crowded her thoughts. For a time last night she had started to believe Charlie's vindictive words, which fed on the fear that she was somehow responsible for her mother's death, which had haunted her ever since that awful day. When a tear escaped, despite her determination not to cry, she wiped it aside angrily and forced herself to concentrate on the recipe. Rehashing the details of last night only upset her, so she soundly rejected any more introspection on the subject.

As promised, Breed returned less than an hour later.

A hand on each of her shoulders, he kissed her lightly on the cheek. He looked wonderful, his hair still wet from his shower.

"Hmm...something smells good."

"I baked some muffins," she said as she led the way into the kitchen. Her culinary efforts were cooling on a rack on top of the counter. "I don't know how they taste. The cookbook said they were great to take camping."

"Are you thinking of taking me into the woods and ravaging my body?" he joked as he lifted a muffin from the cooling rack. It burned his fingers, and he gingerly tossed it in the air several times until, laughing, she handed him a plate.

"You might have told me they were still hot."

"And miss seeing you juggle? Never." Her mood had lightened to match his. Sitting beside him at the circular table, she peeled an orange and popped a section into her mouth.

"How about a trip to our beach today?" he suggested, and his mouth curved into a sensuous smile.

"Sure." Her glance caught sight of his massive hands. A slight swelling in one of the knuckles captured her attention. Had he been fighting? Showering wouldn't have taken him an hour. Immediately the thought flashed through her mind that he'd gone to see her brother. "Breed..." Her eyes sought his as she swallowed past the thickness lodged in her throat. "Give me your hand."

The teasing glitter didn't leave his eyes, and he didn't seem to notice the serious light in hers. "Is this a proposal of marriage?"

"Let me see your hand," she repeated.

He went completely still. "Why?"

"Because I need to know that you didn't do anything…dumb."

He smiled briefly and pushed his chair away from the table, then stood and walked to the other side of the room, folding his arms across his massive chest. Expelling an explosive breath, he replied, "I didn't, although the temptation was strong. While I live, no man will ever treat you that way again."

"I appreciate the chivalry," she said evenly, "but I wish you hadn't."

"I found it…necessary." The hard set of his features revealed the tight hold he was keeping on both his temper and his emotions.

Her composure cracked. "I'm not defending him…."

"I should hope not." He shook his head grimly.

"But I don't want you involved," she said.

"I'm already involved."

She stood and, with her own arms folded around her narrow waist, paced the kitchen. The room was filled with Breed. His presence loomed in every corner. "Please understand, I don't want to argue with you."

His eyes narrowed as he moved into the other room and sat on the arm of the sofa. "I've never met anyone like you, Beth. Those two deserve to have the stuffing kicked out of them."

"He's my brother!" she cried defensively. "He may not be a very nice guy, but he's the only one I've got."

He moved into the living room, his back to her. When he turned to face her again a moment later, his grim look had vanished. "Are we going to the beach or not?"

Numbly, she nodded.

"Good." With long strides he crossed the distance separating them. Then he took her by the shoulders and sweetly kissed her. "Let's hurry. It's isn't every day that I get you all to myself."

They rode in his silver sedan, and again she wondered why he no longer drove Hilda. Maybe the Jeep needed repairs and he couldn't afford to have them done until his finances improved. She wished there was some way she could take care of things like that for him without his knowing. Offering him money wasn't the answer, only a sure way of crushing his male ego. Even so, what was the use of having money if she couldn't spend it the way she wanted?

The surf rolled gently against their bare feet as they strolled along the smooth beach, their arms entwined.

"Tell my about your childhood," he asked curiously after a lengthy, companionable silence.

Under other circumstances she might have had the courage to reveal her wealth. But not today. She'd faced enough upheaval in the last twenty-four hours to warrant caution. Her mouth tightened with tension before she managed to speak.

"What's there to tell? I was born, grew up, went to

school, graduated, went to school some more, dropped out, and traveled a little."

"Nicely condensed, I'd say."

"Have you been to Europe?" she asked, to change the subject.

"No, but I spent six months in New Zealand a few years back." His response told her he knew exactly what she was doing.

"Did you enjoy it?" Relieved, she continued the game.

"I'd say it was the most beautiful country on earth, but I haven't done enough traveling to compare it with the rest of the world."

She recalled her own trip to the South Pacific. Her time in New Zealand had been short, but she'd shared his feelings about the island nation.

"My mother used to love to travel," she commented, mentally recalling the many trips they'd taken together.

"How long has she been gone?" he asked, his hand reaching for hers.

She swallowed with difficulty and forced her chin up in a defensive stance. "She died two years ago," she explained softly. "Even after all this time, I miss her."

He paused, and traced a finger over her jaw and down her neck. "I'm sorry, Beth. You must have loved her very much."

"I did," she whispered on a weak note.

"Did your family ever go camping?" The question came out of the blue and was obviously meant to change the mood.

"No." She had never slept in a tent in her life. Back-to-nature pursuits had never been among her father's interests.

"Would you like to sometime?"

"Us?"

"I was thinking of inviting Gilly along." Gently, his hand closed over hers. "And Peter," he added as an afterthought.

"Peter? You devious little devil."

"Of course, that will take some finagling," he admitted.

"Finagling or downright deception?"

"Deception," he immediately agreed.

"You shock me, Andrew Breed. I wouldn't have guessed that you had a sneaky bone in your body."

His gaze slid past her to the rolling waves that broke against the sand. "I suspect a lot of things about me would shock you," he murmured, and her thoughts echoed his.

"What really irritates me," Gilly continued her tirade as she hauled another box of cooking utensils out from the kitchen, "is the fact that I bare my heart to Peter and then he—he just disappears. It's been three days since I've heard from him. Count 'em, Beth, three long days."

"Well, you slammed the door in his face last time he came over, and you hang up on him whenever he calls."

"Well, he deserves it."

Hands on hips, Gilly surveyed the living-room floor. Half of the contents of their kitchen had been packed into cardboard boxes in anticipation of the weekend camping trip. "Is that everything?"

"Well, I certainly hope so." Elizabeth couldn't believe that people actually went through all this work just for a couple of days of traipsing around the woods.

When Breed arrived he looked incredulously at the accumulated gear.

"Before you complain, I only packed what was on your list," Elizabeth said as she flashed him an eager smile. She was ready for this new adventure, although she was suffering a few qualms about not telling Gilly that Peter had been invited. In fact, he had left the night before and claimed a space for them in the Samuel P. Taylor State Park, north of the city.

"Well, maybe we packed a few things not on your meager list," Gilly amended. "You left off several things we might need."

"I don't know how Hilda's going to carry all this," Breed mumbled under his breath.

"Hilda," Elizabeth cried happily. "We're taking Hilda?" Before Breed could stop her, she rushed down the stairs to the outdated Jeep parked at the curb. Gingerly she climbed into the front seat and patted the dashboard. "It's good to see you again," she murmured affectionately.

"Will someone kindly tell me what's going on?" Gilly stood, one hand placed on her hip, staring curiously at her friend.

"It's a long story," Breed murmured, lifting the first box on board.

Admittedly it was a tight squeeze, but they managed to fit everything.

The radio blared, and they were all singing along as they traveled. When the news came on, they paused to listen. From her squashed position in the backseat, Gilly leaned forward. "Hey, Breed, I don't see any tent back here."

"There isn't one," he said with a smile, glancing at Elizabeth.

"I thought we were going camping?"

"We are," he confirmed.

"With no tent?"

Elizabeth didn't want to carry the deception any further. "Peter pitched the tent yesterday."

"Peter!" Gilly exploded. "You didn't say anything about Peter coming on this trip."

Elizabeth turned and faced her friend. "Are you mad?"

Gilly's gaze raked Elizabeth's worried face. Folding her arms, she resolutely stared out the window. "Why should I be mad? My best friend in the world has just turned traitor."

"If I'm your best friend, then you have to believe I wouldn't do anything to hurt you," Elizabeth returned with quiet logic.

"I'm not answering that."

"Because I'm right," Elizabeth argued irrefutably.

"Peter loves you," Breed inserted, matching Gilly's clipped tones. "And if it means kidnapping you so that he has the chance to explain himself, then I don't consider that much of a crime."

"I suppose you think that someday I'll thank you for this."

"I want to be maid of honor," Elizabeth said with a romantic sigh.

Gilly ignored her and sat in stony silence until Breed turned off the highway and entered the campgrounds. Peter had left word of his location at the ranger station, and within a matter of minutes they were at the campsite.

"I hope you realize that I don't appreciate this one bit," Gilly said through clenched teeth.

"I believe we got the picture." Breed's mouth curved in a humorous smile.

"Really, Gilly, it won't be so bad. All we want is for you to give the poor guy a chance."

Gilly ignored her friend and turned her attention to Breed. "Did you know Beth once called you Tarzan?" she informed him saucily.

"Tarzan?" Breed's large eyes rounded indignantly, and he turned to Elizabeth with a feigned look of outrage. "Beth, you didn't."

She forced herself to smile and nodded regretfully.

"In that case, will you be my Jane?"

"Love to," she returned happily, placing her hand in his.

Peter had the tent pitched and a small fire going when they arrived. Breed and Elizabeth climbed out of the front seat and stretched. Gilly remained inside, her arms folded as she stared defiantly ahead.

"Hi, Gilly," Peter said as he strolled up to the Jeep, his hands buried in his pockets.

Silence.

Peter continued, "I've always been one to lay my cards on the table, so you're going to listen to me. There's no place to run now."

More silence.

He went on, "You once told me that you loved me, but I'm beginning to have my doubts about that." He levered himself so that he was in the driver's seat and turned to face her. "I was so shocked at your announcement that I must have said and done the worst possible things." He hesitated slightly. "The thing was, I had no idea how you felt."

"Your reaction told me that." Gilly spoke for the first time, her words tight and low.

"You see, I'd realized earlier how much you'd come to mean to me. I'd been trying to work up enough nerve to tell you my feelings had changed."

"Don't you dare lie to me, Peter."

"I'm not," he returned harshly. "For too long I've had doors shut in my face, phones slammed in my ear. I've about had it, Gillian Haggith. I want you to marry me, and I want your answer right now."

Feeling like an intruder, Elizabeth leaned against the picnic table with Breed at her side. Fascinated, she watched as Gilly's mouth opened and closed incredulously. For the first time in recent history, her friend was utterly speechless.

"Maybe this will help you decide," Peter mumbled, withdrawing a small diamond ring from his jeans pocket.

"Oh, Peter!" Gilly cried, and she threw her arms around him as she burst into happy tears.

Eight

"Shall we give the lovebirds some time alone?" Breed whispered in Elizabeth's ear.

Her nod was indulgent. "How about giving me a grand tour of the grounds."

"Love to."

"I'm especially interested in the modern technological advances."

His thoughtful gaze swept over her face. "Beth, we're in the woods. There are no technological wonders out here."

"I was thinking of things that go flush in the night."

"Ahh, those." The corners of his mouth twitched briefly upward. "Allow me to lead the way."

He set a comfortable pace as they wandered around the campgrounds, taking their time. The sky couldn't have been any bluer, and the air was filled with the scent of pine and evergreen. A creek bubbled cheerfully down its meandering course, and they paused for a few quiet moments of peaceful introspection. Elizabeth's thoughts drifted to her father. Their showcase home in Boston, with all its splendor, couldn't compare to the tranquil beauty of this forest. If he could see this place, she was confident, he would experience the serenity that had touched her in so brief a time.

Gilly had lunch cooking by the time Breed and Elizabeth returned. The two of them smiled conspiratorially, having agreed to pretend ignorance of the conversation they'd overheard earlier. With an efficiency Elizabeth hardly recognized in her friend, Gilly set out the paper plates, a pan of hot beans, freshly made potato salad, and grilled hot dogs with toasted buns.

"I'll do the dishes," Elizabeth joked as she filled her paper plate. Gilly sat beside Elizabeth at the picnic table.

"I'm sorry about what I said earlier," Gilly murmured as telltale color crept up her neck. "It was childish and immature of me to tell Breed that you once referred to him as Tarzan." She released her breath with a thin edge of exasperation. "Actually, it was probably the stupidest thing I've ever done in my entire life. How petty can I get?"

"You had a right to be angry." Even so, Elizabeth appreciated her friend's apology. "Not telling you that Peter was coming here was underhanded and conniving."

Breed lifted his index finger. "And my idea. I take credit."

Elizabeth's eyes captured his, and her gaze wavered slightly under his potent spell. "But if it had backfired, the blame would have been mine. I'm learning a lot about the workings of the male mind."

"Do you have to sit across the table from me, woman?" Peter complained as he settled next to Breed.

"I'll be sitting next to you for the rest of my life," Gilly returned with a happy note. "Besides, at this angle you can feast upon my unspoiled beauty."

The diamond ring on her finger sparkled almost as brightly as the happiness in her eyes. Things couldn't have worked out better. Elizabeth realized how miserable her friend had been the last few days and felt oddly guilty that she had been so involved in her own problems.

"Do you two have an announcement to make?" Breed asked as he stared pointedly at Gilly's left hand.

"Gilly and I are getting married," Peter informed them cheerfully.

"We haven't set a date yet," Gilly inserted. "Peter thought we should talk to my parents first. And my church has a counseling class for engaged couples. I thought we should take it. Plus, knowing my mother, she'll want a big wedding, which will take a while to plan. So the earliest we could set the date would be autumn. Maybe early November."

"I was hoping for a quiet wedding on the beach just before dawn with our parents and close friends. Preferably next month sometime," Peter said.

"Next month?" Gilly choked. "We can't do that. My mother would never forgive me."

"I thought it was me you were marrying, not your mother," grumbled Peter.

Setting the palms of her hands on the tabletop, Gilly half rose from her seat and glared jokingly at Peter. "Are you trying to pick a fight already?" she asked with a saucy grin.

"It's my wedding, too," Peter challenged. "I think, in the interest of fairness to your future husband, you should consider my ideas."

Gilly mumbled something under her breath, and reached for the potato salad.

Holding back a smile, Elizabeth glanced at Breed, who seemed to be enjoying the moment. She felt as if she could read his thoughts, and she agreed. Gilly and Peter fought much more now that they were in love.

They finished their meal, then got serious about setting up camp.

"I'll unload Hilda," Breed said as he stood.

"I'll help," Peter offered, pointing to Gilly. "The wedding will be next month, on the beach at sunrise."

"Thanks for the invitation, big shot. I hope I can make it."

"I'm doing the dishes," Elizabeth reminded them, and she hurriedly swallowed the last bite of her meal. Everyone was suddenly busy, and she didn't want to sit idle.

The paper plates were easily disposed of in a garbage container. She placed the potato salad and other leftovers in the cooler. The only items left were the plastic forks and a single saucepan.

With a dish towel draped around her neck, and the plasticware, liquid soap and rag dumped inside the saucepan, she headed toward the creek she'd discovered with Breed.

"Hey, where are you going?" Gilly called out as Elizabeth left.

"To wash these." She held up the pan. "I'll be right back. Breed said something about taking a hike."

Gilly's smile was crooked. "Yes, but I think he was referring to me and Peter. If we don't quit fighting, I have the feeling we may have to walk home."

Elizabeth located the stream without a problem and knelt on the soft earth beside the water, humming as she rubbed the rag along the inside of the aluminum pan. A flash of color caught her attention, and she glanced upward. A deer was poised in a meadow on the other side of the water. Mesmerized, she watched the wild creature with a powerful sense of awe and appreciation.

Slowly, she straightened, afraid her movements would frighten off the lovely animal. But the doe merely raised its regal head, and she stared into its beautiful dark eyes. The animal didn't appear to be frightened by her presence.

Wondering how close she could get, she crossed the burbling water, stepping carefully from one stone to another. When she reached the other side, the doe was gone. Disappointed, she walked to the spot where the animal had been standing and saw that it had gone farther into the forest, and now was barely visible. She decided to follow it, thinking she might be able to catch a glimpse of a fawn. She wished she'd thought to bring her camera. But she hadn't expected to see anything like this.

Keeping a safe distance, she followed the deer, rather proud of her ability to track it. She realized that the animal wasn't trying to escape or she wouldn't have had a chance of following it this far.

The lovely creature paused, and she took the opportunity to rest on a felled tree while keeping an eye on the deer. A glance at her watch told her that she'd been away from camp almost an hour. She didn't want to worry anyone, so even though the chase was fun, she felt forced to abandon it. With bittersweet regret, she stood and gave a waving salute to her beautiful friend.

An hour later, she owned up to the fact that she was lost. The taste of panic filled her mouth, and she took several deep breaths to calm herself.

"Help!" she screamed, as loudly as she could. Her voice echoed through the otherwise silent forest. "I'm here!" she cried out, a frantic edge to her words. Hurrying now, she half ran through the thick woods until she stumbled and caught herself against a bush. A thorny limb caught on the flesh of her upper arm and lightly gouged her skin.

Elizabeth yelped with pain and grabbed at her wound. When her fingers came away sticky with blood, a sickening sensation attacked her stomach.

"Calm down," she told herself out loud, thinking the sound of her own voice would have a soothing effect. It didn't, and she paused again to force herself to breathe evenly.

"Breed, oh, Breed," she whispered as she moved through the dense cover, holding her arm. "Please find me. Please, please find me."

Her legs felt weak, and her lungs burned with the effort to push on. Every step cost her more than the previous one.

She tried to force the terror from her mind and concentrate on happy thoughts. The memory of her mother's laughter took the edge of exertion from her steps. The long walks with Breed along the beach. She recalled their first argument and how she'd insisted that she could find the way back. Without him, she would have been lost then, too. His words from that night echoed in her tired mind. *If you ever get lost, promise me you'll stay in one place.* She stumbled to an abrupt halt and looked around her. Nothing was familiar. She could be going in the opposite direction from the campground for all she knew. She was dreadfully tired and growing weaker every minute, the level of her remaining endurance dropping with each step.

If she was going to stop, she decided, she would find a place where she could sit and rest. She found a patch of moss that grew beside a tree and lowered herself to a sitting position. Her breath was uneven and ragged, but she suspected it was more from fear than anything.

Someone would find her soon, she told herself. Soon. The word repeated in her mind a thousand times, offering hope.

Every minute seemed an hour and every hour a month as she sat and waited. When the sun began to set, she realized she would probably be spending the night in the woods. The thought couldn't frighten her any more than she was already. At least not until darkness settled over the forest.

Not once did she doze or even try to sleep, afraid she would miss a light or the sound of a voice. Tears filled her eyes at the darkest part of the night that preceded dawn and she realized she could die out here. At least, she was convinced, her mother was waiting for her on the other side of life.

Of course, she had regrets—lots of them. Things she had wanted to do in her lifetime. But her biggest regret was that she had never told Breed how much she loved him.

She stood up gratefully when the sun came over the horizon, its golden rays bathing the earth with its warmth. She was so cold. For a time she had been convinced she would freeze. Her teeth had chattered, and she'd huddled into a tight ball, believing this night would be her last.

Her stomach growled, and her tongue had grown thick with the need for water. For a long time she debated whether she should strike out again and look for something to drink or stay where she was. Every muscle protested when she decided to search out water, and she quickly sat back down, amazed at how weak she had become.

She tried to call out, but her voice refused to cooperate, and even the attempt to shout took more energy than she could muster.

With her eyes closed, her back supported by the tree trunk, she strained her ears for the slightest sound. The day before, while walking with Breed, she had thought the woods were quiet and serene. Now she was astonished at the cacophony that surrounded her. The loud squawk of birds and the rustle of branches in the breeze filled the forest. And then there were the other noises she couldn't identify.

"Beth." Her name echoed from faraway, barely audible.

With a reserve of energy she hadn't known she possessed, Elizabeth leaped to her feet and screamed back. "Here…I'm here!" Certain they would never hear her, she ran frantically toward the sound of the voice, crying as she pushed branches out of her way. They would search in another area if she couldn't make herself heard. She couldn't bear it if she had come so close to being found only to be left behind.

"Here!" she cried again and again, until her voice was hardly more than a whisper.

Breed saw her before she saw him. "Thank God," he said, and the sound of it reached her. She turned and saw the torment leave his face as he covered the distance between them with giant strides.

Fiercely, she was hauled into his arms as he buried his face in her neck. A shudder ran through him as she wrapped her arms around him and started to weep with relief. Huge tears of happiness rolled down her face, making wet tracks in the dust that had settled on her cheeks. She was so relieved that she didn't notice the other men with Breed until he released her.

Some of the previous agony returned to Breed's eyes as he ran his finger down the dried blood that had crusted on her upper arm.

A forest ranger handed her a canteen of water and told her to take small sips. Another man spoke into a walkie-talkie, advising the members of the search party that she had been found and was safe.

The trip back to camp was hazy in Elizabeth's memory. Questions came at her from every direction. She answered them as best she could and apologized profusely for all the trouble she had caused.

The only thing that stood out in her mind was how far she had wandered. It seemed hours before they reached the campground. Breed took over at that point, taking her in his arms and carrying her into the tent.

The next thing she knew, she was awake and darkness surrounded her. She sat up and glanced around. Gilly lay sleeping on one side of her, Breed on the other. Peter was beside Gilly.

Breed's eyes opened, and he sat up with her. "How do you feel?" he whispered.

"A whole lot better. Is there anything to eat? I'm starved."

He took her hand and helped her out of the sleeping bag. Sitting her at the picnic table, he rummaged around and returned with a plate heaped with food.

He took a seat across the table from her—to gaze

upon her unspoiled beauty, he told her, laughing. A lantern that hung from a tree dimly lit the area surrounding the tent and table. His features were bloodless, so pale that she felt a surge of guilt at her thoughtlessness.

She set her fork aside. "Breed, I'm so sorry. Can you forgive me?"

He wiped a hand across his face and didn't answer immediately. "I've never been so happy to see freckles in my life."

"You look terrible."

He answered her with a weak smile. "You're a brave woman, Beth. A lot of people would have panicked."

"Don't think I didn't," she told him with a shaky laugh. "There were a few hours there last night when I was sure that I'd die in those woods." She glanced lovingly at him. "The craziest part of it was that I kept thinking of all the things I regret not having done in my life."

"I suppose that's only natural."

"Do you want to know what I regretted the most?"

"What?" he asked with a tired sigh, supporting his forehead with the palms of his hands, not looking at her.

"I kept thinking how sorry I was that I'd never told you how much I love you."

Slowly, Breed raised his gaze to hers. The look in his tired amber eyes became brilliant as he studied her.

"Well, say something," she pleaded, rubbing a hand across her forehead. "I probably would have told you long ago except that I was afraid the same thing would happen to me as happened to Gilly." She paused and inhaled a deep, wobbly breath. "I know you love me in your own way, but I—"

"In my own way?" Breed returned harshly. "I love you so much that if we hadn't found you in those woods I would have stayed out there until I died, looking for you." He got up from the picnic table and walked around to her. "You asked me if I can forgive you. The answer is yes. But I don't think my heart has recovered yet. We're bound to have one crazy married life together, I can tell you that. I don't think I can take many more of your adventures."

"Married life...?" she repeated achingly.

Breed didn't answer her with words, only hauled her into his arms and held on to her as if he couldn't bear to let her go.

"If this is a dream, don't wake me," she said.

"My love is no fantasy. This is reality."

"Oh, Breed," she whispered as tears of happiness clouded her eyes. She slipped her arms around his neck and pressed her face into his strong, muscular chest.

"Are we going to argue like Peter and Gilly? Or can we have a quiet ceremony with family and a few friends?"

She brushed his lips with a feather-light kiss. "Anything you say."

"Aren't you agreeable!"

She curled tighter in his embrace. "Just promise to love me no matter what." She was thinking of what his reaction would be to her family's wealth and social position. He had a right to know, but telling him now would ruin the magic of the moment. As for not having said anything in the past, she was pleased that she hadn't. Breed loved her for herself. Money and all that it could buy hadn't influenced his feelings. Maybe she was anticipating trouble for no reason.

His smile broadened. The radiant light in his amber eyes kindled a soft glow of happiness in her. His fingers explored her neck and shoulders, holding her so close that for a moment it was impossible to breathe normally. When he moved to kiss her, she slid her hands over his muscular chest and linked them behind his neck. He allowed her only small gasps of air before a new shiver of excitement stole her breath completely.

Her parted lips were trembling and swollen from Breed's plundering kisses when he finally groaned, pulled himself away and sat up straight. "I think the sooner we arrange the wedding, the better." He sighed. "I'd prefer a tent built for two." He ran a hand over his eyes. "And this may be old-fashioned, but I'd like to be married when we start our family."

Elizabeth knew the music in her heart would never fade. Not with this man. He didn't sound old-fashioned to her but refreshingly wonderful.

"I'm so glad you want children." Her voice throbbed with the beat of her heart.

"A houseful, at least." His husky voice betrayed the tight rein he held on his needs. "But for now I'd be content to start with a wedding ring."

"Soon," she promised.

"Tomorrow we'll go down and get the license."

"Tomorrow?" The immediacy frightened her. She wanted to get married, but she couldn't see the necessity of rushing into it quite *that* quickly.

"Maybe we should pack up and drive to Reno and get married immediately."

"No." Elizabeth didn't know why she felt so strongly about that. "I want to stand before God to make my vows, not the Last Chance Hitching Post."

She could see Breed's smile. "You're sure you want to marry me?" he said.

In response, she leaned over and teased him with her lips. "You'll never need to doubt my love," she said, and playfully nipped at his earlobe.

"Who would have believed you'd get lost in the woods?" Gilly commented late the next night as they unpacked the camping gear in the apartment kitchen.

"Who would have believed we'd both become engaged in one weekend?"

"Elizabeth, I can't tell you how frantic we all were," Gilly said tightly. "Breed was like a man possessed. When you didn't come back, he went to find you. When he didn't return, Peter and I went to look for you both."

Color heated Elizabeth's face. "I was so stupid." Her inexperience had ruined their trip. After a good night's sleep, they'd packed up and headed straight back to San Francisco.

"Don't be so hard on yourself. This was your first time camping. You didn't know."

"But I feel so terrible for being such an idiot."

Gilly straightened and brushed the hair off her forehead. "Thank God you're safe," she said, staring into the distance. "I don't know what would have happened to Breed if we hadn't found you. Beth, he was like a madman. I don't think there was anyone who didn't realize that Breed would have died in the attempt to find you."

Leaning against the counter, Elizabeth expelled a painful sigh. "On the bright side of things, getting lost has done a lot for Breed and me. I wonder how long it would have been otherwise before we admitted how we felt."

"It's taken too long as it is. I knew almost from the beginning that you two were meant for each other."

Elizabeth attempted to disguise a smile. "We don't all have your insight, I guess."

Gilly seemed unaware of the teasing glint in her roommate's eye. "Peter's coming to get me in a few minutes. We're going to go talk to my parents. Will you be safe all by yourself, or should I phone Breed?"

"He's coming over in a while. I'm cooking dinner."

Breed arrived five minutes after Gilly left with Peter. He kissed her lightly on the cheek. "How do you feel?"

"Hungry," she said with a warm smile. "Let's get this show on the road."

"I thought you were cooking me dinner."

"I am. But we left the food in Hilda, which means it's at your place. If I'm going to share my life with you, then the least you can do is introduce me to your kitchen."

That uneasy look came over his features again. "We could go out just as well."

"Breed," Elizabeth intoned dramatically, "how many times do we have to argue about this apartment of yours? It's so obvious you don't want me there."

His mouth tightened grimly. "Let's go. I don't want another argument."

"Well, that's encouraging."

The brisk walk took them about fifteen minutes. His apartment was exactly as she remembered it. No pictures or knickknacks that marked the place as his. That continued to confuse her, but she couldn't believe that he would hide anything from her.

There wasn't much to work with left from their trip, and his cupboards were bare, but she assumed this was because he ate most of his meals out.

"Spaghetti's my specialty," she told him as she tied a towel around her waist.

"That sounds good."

He hovered at her elbow as she sautéed the meat and stood at her side while she chopped the vegetables. He shadowed her every action, and when she couldn't tolerate his brand of "togetherness" another second, she turned and ushered him into the living room.

"Read the paper or something, will you? You're driving me crazy."

His eyes showed his indecision. He glanced back into the kitchen, then nodded as he reached for the newspaper.

Singing softly as she worked, Elizabeth mentally

reviewed her cooking lessons from school. The sauce was simmering and the pasta was boiling. She decided to set the table. A few loose papers and mail littered the countertop. Humming cheerfully, she moved them to his desk on the far side of the kitchen. The top of the desk was cluttered with more papers. As she set down his mail, she noticed a legal-looking piece of paper. She continued to hum as idly she glanced at it and realized it was a gun permit. *Breed carried a gun.* A chill shot up her spine. The song died on her lips. Breed and firearms seemed as incongruous as mixing oil and water. She would ask him about it later.

"Anything I can do?" he volunteered, seeming to have relaxed now.

"Open the wine."

"Wine?"

"You mean you don't have any?" she asked as she stirred the pasta. "The flavors in my sauce will be incomplete without the complement of wine."

"I take it you want me to buy us a bottle."

"You got it."

"Okay, let's go." He stood and tucked in his shirttails.

"Me? I can't go now. I've got to drain the pasta and finish setting the table."

He hesitated.

"Honestly, Breed, there's a grocery just down the street. You don't need me to hold your hand."

He didn't look pleased about it, but he turned and walked out.

The minute the door was closed, Elizabeth returned

to his desk. She knew she was snooping, but the gun permit puzzled her, and she wanted to look it over. The permit listed a different address, confirming her suspicions that he hadn't been in this apartment long. The paper felt like it was burning her fingers, and she set it aside, hating the way her curiosity had gotten in the way of her better judgment.

She could ask him, of course, but she felt uneasy about that. Where would he keep a lethal weapon in this bare place? She wondered about the kind of gun he carried. With her index finger she pulled out the top desk drawer. It wasn't in sight, but a notebook with her full name written across the top caught her gaze. Fascinated, she pulled it from the drawer and flipped it open. Page after page of meticulous notes detailed her comings and goings, her habits and her friends. *Breed had been following her since she arrived!* But whatever for? This was bizarre.

Coiled tightness gripped her throat as she pulled open another drawer. Hurt and anger and a thousand terrifying emotions she had never thought to experience with regard to Breed filled her senses. The drawer was filled with correspondence with her father. Andrew Breed had been hired by her family as her bodyguard.

Nine

Elizabeth backed away from the drawer. Her hand was pressed against her breast as the blood drained from her face. Her heart was pounding wildly in her ears, and for several seconds she was unable to breathe. So many inconsistencies about Breed fell into place. She was amazed that she could have been so blind, so utterly stupid. His cover had been perfect. Dating her had simplified his job immeasurably.

Her stomach rolled, and she knew she was going to be sick. She closed the drawer and staggered into the bathroom. It was there that Breed found her.

"Beth." His voice was filled with concern. "You look terrible."

She didn't meet his eyes. "I'm…I'm all right. I just need a moment."

He placed his arm across her back, and the touch, although light, seemed to burn through the material of her shirt, branding her. Leading her into the living room, he sat her down on the sofa and brought in a cool rag.

"I was afraid something like this might happen," he murmured solicitously. "You're probably having a delayed reaction to the trauma of this weekend."

She closed her eyes and nodded, still unable to look at him. "I want to go home." Somehow the words managed to slip past the stranglehold she felt around her throat.

Not until they were ready to leave did she glance out Breed's window and realize that, thanks to the city's hills, her apartment could be seen from his. No wonder he was able to document her whereabouts so accurately. Mr. Andrew Breed was a clever man, deceptive and more devious than she could have dreamed. And he excelled at his job. She didn't try to fool herself. She was a job to him and little or nothing more than that.

It was no small wonder he'd suggested they go to Reno and get married right away. He wanted the deed accomplished before they confronted her father. He knew what her family would say if she were to marry a bodyguard. Her emotions when her purse had been taken had been a small-scale version of what she felt now. A part of her inner self had been violated. But the pain went far deeper. Deep enough to sear her soul. She doubted that she would ever be the same again.

Concerned, Breed helped her on with her sweater and gripped her elbow. Several times during the short drive to her apartment he glanced her way, a worried look marring his handsome face. After he had unlocked her apartment and helped her into her room, she changed clothes, took a sleeping pill and climbed into bed. But the pill didn't work. She lay awake with a lump the size of a grapefruit blocking her throat. Every swallow hurt. Crying might have helped, but no tears would come.

She didn't know how long she lay staring at the shadows on the ceiling. The front door clicked open, and she heard Breed whisper to Gilly. She was mildly surprised that he'd stayed, then grinned sarcastically. Of course he would; he'd been paid to baby-sit her. And knowing her father, the fee had been generous.

The front door clicked again, and she heard Gilly assure Breed that she would take care of Elizabeth. The words were almost ludicrous. These two people whom she'd come to love this summer had given her so much. But they had taken away even more. No, she thought. She didn't blame Gilly. She was grateful to have had her as a friend. Gilly might have been in on this scheme, but she doubted it.

Finally Elizabeth heard Gilly go into her bedroom. An hour later, convinced her friend would be asleep, she silently pushed back the covers and climbed out of bed. Dragging her suitcases from the closet, she quickly and quietly emptied her drawers and hangers. She only took what she had brought with her from Boston. Everything else she was leaving for her roommate.

The apartment key and a note to Gilly were left propped against a vase on the kitchen table. A sad smile touched Elizabeth's pale features as she set a second note, addressed to Breed, beside the first. She picked it up and read over the simple message again. It read: *The game's over. You lose.*

The taxi ride to the airport seemed to take hours. Elizabeth kept looking over her shoulder, afraid Breed was following. She didn't want to think of how many times this summer he had done exactly that. The thought made her more determined than ever to get away.

There wasn't a plane scheduled to leave for Boston until the next morning, so she took the red-eye to New York. Luckily, the wait was less than two hours. Her greatest fear was that Gilly would wake up and go to check on her. Finding her gone, she would be sure to contact Breed.

Restlessly, Elizabeth walked around the airport. She knew that she would never forget this city. The cable cars, the sounds and smells of Fisherman's Wharf, sailing, the beach... Her musings did a buzzing tailspin. No, thoughts of San Francisco would always be irrevocably tied to Breed. She wanted to hate him, but she couldn't. He'd given her happy memories, and she would struggle to keep those untainted by the mud of his deception.

The flight was uneventful. The first-class section had only one other traveler, a businessman who worked out of his briefcase the entire time.

Even though it was only 10:00 a.m. when her plane landed, New York was sweltering in an August heat wave. The limousine delivered her to the St. Moritz, a fashionable uptown hotel that was situated across the street from Central Park South.

Exhausted, she took a hot shower and fell asleep almost immediately afterward in the air-conditioned room.

When she awoke, it was nearly dinnertime. Although

she hadn't eaten anything in twenty-four hours, she wasn't hungry.

A walk in Central Park lifted her from the well of overwhelming self-pity. She bought a pretzel and squirted thick yellow mustard over it. As she lazily strolled beside the pond, goldfish the size of trout came to the water's edge, anticipating a share of her meal. Not wanting to disappoint them, she broke off a piece of the doughy pretzel and tossed it into the huge pond.

A young bearded man, strumming a ballad on his guitar, sat on a green bench looking for handouts. She placed a five-dollar bill in the open guitar case.

"Thanks, lady," he sang, and returned her wave with a bob of his dark head.

Most of the park benches were occupied by a wide range of people from all walks of life. She had taken a two-day trip to the Big Apple the previous year and stayed at the St. Moritz, but she hadn't gone into Central Park. The thought hadn't entered her mind.

Today she strolled around the pond, hoping that the sights and sounds of the vibrant city would ease the heaviness in her heart. Unfamiliar settings filled with anonymous faces were no longer intimidating. San Francisco had done that for her.

An hour later she stepped into the cool hotel room and sighed. Reaching for the phone, she dialed Boston.

"Hello, Dad," she said when he picked up, her voice devoid of emotion.

"Elizabeth, where are you?" he demanded instantly.

"New York."

"Why in heaven's name did you run off like that?"

His question drew a faint smile. "I think you already know why," she answered softly, resignedly. "How often have you hired men to watch me in the past?"

"Did he tell you?" her father responded brusquely.

"No. I found out on my own."

"The fool," he issued harshly under his breath.

She disagreed. The only fool in this situation had been herself, for falling in love with Breed.

A strained silence stretched along the wires.

"How often, Dad?" she finally asked.

"Only a few," he answered after a long moment.

"But why?" she asked, exhaling forcefully. The pain of the knowledge was physical as well as mental. Her stomach ached, and she lowered herself into the upholstered wing chair in her suite and leaned forward to rest her elbows on her knees.

"That's a subject we shouldn't discuss over the phone. I want you at home."

"There are a lot of things *I* want, too," she returned in a shallow whisper.

"Elizabeth, please. Be reasonable."

"Give me a few days," she insisted. "I need time to think."

Her father began to argue. She closed her eyes and listened for a few moments. Then she whispered, "Goodbye, Dad," and hung up.

The next morning she checked out of the hotel, rented a car and headed north. Setting a leisurely pace, she stopped along the way to enjoy the beauty of the Atlantic Ocean. It took her three days to drive home.

She recognized that her father would consider her actions immature, but for her, this time alone with her thoughts had been vital. The long drive, the magnificent coastline, the solitude, gave her the necessary time to come to terms with her father's actions. Decisions were made. Although her father hadn't asked for it, she gave him her forgiveness. He had only been doing what he thought was best.

The thing that shocked her most had been her own stupidity. How could she have been so gullible? All the evidence of Breed's deceit had been there, but she had been blinded by her love. But no more. Never again. Loving someone only caused emotional pain. She had been naive and incredibly foolish.

She wouldn't allow her father to interfere in her life that way again. Once she got home, she would make arrangements to find a place of her own. Breaking away had been long overdue. This summer she'd proved to her father and herself that she was capable of holding a job. And that was what she decided to do: get a job. She spoke fluent French, and enough German and Italian to make her last visit to Europe trouble-free. Surely there was something she could do with those skills.

Not once during the drive home did she allow bitterness to tarnish her memories of Breed. Ultimately, the special relationship they'd shared led to heartache. But she was grateful to him for the precious gift that he'd so unwittingly given her.

One thing she couldn't accept was his calculated deception. Maybe forgiveness would come later, but right now the pain cut so deep that she knew it would take a long time, and maybe it would never come.

It was midafternoon when she pulled up in front of the huge family home.

The white-haired butler opened the door and gave her a stiff but genuine smile.

"Welcome home, Miss Elizabeth." His head dipped slightly as he spoke.

"Hello, Bently."

"Your father's been expecting you, miss. You're to go directly to the library."

Although he hadn't said as much, she knew he was warning her that her father wasn't pleased.

"I'll see to your luggage," he continued.

"Thank you, Bently."

Her elderly ally inclined his head in silent understanding.

Elizabeth stood in the great entry hall and looked around with new eyes. The house was magnificent, a showpiece, but it felt cold and unwelcoming. The heart of this home had died with her mother.

Knocking politely against the polished mahogany door that reached from the ceiling to the floor, Elizabeth waited with calm deliberation.

Charles Wainwright's reply was curt and impatient. "Come in."

"Hello, Father," she said as she walked through the door.

"Elizabeth." He raised himself out of his chair. Relief relaxed the tightness in his weathered brow and he gave her a brief, perfunctory hug. "Now, what's all this nonsense of needing time away?"

She was saved from having to reply by the arrival of Helene. The maid seemed to appear noiselessly, carrying a silver tray with a coffeepot and two delicate china cups.

Both Elizabeth and her father waited to resume their conversation until Helene had left the room.

"I have a few unanswered questions of my own," she said as she stood and dutifully filled the first cup. She handed it to her father. Charles Wainwright's hair was completely white now, she noted as he accepted the steaming cup from her hand. Once, a long time past, her father's hair had been the same sandy shade as her own. The famous Wainwright blond good looks. Charlie was dark like her mother. But other than her coloring, Elizabeth felt as if she had nothing in common with this man. He wasn't affectionate. She couldn't ever recall him bouncing her on his knee or telling her stories when she was a child. The only time she recalled seeing deep emotion from him had been after her mother's funeral.

Her reverie was interrupted by coffee that dripped from the spout of the silver service and scalded her fingertips. She managed to set the pot aside before giving an involuntary gasp of surprise. Tears filled her eyes, but not from physical pain.

"Elizabeth." Charles Wainwright leapt to his feet. "You've burned yourself." He turned aside. "Helene!" he shouted. Elizabeth couldn't remember hearing that much emotion in his voice for a long time. "Bring the first-aid kit."

"I'm fine," she struggled to reassure him between sudden sobs. She hadn't wept when she learned of Breed's deceit. Nor had she revealed her grief at her mother's funeral. After all, she was a Wainwright, and tears were a sign of weakness. Now she was home, with possibly the only person alive who loved her for herself, and they sat like polite acquaintances, sharing coffee and shielding their hearts. A dam within her burst, and she began to sob uncontrollably.

She could see by the concerned look on his face that her father didn't know how to react. He raised and lowered his hands, impotently unsure of himself. Finally he circled his arms around her and patted her gently on the back as if he were afraid she was a fragile porcelain doll that would break.

"Princess," he whispered, "what is it?"

Helene burst in the door, and Charles dismissed her with a wave of his hand.

"Who's hurt you?"

Between a fresh wave of sobs, she shook her head.

Her father handed her his starched and pressed linen handkerchief, and she held it to her eyes.

"My dear," he said, smoothing her back. "You have the look of a woman in love."

"No." She pulled free of his loose embrace and violently shook her head. "I can't love him after what he's done," she choked out between sobs.

"And what did he do?"

She sniffled. "Nothing. I...can't talk about it. Not now," she whispered in painful denial. "I apologize for acting like an idiot. I'll go upstairs and lie down for an hour or so, and I'll be fine."

"Princess, are you sure you won't tell me?"

Fresh tears squeezed through her damp lashes. "Not now." She turned toward the great hall. "Dad," she said with her back to him, "I'll probably be leaving for Europe within the week."

Her father was silent for a moment. "Running away won't solve anything." His haunting voice, gentle with wisdom, followed her as she left the library.

One suitcase was packed and another half-filled. She'd realized after one night that she couldn't remain in this house. Once the tears had come, the aching loneliness in her heart had throbbed with its intensity. Her father was right when he told her running away wouldn't heal the void. But escaping came naturally; she had been doing it for so long. Last night she hadn't gone down to dinner, and she'd been shocked when her father brought her a tray later in the evening. She had pretended to be asleep. She regretted that now, and decided to go downstairs and say goodbye to him.

Tucking her passport in her purse, she examined the contents of her suitcases one last time before securing the locks and leaving them outside her door. The reservations for her flight had been made earlier that morning, and plenty of time remained before she needed to leave for the airport. But already she was restless. Forcing a smile on her pale features, she descended the stairs.

She was only halfway down the staircase when she heard Bently engaged in a heated argument with someone at the front door. The other voice was achingly familiar. Breed.

That he was angry and impatient was apparent as his raised voice echoed through the hall. She took another step, and then her father appeared in the foyer.

"That'll be all, Bently," her father said with calm authority. "I'll see Mr. Breed."

She restrained a gasp and drew closer to the banister. Clearly neither man was aware of her presence.

Breed stepped into the house. His deeply tanned features were set in hard lines as he approached her father.

"I appreciate the fact that you're seeing me." His voice was laced with heavy sarcasm. "But I can assure you that I was prepared to wait as long as it took."

"After four days of pounding down my door, I can believe that's a fair assumption," her father retorted stiffly. "But now that you have my attention, what is it you want?"

"Elizabeth," Breed said without hesitation. "Where is she?"

"Your job of protecting my daughter was terminated when she left San Francisco. I believe you've received your check."

She watched, fascinated and shocked, as Breed took an envelope from his pocket and ripped it in two. "I don't want a dime of this money. I told you that before, and I'm telling you again."

"You earned it."

Every damn penny, Elizabeth wanted to shout at him.

"I kept my word, Wainwright," Breed explained forcefully. "I didn't tell Beth a thing. But I hated every minute of this assignment, and you knew it."

"Why? I thought this type of work was your specialty. You came highly recommended," her father said quietly.

Breed rubbed a hand across his eyes, and she knew the torment she saw in his features was mirrored in her own. When he lowered his hand, he must have caught a glimpse of her from out of the corner of his eye. He hesitated and turned toward her.

"Beth." He said her name softly, as though he was afraid she would disappear again. He moved to the foot of the stairs. The tightness eased from his face as he stared up at her.

"Mr. Wainwright," Breed said, and the anger was gone from his voice as he glanced briefly at her father, "I love your daughter."

"No," Elizabeth said in agitation. "You don't know the meaning of the word. I was nothing more than a lucrative business proposition."

Breed pulled another envelope from his shirt and handed it to her father. His eyes left her only briefly. "While we're on the subject of money..."

Her gaze wavered under the blazing force of his.

"This paper proves that I'm not a poor man. I own

a thousand acres of prime California timberland. The land has been in my family for a hundred years," Breed stated evenly, then turned toward her father. "I have no need of the Wainwright money. From the first day I met your daughter, it's stood between us like a brick wall."

He turned back to the stairs, and his look grew gentle. "I love you, Beth Wainwright. I've loved you from the moment we went swimming and I saw you for the wonderful woman you are."

Her heart was crying out for her to run to Breed. But the feelings of betrayal and hurt kept her rooted to the stairs. Her hand curved around the polished banister until she was sure her fingernails would dent the wood.

At her silence, he returned his attention to her father. "Mr. Wainwright, I'm asking for your permission to marry your daughter—"

"I won't marry you," she interrupted in angry protest. "You lied to me. All those weeks you—"

"You weren't exactly honest with me," he returned levelly. "And there was ample opportunity for you to explain everything. You have no right to be mad at me." He paused, and the hardness left his chiseled features. "I'll say it again. I love you, Beth. I want you to share my life."

Indecision played across her face, and her gaze met her father's. Breed's eyes followed hers, and a proud look stole over them.

"I'm asking for your permission, Wainwright," Breed said coolly. "But I'll be honest. I plan to marry your daughter with or without it."

A hint of mirth brightened her father's face. "That's a brash statement, young man."

"Daddy!" Elizabeth called, knowing what her father would say to someone like Breed. Her heart and her pride waged a desperate battle.

Charles Wainwright ignored his daughter. "As it is, I realize that Elizabeth loves you. I may be a crusty old man, but I'm not too blind to see that you'll make her happy. You have my permission, Andrew Breed. Fill this house with grandchildren and bring some laughter into its halls again."

Breed appeared as stunned as Elizabeth.

"Go on." Charles Wainwright flicked his wrist in the direction of his daughter. "And don't take no for an answer."

"I have no intention of doing so," Breed said as he climbed the stairs two at a time.

Elizabeth felt the crazy desire to turn and run, but she stayed where she was, her body motionless with indecision. She bit into her trembling bottom lip as her pride surrendered the first battle.

"Your money will go into a trust fund for our children, Beth," Breed began with a frown. "I don't want a penny of what's yours. There's only one thing I'm after."

"What's that?" she asked in a quiet murmur, battling with the potency of his nearness.

He slid his hands around her waist and pulled her into the circle of his arms. "A wife."

Her breath came in small flutters as he lowered his mouth and paused a scant inch above hers. Their breath

YOUR PARTICIPATION IS REQUESTED!

Dear Reader,

Since you are a lover of romance fiction – we would like to get to know you!

Inside you will find a short Reader's Survey. Sharing your answers with us will help our editorial staff understand who you are and what activities you enjoy.

To thank you for your participation, we would like to send you 2 books and 2 gifts – **ABSOLUTELY FREE!**

Enjoy your gifts with our appreciation,

Pam Powers

SEE INSIDE FOR READER'S SURVEY

For Your Romance Reading Pleasure...

Get 2 FREE BOOKS that will fuel your imagination with intensely moving stories about life, love and relationships.

We'll send you 2 books and 2 gifts
ABSOLUTELY FREE
just for completing our Reader's Survey!

YOUR READER'S SURVEY
"THANK YOU" FREE GIFTS INCLUDE:

▶ **2 Romance books**
▶ **2 lovely surprise gifts**

PLEASE FILL IN THE CIRCLES COMPLETELY TO RESPOND

1) What type of fiction books do you enjoy reading? (Check all that apply)
- ○ Suspense/Thrillers
- ○ Action/Adventure
- ○ Modern-day Romances
- ○ Historical Romance
- ○ Humour
- ○ Paranormal Romance

2) What attracted you most to the last fiction book you purchased on impulse?
- ○ The Title
- ○ The Cover
- ○ The Author
- ○ The Story

3) What is usually the greatest influencer when you <u>plan</u> to buy a book?
- ○ Advertising
- ○ Referral
- ○ Book Review

4) How often do you access the internet?
- ○ Daily ○ Weekly ○ Monthly ○ Rarely or never.

5) How many NEW paperback fiction novels have you purchased in the past 3 months?
- ○ 0 - 2
- ○ 3 - 6
- ○ 7 or more

YES! I have completed the Reader's Survey. Please send me the 2 FREE books and 2 FREE gifts (gifts are worth about $10) for which I qualify. I understand that I am under no obligation to purchase any books, as explained on the back of this card.

194/394 MDL FS76

FIRST NAME	LAST NAME

ADDRESS

APT.#	CITY

STATE/PROV.	ZIP/POSTAL CODE

© 2012 HARLEQUIN ENTERPRISES LIMITED
® and ™ are trademarks owned and used by the trademark owner and/or its licensee. Printed in the U.S.A.
SUR-ROM-12

The Reader Service — Here's How It Works:

Accepting your 2 free books and 2 free gifts (gifts valued at approximately $10.00) places you under no obligation to buy anything. You may keep the books and gifts and return the shipping statement marked "cancel." If you do not cancel, about a month later we'll send you 4 additional books and bill you just $5.99 each in the U.S. or $6.49 each in Canada. That is a savings of at least 25% off the cover price. It's quite a bargain! Shipping and handling is just 50¢ per book in the U.S. and 75¢ per book in Canada.* You may cancel at any time, but if you choose to continue, every month we'll send you 4 more books, which you may either purchase at the discount price or return to us and cancel your subscription.

*Terms and prices subject to change without notice. Prices do not include applicable taxes. Sales tax applicable in N.Y. Canadian residents will be charged applicable taxes. Offer not valid in Quebec. Books received may not be as shown. All orders subject to credit approval. Credit or debit balances in a customer's account(s) may be offset by any other outstanding balance owed by or to the customer. Please allow 4 to 6 weeks for delivery. Offer available while quantities last.

If offer card is missing write to: The Reader Service, P.O. Box 1867, Buffalo, NY 14240-1867 or visit: www.ReaderService.com

BUSINESS REPLY MAIL
FIRST-CLASS MAIL   PERMIT NO. 717   BUFFALO, NY

POSTAGE WILL BE PAID BY ADDRESSEE

THE READER SERVICE
PO BOX 1341
BUFFALO NY 14240-8571

NO POSTAGE
NECESSARY
IF MAILED
IN THE
UNITED STATES

merged. She swayed against him, her hands moving over his chest. The entire time her pride urged her to break free and walk away. But her heart held her steadfast.

"Don't fight me so hard," he whispered, claiming her lips in a kiss so tender that she melted against him.

"Together we'll build a lumber kingdom," he whispered into her hair.

"I don't know," she faltered. "I need time to think. I'm confused." She wanted him so much. It was her pride speaking, not her heart.

"Elizabeth," her father called from the hall. "I think it's only fair to tell you that your Andrew came to me a few weeks back and asked to be relieved of this case. Naturally, I declined and demanded that he maintain his anonymity."

Her eyes met Breed's. "Your business trip?"

He nodded and placed his hands on her shoulders. "Is it really so difficult to decide?" he asked in a husky whisper.

She stared at the familiar features and saw the pain carved in them. "No, not at all."

For a breathless moment they looked at one another.

Then Elizabeth's pride surrendered to her heart as she pressed her mouth to his.

* * * * *

NO COMPETITION

One

Carrie Lockett carefully backed the fifteen-year-old minivan up to the rear entrance of Dove's Gallery. Shifting into Park, she hopped out the side door and raised the hatchback of the van to take out the large canvas. She didn't like what she was doing, but the portrait of Camille grinning at her every time she entered her work room was driving her up the wall. All right, she openly admitted it: she was insecure. But who wouldn't be, with a twin sister who looked like Camille?

"Darn you, Camille," she muttered disparagingly, though she knew she had nothing to blame but her own insecurities.

As an artist, Carrie had yearned to paint her fine-boned, fine-featured sister. Camille was lovely in a delicate, symmetrical way that had brought her admirers in droves. No one could look at Camille without being arrested by her beauty.

Awkwardly balancing the canvas with one hand, Carrie pounded on the rear door of the gallery.

Elizabeth Brandon opened it for her. The older woman's astute gaze narrowed on the dilapidated minivan. "Darling, are you still driving that…thing?"

It was Elizabeth's opinion that a woman of talent shouldn't be seen in anything so mundane. If it were up to her friend, Carrie would be seated behind the wheel of a Ferrari. Carrie had no objections to that, but the middle-aged vehicle was all she could afford. "It's the only car I have."

"I hope you realize that if that 'thing' was a horse, they'd shoot it."

Carrie managed to smother a laugh. "I suppose. Now, do you want to lecture me about my car or look at this portrait?"

Already Elizabeth's keen eyes were examining the painting. "Darling," she breathed out slowly, "she's exquisite."

"I know," Carrie grumbled. No one would ever guess that the stunning woman in the portrait was the artist's twin. Camille's dark hair shone with a luster of the richest sable. Carrie's own mousy reddish-blond hair looked as though Mother Nature couldn't decide what color it should be. Even worse, Carrie had been cursed with a sprinkling of freckles across her nose that stood out like shiny new pennies the minute she hit sunlight. Camille's complexion had been peaches and cream from the time she was a toddler.

"Look at those eyes," Elizabeth continued, her hand supporting her chin. "Such a lovely shade of blue."

Carrie lowered her own greenish-gray eyes. Camille's

eyes resembled the heavens, and Carrie's looked like dirty swamp water.

"She's intriguing."

Camille was that, all right.

"But I sense a bit of a hellion under all that beauty."

Elizabeth had always been a perceptive woman. One didn't become the proprietor of San Francisco's most elite art gallery without a certain amount of insight.

"Is she anyone I know, darling?"

The way Elizabeth called everyone "darling" continually amused Carrie. She struggled to hold back a smile. "No, I don't think you would."

"She owes you money?"

"No."

Elizabeth's astute eyes looked directly into Carrie's as a gradual grin formed, bracketing the older woman's mouth. "You've outdone yourself this time. She's fascinating."

"Will it sell?" The question was posed to change the subject. At the moment, Carrie was more concerned with doing away with the irritating portrait than any financial reward.

"I think so."

"Quickly?"

"Someone's coming in this afternoon who might be interested. He's bought several of your other pieces."

Carrie sat on the corner of the large oak desk while Elizabeth directed a young employee to hang the portrait out front.

"This 'someone' who's coming in this afternoon…
Is it anyone I know?"

"I don't believe so. Have you heard of Shane Reynolds?"

Carrie wrinkled her nose. The name was oddly familiar, but she couldn't remember where she'd heard it.
"Yes, I think I have."

"He's the architect who designed the new Firstbank building."

"Of course. Didn't he just win a plaque or something for that?" She idly rolled a pencil between her fingers, trying to put a face with the name. None came. If his picture had been in the paper, she had missed it.

"Oh, darling, you amaze me. Shane was presented the Frank Lloyd Wright annual award. It's the most prestigious honor given to an architect."

"Then he must be good."

"He's single." The statement was accompanied by two perfectly shaped brows arching suggestively.

Carrie shrugged. "So?"

"So let me introduce you."

"Now?" Shock echoed in Carrie's voice. "No way, Elizabeth. Look at me." She pushed back the headband that held her curly hair at bay and rubbed her hand down her jeans-clad thigh. "I'm a mess."

"Hurry home and pretty yourself up."

"He hasn't got that much time."

Tapping her foot in unspoken reprimand, Elizabeth continued, "I wish you'd stop putting yourself down."

"I'm calling a spade a spade."

"I don't know why you're still single. There are plenty of eligible young men in San Francisco. You're an attractive young woman."

"Good try, but I happen to pass a mirror every now and then. If you want classic beauty, then look at the woman in that portrait."

"A man like Shane Reynolds wouldn't be romantically interested in someone like the woman in your painting."

"I know from experience that you're wrong. You stand the two of us together and there's no competition. No man in his right mind would choose me over…her." Carrie nearly spilled out Camille's name which would have been a mistake. During the few years that Carrie had been doing business with the Dove Gallery she'd gone to great lengths to keep her personal life separate from her professional one.

"Shane isn't like other men." Amusement danced briefly in the older woman's gaze, while the rest of her face remained expressionless.

"Ha," Carrie snorted. "When it comes to a beautiful woman, all men react the same way."

"Have I ever before suggested you meet a collector?"

Carrie hedged. Elizabeth wasn't a matchmaker. The other woman's persistence surprised her. "No," she admitted reluctantly.

"There's something about Shane Reynolds I think you'll like. He's enthralled with your work."

"Oh?"

"Besides, he's a bit of a free spirit himself."

Carrie admitted she was intrigued, but she wouldn't willingly meet any man looking the way she did now. "Another time, maybe."

"I'm having a party Friday night."

"Tomorrow?" Carrie groaned inwardly and offered the oldest excuse in the world. "I don't have a thing to wear. Besides, you know I hate those things."

"Buy something."

For one crazy instant Carrie actually considered it. This late in the month she was traditionally low on ready cash, but there were always her credit cards. She made a quick decision.

It could be that Elizabeth was right about Shane. If he was everything her friend seemed to think, Camille's portrait really *wouldn't* interest him. A free spirit who appreciated her art had to have some redeeming qualities.

Then again, if Shane Reynolds bought the portrait, Carrie would know not to bother with him. But maybe, just maybe, for once in her life she could find a man who saw beyond the deceptive beauty of her sister.

"Well?" Elizabeth pressed.

"I don't know. Let me think about it."

"Don't take too long. A man like Shane Reynolds won't be single forever."

"I'll let you know."

"Do that."

The receptionist joined the two women and smiled cordially before handing Elizabeth a business card. "Mr. Reynolds is here for his appointment."

Elizabeth held Carrie's eyes. "You're sure you won't meet him?"

"Maybe Friday."

The older woman nodded. "As you wish. And, darling, do me a favor and check into buying a new car. I fear for your life in that…contraption." Elizabeth stopped abruptly. "By the way, do you have a title for the portrait?"

Unconsciously, Carrie nibbled on her bottom lip as she quickly decided. "How about *No Competition?*"

"Perfect." Elizabeth turned, prepared to enter the gallery and greet her customer. "There aren't many women in the world who would want to compete against her."

"You're right about that," Carrie murmured.

Already Elizabeth's mouth had curved into a warm smile meant for her customer, and Carrie doubted that her friend had heard her. She jumped down from the edge of the desk and drew a steadying breath. Elizabeth had succeeded in arousing her curiosity. Shane Reynolds must be someone special to have Elizabeth singing his praises. Briefly she allowed a mental image to form in her mind. If beauty didn't impress him, it must be the result of some unattractive feature of his own. Men with imperfections were often willing to overlook the flaws in others. Perhaps he was short and balding. The thought served only to pique her curiosity. If he was inside an office all day, then he'd probably gone flabby. That sometimes happened to busy men who ate on the run and didn't take time to exercise or worry about proper nutrition.

As she prepared to leave, Carrie's hand was on the doorknob when she gave in to her niggling curiosity. If Shane Reynolds was standing in the other room, all she had to do was take a peek. No one would be the wiser.

Feeling a little like a cat burglar, she opened the door and glanced through the crack. Tiny shock waves coursed through her body as her mental image went crashing to the floor. At first all she could see was a full head of gray hair. No, not gray but a fantastic shade of silver, as burnished as a new coin. Her thought was that he was older, possibly nearing middle age. But then he turned around, and her heart tripped out a staccato beat of surprised disbelief. The silver was premature. This wasn't some old, dignified architect, but a rawly virile man in his early thirties. One who was suntanned and vigorously provocative. His sports jacket and dark pants revealed discriminating good taste and made for a distinguished impression. The top two buttons of his shirt were unfastened to display hard, tanned flesh. Carrie tried to tell herself he'd gotten that deep bronze from a tanning bed, but in her heart she knew she was wrong. This man didn't have the time for such vanity. He couldn't be termed classically handsome, but everything about him breathed overwhelming masculinity.

A curious ache grabbed her between the shoulder blades. Elizabeth was right. There was something about Shane Reynolds she liked. An awareness gripped her that was so strong her body went rigid. Rarely had the sight of a man affected her this way. It frightened her and, in the same heartbeat, exhilarated her beyond anything else in her twenty-seven years.

Attaining a grip on her emotions, Carrie turned and quietly slipped out the back door. She prayed fervently that Shane wouldn't buy the painting. If he appreciated Camille's flagrant beauty, he would be like all the others. Desperately, she hoped he wasn't. For once in her life, she wanted a man who could look beyond her glaring imperfections and discover the warm woman inside who was ready to burst out and be discovered. Her stomach churning with hope and expectation, she headed toward her minivan.

Thirty minutes later, when Carrie pulled into her driveway, her hands felt clammy. Her small, one-bedroom cottage sat on a cliff high above the rolling Pacific Ocean. The price had been outrageous. It was ironic that the one great love of her life would be a narrow strip of rocky beach and not a man. Camille collected men, while Carrie boldly etched her emotions across bare canvas, revealing the innermost secret places of her heart.

She breathed in the fresh clean scent of the ocean and experienced an unshakable freedom. Someday she would like to build a bigger home, but for now the cottage suited her perfectly.

Smiling to herself, she unlocked the front door and tossed her purse aside. She paced the living room once, then moved directly to the phone in the kitchen and punched out a number with an impatience she rarely experienced.

"Dove Gallery," came the soft voice of the receptionist.

"This is Carrie Lockett for Elizabeth Brandon," she said as calmly as she could manage, swallowing down her uncertainty. From the minute she left the gallery, she hadn't stopped thinking about Shane. Already she'd made a decision.

"Could you hold the line a minute?"

"Yes."

"Darling," Elizabeth answered a moment later. "It's that car, isn't it? You've had an accident."

"Of course not." Carrie laughed, and added without preamble, "Did he buy the painting?"

"Shane Reynolds?"

Who else did Elizabeth think she was referring to? Carrie mused with a hint of irritation. "Yes, Shane Reynolds."

"He was impressed with it. In fact, *No Competition* has been the center of interest all afternoon."

Her lashes fluttered down with distress. "But did he buy it?"

Carrie heard Elizabeth's sigh. "I'm afraid you're going to be disappointed, but he didn't. I felt sure he would. Do you need the money? I could probably—"

"No...no," she gasped, too happy to think about something as mundane as food or house payments or anything else. Her voice was remarkably even when she spoke. "Don't worry about me. And, Elizabeth, about that party Friday night—count me in. I'd enjoy coming."

"What a pleasant surprise. Shane will be there. I'll introduce you, if you like."

"I'd like that very much." Already she felt hope stirring within her breast. It had been a lot of years since she'd experienced such a strong sense of expectation.

"I'll see you Friday at seven, then."

"At seven," Carrie repeated, and after a cordial farewell, she replaced the telephone receiver.

She shouldn't feel this excited. She was behaving like an adolescent and setting herself up for a big disappointment. She didn't care. A surge of exhilarated expectancy washed through her. Something wonderful was about to happen. She could feel it all the way to the marrow of her bones.

Although she hadn't eaten since early morning, she wasn't hungry. But past experience dictated that she fix herself some dinner or she would be out of sorts later. Warming up a can of tomato soup and popping half an English muffin in the toaster, she hummed cheerfully as she worked in the cozy kitchen.

The front door clicked open, and Carrie glanced up to see her twin sister saunter into the house.

"Hi." Camille was dressed in a pale pink sundress that showed off the ivory perfection of her bare shoulders. "Something smells good."

"Tomato soup. Do you want some?"

"No thanks. Bob's taking me to dinner later."

"You've been seeing quite a bit of him lately, haven't you?" Camille had been dating Bob for a couple of months. Perhaps she was feeling that the time had come to start thinking about marriage and a family. Naturally, Camille would marry first.

"Bob's all right." She helped herself to an apple from the basket on the kitchen table. "He's rich, you know."

"I didn't." But knowing Camille, money wouldn't necessarily enhance a man's attraction. For that matter, it didn't mean all that much to Carrie, either. The two of them were so different outwardly, but shockingly alike in other ways.

"He's in exports," Camille elaborated.

"That's interesting." For the moment, the only thing that concerned Carrie was why the toaster was taking so long to produce a crisp muffin.

"I think he might ask me to marry him." Camille said it as though the idea of marriage utterly bored her. She sat on an oak chair with webbed seating and crossed her long, shapely legs.

Caught off guard by the disinterested announcement, Carrie turned to face her sister. "Will you accept?"

"I don't know. Bob's really nice, but if I'm going to settle down, there are certain things I want in a man."

"Oh?" Carrie was surprised. She didn't think her sister had given the matter of what she wanted in a marriage partner anything more than a fleeting consideration. "What qualities are you looking for?" Carrie's own wants were specific. She wanted a husband who would be her best friend, her shock absorber and, in some ways, her compass.

Camille bit into the apple. A tiny drop of juice ran down her chin, and she lazily wiped it away. "Money isn't all that important. It's nice, I suppose, but there are so many other qualities I want more."

"Like?"

"He should want a family," Camille said thoughtfully.

"I want a husband with integrity and tenderness," Carrie offered.

"But I don't think he should want a large family."

"Why not?" Carrie couldn't understand her sister's thinking on that one.

"I only want one child," Camille explained.

The soup started to simmer, and Carrie removed it from the burner. "Why only one?"

"Babies fluster me. You're the motherly type. Not me."

Maybe that was because Carrie had taken over the role so early in life. Their mother had died unexpectedly when they were twelve, and Carrie had assumed many of the duties around the house. Their father worked a lot of overtime, and the twins were often left to their own devices. First thing after school, Carrie started the evening meal while Camille did homework. For Carrie, studying was a breeze. On the other hand, Camille had a difficult time with schoolwork. She often lamented her inability to "remember things the way Carrie does." Consequently it was Carrie who cooked, cleaned and struggled to maintain a balance for everything else in their lives.

"I took your portrait into the gallery today."

Camille didn't look surprised. "I imagine someone

will buy it quickly." She said it with absolute certainty, but Carrie wasn't sure if this was a back-handed compliment to the work she'd done on the portrait or if Camille felt few could resist her beauty.

"It's already causing some stir." The exaggeration was only a slight one. Elizabeth would have it sold by the end of the week, and Camille's flawless beauty would be intriguing men for years to come. Few would give a moment's thought to the artist, and Carrie actually preferred it that way. Camille belonged in the spotlight, while she herself was strictly a background player.

"You're a good artist, Carrie."

Her twin's compliment came as a surprise. "Thank you. But usually it's the subject that causes a painting to sell."

A small smile revealed Camille's perfect white teeth. "Are you telling me the subject will help *this* painting to sell?"

"Undoubtedly."

"Good." Camille took another bite of the apple, pleased with herself.

The English muffin popped up from the toaster, and Carrie reached for it, piling tuna fish over the top and placing a sliced tomato over that. She carried her meal to the table and sat down opposite Camille.

"I'm happy to hear the portrait will sell soon."

Carrie spread a paper napkin across her lap. This was the second time her sister had alluded to money. "Is there something you needed?"

Camille straightened and cocked her head to one

side. "I was wondering if you could float me a loan. You know I'll pay you back."

Carrie knew her sister would, but borrowing money to hold her over until pay day was becoming increasingly common. Camille's job as a beauty consultant for a large downtown store paid well. Unfortunately, she had never learned to budget. Things were tight this month for Carrie, as well, and she was hoping to buy a new dress for Elizabeth's party. "I suppose I could loan you some, but not much." She had been rescuing Camille from the time they'd lost their mother. Old habits died hard.

"You don't sound that eager," Camille returned. "You know how I struggle to make ends meet."

"We all do." Carrie stood and reached for her wallet, then handed Camille a fifty dollar bill, which left her with the loose change in the bottom of her purse.

"Thanks." An irresistible smile lit up Camille's baby blue eyes. "I'll talk to you later." Already she was on her way out the front door.

"Right. Later." With a grumble, Carrie returned to her soup. It happened every time. Camille asked and Carrie gave.

That night Carrie dreamed that Shane Reynolds was walking along the beach with her. The salty breeze buffeted them as their feet made deep indentations in the wet sand. He slipped a casual arm around her shoulders and smiled into her eyes with a love so strong that it would span a lifetime. In the morning, she woke feel-

ing warm and wonderful. And a bit foolish. She wasn't
a young girl to be swayed by romantic dreams, nor did
she waste her time on fantasies. She was a woman with
a woman's heart. And for the first time in months, she
felt the longing for a man who would share her life.

Sitting up, she looped her arms around her knees
and rested her chin there. She was determined to attend
Elizabeth's party Friday night and meet Shane Reynolds. The first hurdle had already been passed. He'd
seen Camille's sleek elegance and hadn't been lured
by all that untarnished beauty. Elizabeth had claimed
he wouldn't be, but experience had taught Carrie otherwise.

Her first order of the day was to shop. After spending a fruitless morning downtown, she found the perfect
dress in a small boutique tucked away from the main-
stream of the large downtown shopping complexes. The
pale green dress was the most expensive thing she'd
ever owned. The smooth silk whispered over her skin
and clung in all the right places, giving an illusion of
beauty. Wearing this dress and standing in the right
light, she felt that someone might actually be able to
detect the fact that Camille was her sister.

The color did something fantastic for her eyes. No
longer did they resemble dirty swamp water. Unexpectedly, they held flashes of jade and a touch of emerald.
The dress was definitely worth the price, she reasoned,
signing the charge slip.

On Friday evening she arrived at Elizabeth's party
feeling light-headed and a little nervous. Her stomach

felt as if she'd been on a roller coaster all afternoon, pitching and heaving with every turn. She'd been extra careful with her makeup and pinned her hair away from her face. Her mother's pearls graced her slender neck and ears. Normally she avoided the mirror, but this evening she had stood in front of it so long that she was half tempted to ask it who was the fairest in the land. But she already knew the answer. Tonight she could give Camille a run for her money.

Still, her smile trembled when the maid answered the door and took her lace shawl. Her pulse soared at the sound of laughter, tinkling ice and the hum of conversation that drowned out the piano player.

Her eyes scanned the crowded room, seeking only one person and experiencing keen disappointment when she couldn't locate Shane Reynolds. It was still early, and he probably hadn't arrived yet. People were everywhere, sipping champagne and chatting easily, but she had never been good at making small talk. The roller coaster dipped, and she placed a hand on her stomach to calm it.

From across the room Elizabeth raised her hand in greeting and hurried to greet her. "Carrie, darling, you're positively stunning."

"Don't look so surprised," Carrie teased, her eyes gleaming. She knew she looked good. Her best. She wanted to make her meeting with Shane Reynolds a memorable one.

"But I *am* surprised," Elizabeth countered. "I've never seen you in a dress."

"I've been known to don one now and again."

"You should do it more often," Elizabeth chastised lightly. "You're really very lovely."

The compliment was so sincere that Carrie blinked. Her first inclination was to make excuses for the way she normally dressed. She quickly suppressed the idea, astonished at her own lack of self-confidence. Instead she said only "Thank you." She didn't mention that Camille had always been the one for dresses.

"Now come, there are several people you must meet." Elizabeth made it sound as though the entire party had been waiting for Carrie's arrival, as if she were the guest of honor.

Elizabeth led the way across the room. As Carrie followed, she let her gaze skid around the elegant space, thinking perhaps she had merely missed seeing Shane the first time.

Before she could make a thorough inspection, Elizabeth introduced her to a long list of her most intimate and dearest friends. Many had bought Carrie's paintings, and she spent the next half hour answering questions and making what she hoped was stimulating conversation. A glass of champagne was handed to her. As she raised it to her lips, she spotted a flash of silver across the room. The bubbly liquid stayed on her tongue as her eyes collided with Shane Reynolds's deep blue gaze.

A slow, sensuous grin lifted the corners of his mouth, and he slowly raised his own glass in a silent salute.

The champagne stuck halfway down Carrie's throat.

Tingling bubbles tickled the back of her tongue until she gulped the liquid down, nearly choking. Because she didn't know what else to do, she looked away. It had been years since any man had interested her as much as Shane Reynolds did. Cursing herself for her inability to flirt, she quickly looked back again. His smile was brilliant and directed solely at her. The palms of her hands felt clammy. The roller coaster unexpectedly left its tracks, plummeting downwards.

"Carrie, there's someone you must meet," Elizabeth was saying, and Carrie turned her attention to another group of guests.

Even so, she felt Shane's eyes follow her. Drawn to him by a force stronger than any magnet, she sought him out again. From across the width of the room their gazes met and locked. This time he grinned boldly. She returned his smile and, feeling extraordinarily fearless, winked.

"Carrie, have you met Ashley Wallingford?"

"I don't believe I have," she returned, reluctantly pulling her gaze from Shane's. The first thing she noticed about the elderly woman was her exquisite eyes. Deep blue, shrewd, and perhaps a little calculating. This woman had lived a hard life, and it showed in the network of wrinkles across her intelligent face.

"I understand you do portraits," Mrs. Wallingford said conversationally.

"Some."

"Mrs. Wallingford was in this morning to see *No*

Competition," Elizabeth added. "She was quite taken with it."

"You managed to portray an elegant, sometimes vain woman in a flattering light. I wonder if you always read your subjects so well."

Carrie sucked in her breath. "And I wonder if you're always so perceptive," she returned. Ashley Wallingford was a marvel.

"I try to be." A hint of amusement showed in those clear blue eyes.

Painting this woman would be a challenge and a treat. Already Carrie's fingers itched for a pencil.

"I would have purchased it," Mrs. Wallingford continued, "but unfortunately I was too late."

"It sold?" Carrie turned to Elizabeth.

Elizabeth's eyes brightened. "I thought you'd be pleased."

Mrs. Wallingford touched her arm. "I'd like to talk to you again, Carrie Lockett. You're an excellent artist. I'm hoping we can do business some day. Now if you'll excuse me?"

"Of course."

"Then I'll be getting in touch with you soon."

"I'll look forward to it."

As soon as the older woman had departed, Carrie turned her attention to Elizabeth.

"You're pleased about the portrait, aren't you?" the older woman asked.

"Very. I didn't expect it to go so quickly."

"I was rather shocked myself. First thing this morning. I hadn't been open five minutes when…"

Carrie knew. In one horrible minute she knew. Her eyes darted across the room to Shane. The dream died as quickly as it had been conceived. And with it something young and vital shriveled up and wept inside of her.

"Shane Reynolds came into the gallery. He said he hadn't been able to stop thinking about the portrait all night. He didn't care about the price, he wanted it."

The fragile smile curving Carrie's soft mouth cracked. "I see."

"I don't think you do." Elizabeth's soft lilting voice rose with excitement. "Not only is he crazy about the picture, he's dying to meet you."

Two

"No," Carrie stated, shaking her head.

"What do you mean, no?" Elizabeth's eyebrows shot up in surprise.

"I refuse to meet Shane Reynolds."

"But…why? Carrie, darling, are you feeling ill? You're quite pale."

"You're right, I'm not well. I shouldn't be here." She'd been an idiot to entertain the idea that someone as handsome as Shane Reynolds would ever appreciate her. She swallowed her disappointment. She'd been an idealistic, romantic fool, and worse, it hadn't been the first time.

"Carrie…" Elizabeth gently placed a hand on Carrie's forearm.

"Thank you for inviting me," she said, taking a step back with each word. "I'm sorry to leave so quickly."

"But you just got here. Perhaps if you lie down for a few minutes…?"

"No…no." Carrie bumped into someone and turned

around sharply to apologize. "Please excuse me. I'm sorry, really sorry."

The man looked at her as though seeing someone drop in from outer space. The floor pitched beneath her feet, and Carrie inhaled a calming breath. Abruptly, she headed for the front door.

Elizabeth followed, instructing the maid to bring Carrie her coat. "I'll call you tomorrow," she said, looking concerned.

"Fine." She would have agreed to any terms as long as she could escape quickly.

"I'm sure once you're feeling better you'll reconsider meeting Shane."

Carrie knew there wasn't any possibility she would change her mind, but she lacked the strength to argue. The sooner she was out of there, the better.

It seemed an eternity before the maid returned with her shawl. Carrie wrapped it around her shoulders, gripping it as if an Arctic wind were raging around her. But the cold that ripped through her had nothing to do with the temperature.

"You're sure you'll be all right?"

"Yes, yes." As soon as she left the party, she would be a thousand percent better.

"Thank you for inviting me." Hurriedly she stepped out the door and rushed down the front steps. When she reached her minivan, she looked back to see Elizabeth standing in the open doorway, studying her with a concerned frown.

Carrie gave a brief wave and unlocked her door. Her

fingers trembled as she inserted the key into the ignition. Gripping the steering wheel, she pressed her forehead against the chilly plastic. Would she never learn? What masochistic streak did she possess that made her refuse to accept the simplest facts of life? There were no gallant princes riding around on white stallions ready to rescue her from her fate. From birth, she'd been doomed to stand in Camille's shadow. But she'd been compensated. She had her art. What more could she want?

She released a jagged breath and started the engine. *What more could she want?* The list was so long it would take a lifetime to write it all down.

Once she was home, she stripped off the dress and hung it in the far reaches of her closet so she wouldn't be faced with it every time she opened the door. She wanted only to forget her harebrained scheme.

By morning she felt much better. Her romantic heart had been wounded, but she had an incredible recovery rate. The Shane Reynoldses of this world weren't meant for someone like her. The universe was full of too many beautiful women—like Camille. She had accepted that long ago.

Standing at the kitchen window, she watched the sea gulls swoop down to the beach far below. She softly smiled and poured a cup of coffee, taking in the unspoiled beauty of the morning. White-capped waves crashed against the rocks and left a meandering path of foam across the virgin sand. A feeling of serenity crowded her heart.

Taking her coffee with her, she wandered down

the steep trail that led to the beach. A few minutes of breathing fresh salty air would rejuvenate her.

The wind tugged at her unbound hair and whipped it across her face as she walked along the beach and found her favorite rock, where she sat sipping her coffee. There was something so comforting about being on the beach. It didn't seem to matter what was troubling her; twenty minutes of watching the tide roll in made her feel like a new person, ready to take on the world and its problems.

Time lost meaning. A hundred chores demanded her attention at the house, but nothing was more pressing than her need to sit in the sun.

The sound of her name caused her to turn around. Her breath caught in her throat at the sight of Shane Reynolds. He was walking down the path toward her.

He was the last person she would have expected to see, and she marched away from him, intent on escaping. She didn't want to see or talk to this man. He was trouble, and she knew it.

"Carrie Lockett?"

She trudged on, ignoring him.

The sound of someone running after her caused her to quicken her pace.

"Ms. Lockett?" Shane was out of breath by the time he reached her side. Maybe it was a crazy idea to have come to her like this, but he hadn't been able to resist. Something had happened last night to make her run from the party, and he wanted to know what.

"Yes?" She found it strange how immediately familiar his voice sounded. Cool and commanding, as though he expected an immediate response from her.

"You probably couldn't hear me call you."

Arms swinging at her sides, she continued walking at a furious pace. "I heard you."

He swallowed his irritation. "Then why didn't you stop?"

"Why didn't you get the message?" she demanded, struggling to present a facade of searing indifference. Now that she'd seen him up close, the illusion of virile and overpowering masculinity was all the more pronounced. No wonder he'd purchased the portrait of Camille: he was breathtaking. A man as perfect as Shane would appreciate the extraordinary beauty of her twin.

"What's wrong?" His anger died at the look of hurt in her expressive eyes.

"Nothing," she lied, nearly breathless as she maintained her killing pace.

"I want to talk to you."

"And I'd prefer it if you didn't."

"Why not? I bought your painting. You're a fantastic artist and—"

"Listen," she said, whirling around, her hands on her hips. "You bought my painting. Big deal. I don't owe you anything. Who gave you the right to charge uninvited into my morning?"

His backbone stiffened. She wasn't anything like he'd expected or hoped. "Just a minute here, aren't you the same Carrie Lockett who sashayed into Elizabeth Brandon's party last evening and gave me a wink?"

Oh heavens, she had forgotten that. "I…had something in my eye," she lied.

The robust sound of his laugh echoed around her. "You were blatantly flirting with me. You liked what you saw and said so. For that matter, I was intrigued, too."

"I wasn't flirting." She continued walking, forcing him to keep up with her.

"I want to know what made you suddenly change your opinion of me," he pressed. "All I really wanted to say was how much I appreciate your work."

"You've already told me that. Thank you, I'm grateful. Now you can leave."

He ignored that. "Elizabeth has mentioned you several times." He paused and struggled to maintain his control. He wanted to tell her that the only reason he'd attended Elizabeth's party was so he could meet her. But from her unfriendly stance, he could see that she would refuse to believe that. "I assumed you wanted to meet me," he added.

"Then you assumed wrong." How easy it would be to fall for this man. One look and she sensed danger. But if she got to know Shane, then it would only be a matter of time before he met Camille. And it would be over even before it began. Her fragile heart couldn't afford to trust this man.

"Have lunch with me." The low-pitched request was a surprise.

"No."

Ignoring her refusal, he continued, "I don't know

what I've done to offend you, but I'd like to make it right. Somehow we got started on the wrong foot."

"I'm simply not interested."

"Are you always this prickly?"

"Only with insufferable, arrogant men who bulldoze their way into my mornings."

The cutting quality of his dark eyes grew sharper as she struck a raw nerve. "I've been called a lot of things in my life, but never insufferable and arrogant."

"I trust my instincts." She had nothing more to judge him by.

"Then accept my apology for intruding, Ms. Lockett." His voice dripped with sarcasm. Abruptly, he turned away and walked in the opposite direction. He didn't know what had happened, but he had too much pride to stand around and accept her insults.

Carrie paused as she watched him walk away. Her hands trembled, and she sank onto the sandy beach, her lungs heaving. The wind made a frothy confusion of her hair, and she let it blow around her face. Swallowing the tightness that gripped her throat, she turned her concentration to the angry waves that pounded the beach. She hadn't wanted to be rude and prickly. It would have felt far more natural to smile up at him and share the beauty of this unspoiled stretch of beach than to insult him. But it was better this way. Much better—yet far more difficult than anything she could remember.

Her thoughts troubled, Carrie climbed the steep path back to the small beach house. She tried to convince her sagging self-confidence that she was saving herself a whole lot of heartache. Pausing on the back porch, she unceremoniously stuffed a pile of dirty clothes into the washing machine.

The phone rang just as she was adding the laundry soap. She grabbed it automatically, then returned to her laundry, the receiver held between her ear and her shoulder. "Hello."

"Darling, you survived."

"Elizabeth." Instantly, Carrie's fingers froze on the washer dial. She regretted her panic of the night before. "I'm glad you phoned. I feel terrible about last night. I owe you an apology. My behavior was inexcusable."

"The only thing you owe me is an explanation."

"Yes, well, that could be a bit complicated."

Elizabeth wasn't about to be dissuaded. "I've got all day. I've known you a lot of years, and I've never seen you behave like that."

"Then maybe you don't really know me."

"Carrie, if you'd rather…"

"No, I'll explain." She owed Elizabeth that much. "I have a sister. I guess you can say that you've met her."

"Who is she, darling?"

From the tone of her voice, Carrie could tell that Elizabeth was searching through her memory. "As I recall, you found her intriguing."

"The portrait?" Elizabeth was clearly surprised. "The girl in the portrait is your sister?"

"My twin sister."

"Your twin sister," Elizabeth repeated, still stunned.

Her voice wobbled between two octaves as she struggled to disguise her shock.

"We're nothing alike, believe me."

"I can tell that, darling."

"Then you can also understand why I don't want to meet Shane Reynolds."

A short silence followed. "No, I can't say that I can."

"Elizabeth, think about it. Anyone who appreciates Camille's beauty isn't going to be interested in me. Good grief, people wouldn't even guess we came from the same family. Camille is everything I'm not."

"I thought I explained that Shane Reynolds isn't the type of man to be impressed with beauty."

"Right. That's why he bought the painting."

"He purchased that portrait because you painted it and for no other reason."

"I doubt it, Elizabeth. I sincerely doubt it."

Their conversation ended five minutes later, and with flint-hard resolve Carrie returned to her Saturday morning chores and refused to waste another second thinking about Shane Reynolds. But as the day wasted away, she *did* think about him. She hadn't wanted to be rude. She hadn't wanted to push him away when everything in her yearned to reach out to him. Maybe Elizabeth was right and he *was* different. But she doubted it. She was certain that once he met Camille it would all be over.

Carrie's thoughts were still confused when the doorbell chimed the following afternoon. She was washing her hands, wondering what she should eat for lunch.

All morning she'd been sitting with paper and charcoal, sketching faces. Every one of them was Shane. Even the women and children had a strong resemblance to the silver fox who dominated her thoughts. Her floor was littered with the evidence of her frustration. Drying her hands on a towel, she hurried toward the door. Camille never bothered to knock, so it couldn't be her sister.

On the other side of the door, Shane shifted his weight from one foot to the other. He hadn't stopped thinking about the feisty artist all night. She intrigued him. Outwardly she was as prickly as a cactus, but her work revealed a warm, loving soul. There was obviously something about him she didn't like. Fine, he would find out what it was and take it from there.

Smiling, Carrie unlatched the lock and opened the door. "Hello." The welcome faded from her eyes as her gaze met Shane's. Her heart throbbed at the unexpectedness of seeing him a second time, and she glanced guiltily over her shoulder, as if the charcoal sketches might materialize before her eyes—and his. He'd come back, and, after her rudeness on the beach the day before, she couldn't imagine why.

"Hello." His gaze softened.

Gathering her resolve, she opened her mouth to tell him to leave, but the command in his eyes stopped her.

"Listen, I don't know what was wrong before, but I'd like to talk this out."

"I—"

"Before you argue with me, let me assure you that

I'm really a nice guy. And if you'll listen, I'd like to make a confession."

"What kind of confession?"

"I knew who you were long before Elizabeth's party."

"But how...?"

"You were at the gallery about a month ago, and I saw you leave. Elizabeth pointed you out to me." Remembering the woman he'd seen that afternoon told him something was wrong. That woman and the one on the beach weren't the same person.

Carrie remembered the day. It was one of those rare San Francisco days when the sun was shining, and everything in and about the world was perfect.

"I followed you to Fisherman's Wharf," he continued. "And watched you buy a bright red balloon."

"I didn't get it for me." That was only a small white lie.

"I know. I saw you give it to the little girl, but not until after you'd carried it with you for several blocks."

"I was looking for a *special* little girl." One like herself, plain and unassuming, someone who didn't command the attention of others. A child who walked in the shadow of an attractive brother or sister.

"Then you caught the cable car and—"

"You were spying on me."

"Actually, I was trying to come up with an original way of introducing myself," he admitted with a chagrined smile. "I'd just figured out that the straightforward approach would be best when you jumped on the cable car. I didn't make it."

"Oh." How incredibly inane that sounded.

"Now that I've bared my soul, I'm hoping that you'll share a picnic lunch with me." Surprise showed in her eyes, and Shane knew that half the battle had been won. At least she hadn't told him to leave again.

Carrie had to put a stop to the way her heart reacted to this man. "It looks like rain." Any excuse would do.

"There isn't a cloud in sight," Shane said, contradicting her.

"I don't have anything to pack for lunch."

"I do," he said. "I figured if you wouldn't go out to lunch with me, then I'd bring lunch to you."

"You're very sure of yourself." Her resolve managed one last rally.

"I'm very sure of what I want," he responded with a breathtaking smile that was meant to melt her defenses. He succeeded.

"And what exactly do you want?"

"To get to know you."

"Why?" she asked, lacing her fingers together. He really was something.

"That's the part that confuses me." A frown marred the urbane perfection of his features. He was unsure of his feelings. He didn't usually get much resistance from women. He was successful, wealthy, and reasonably attractive. Women gravitated toward him. After their minor confrontation on the beach, Shane had thought his own attraction to Carrie could be attributed to the challenge she represented. Today he was willing to admit differently. He'd wanted to meet her for weeks.

There was a reason she'd responded to him the way she had. And he was determined to find out why.

"I…don't know." Carrie hesitated, knowing that she'd already lost the inner battle.

"Come on, Carrie, I'm not really all that bad."

With a growing sense of anticipation, she smiled and, with a nod, asked, "Can we haul it down to the beach?"

"I was hoping you'd suggest that."

She followed him out to his car, where he retrieved a small wicker basket and blanket. She still couldn't believe that he'd come back after she'd been so rude and unreasonable. She realized she shouldn't be so glad, but she was. A warning light went off in her head like a traffic light gone berserk, but she chose to ignore it, cursing her foolish heart for wanting this so badly.

Leading the way down the well-worn path to the beach, she commented, "It's a beautiful day, isn't it?"

Shane's warm gaze held hers. "Yes, it is."

A mere smile from this man could charm snakes. He obviously possessed more enchantment than her meager defenses could easily fend off. Her stomach knotted in a tight ball of nerves as she determined that she wouldn't let one picnic with him influence her feelings. No matter how difficult it was, she would remain coolly detached. She had to.

Her smile was wavering by the time they reached the sand.

"This is perfect," he commented when she paused to spread out a blanket. Behind his lazy regard, Carrie felt that he was watching her every move. She struggled to remain unaffected.

"We don't often see bright sunshine so early in the summer," she finally said, then wondered why she was talking to him as though he were a tourist. Anyone who lived in San Francisco knew what the weather was like.

He didn't comment, almost seeming to enjoy her obvious discomfort. "The weather's generally pleasant this time of year."

Silently, she wished he wasn't so damned logical. Surely he could recognize that she was making an effort to be polite. She owed him that much. No doubt few women ignored a man like Shane Reynolds. Unfortunately, the knowledge served only to heighten her awareness of him and his many charms.

"Maybe we should eat now," he suggested.

"Sure," she agreed, eager to change the subject.

Shane handed her napkins and pried the top from a bucket of chicken. They ate in silence.

By the time they'd finished, Carrie was wondering why she'd ever agreed to this.

Stretching his long legs out in front of him, he crossed them at the ankles and rested his weight on the palms of his hands. "Do you feel like talking now?"

"I suppose." She made busy work, picking up the litter. Her gaze avoided his.

"What happened the other morning?" Once he passed that hurdle, he could venture on to Elizabeth's party.

"When you said you wanted to talk, I assumed you meant about the painting."

"Not particularly." His blue eyes smoldered as they studied her.

"Then why'd you come here?"

"I wanted to get to know you."

"I don't understand why." Carrie was embarrassed that her voice trembled.

"Elizabeth told me what a rare talent you are." Shane suspected she would feel more comfortable discussing her art.

"You don't look like the type of man who goes around forcing himself on artists."

"You're right, I'm not. Something happened the night of the party that made you run away almost immediately after I arrived. I want to know what."

"You're imagining things." If she'd known this was going to turn into an interrogation, she never would have agreed to this picnic.

"Maybe I was imagining something at the party," he reasoned. "But Saturday morning you were rude and abrupt."

"Why did you come back, then?"

"I felt that, given time, you'd change your mind about me."

His confidence grated on Carrie. "You've got a big ego."

"Agreed, but in the past it's worked to my advantage."

"Okay, you've met me. Now what?" She wasn't up

to playing verbal games with him. The sooner she discovered why he was so curious about her, the sooner she could deal with her emotions.

"I'm intrigued."

"Don't be. What you see is what you get." She pushed back a thick strand of rusty-colored hair and batted her long lashes at him.

His deep husky laugh floated with the wind. "But I like what I see."

"Then you need bifocals." He wouldn't have bought the painting of Camille if he appreciated someone like her. "Why did you buy the portrait?" she asked bluntly, needing to know.

He smiled lazily, and his handsome features looked years younger. He wondered what it was about that painting that disturbed her, and he weighed his words carefully, not wanting to reveal the true reason just yet. "If you want the truth, I needed something for my office. I was hoping a few of the unwelcome matchmakers I know would view the woman as my current love interest."

"*No Competition* should do the trick." This was even worse than she'd realized. A feeling of disappointment burned through her.

"Who is she?"

It took Carrie a moment to realize Shane was asking about Camille. "A beautiful woman." Her answer was clipped and cool.

"Yes, she's that, but the portrait isn't the first piece of yours that I've seen."

"Oh?" She pretended ignorance, even though Elizabeth had already told her Shane had purchased other paintings of hers.

"I have one of your seascapes and a couple of your earlier watercolors."

"Oh." Her vocabulary had unexpectedly been reduced to words of one syllable.

"You're very good."

"Thanks."

"It's to the point where Elizabeth contacts me the moment you bring in something new."

"I'm flattered."

"The problem is that lately I haven't been able to separate the paintings from the artist."

Startled green eyes met intense blue ones, and Carrie caught her breath before it jammed her throat. If he saw her personality in her work, then he must glimpse her insecurities and all her glaring faults.

"I feel like I already know you, Miss Carrie Lockett."

Her heart was threatening to pound right out of her chest.

"I look at your painting of spring flowers blowing free in the wind, and I sense your love of nature and generosity of spirit. You love with an intensity that few seldom see or experience."

Tight-lipped, she lowered her gaze. Every word he said was distinctly unsettling. He'd blown her up in his mind to be something she wasn't. "I'm not Mother Theresa."

"The seascape taught me that. There's depth to you. You're an anchor while others are sails. I also sense rebellion, and, with this recent portrait, perhaps a hint of jealousy."

Shane Reynolds unnerved her, and Carrie struggled to cover her confusion by responding sharply. "Who wouldn't be jealous? You bought the painting, so you obviously appreciate beauty."

Her own words echoed around her like a taunt, and she closed her eyes to a lifetime of being second best.

"Is that why you called it *No Competition?*" he asked quietly.

"Of course," she came back flippantly.

"But there's no comparison between you and the woman in the painting."

"Exactly." She rose awkwardly and brushed the grains of sand from the backs of her legs. She hoped to hide her confusion by taking a walk along the beach.

He followed. "Do you always walk away when the conversation doesn't suit you?"

"Always." The tension she struggled so hard to disguise threaded its way through her nerves. "Listen, I appreciate the compliment. Any artist would. But you've met me, and now you can see that I'm nothing like you imagined."

"But you are," he interrupted. "And a whole lot more."

"Sorry, wrong girl."

"Correction, right woman." He slipped his hands into his pants pockets. "I want the chance to know you better."

"I'm all out of résumés. Check with Elizabeth."

"I don't want to read about you. Let me take you to dinner."

"No." She hated this, and silently pleaded with him to leave things as they were.

"Why not?"

"Do I have to spell it out for you, Mr. Reynolds? Thanks, but no thanks. I'm simply not interested."

"I don't believe that."

"Have you got such a colossal ego that you believe no woman can turn you down?"

"Maybe so. I'm not giving up on you, Carrie."

"Please." Her voice softened, and her green eyes pleaded with him. "I hate being so rude. I'm simply not interested."

"Give it some thought," he coaxed gently.

"There's nothing to think about." She wanted to cry. "Believe me, I'm flattered, but the answer is no. Plain and simple. N-O. No."

He struggled not to argue with her. He would have to come up with some other way to reach her. "You can't blame a guy for trying."

"No, I don't blame you." She looked out to the sea to avoid his smoldering gaze. "Thank you for the lunch." And everything else, she mused, wondering what it would mean to her life to send him away.

He didn't argue her curt dismissal, only cocked his head slightly and, without a word, turned and walked out of her life.

Shane was the type of man of whom dreams were made, and she was turning him away. But it was more than the fact that he'd bought Camille's picture that had prompted her to dismiss him. Shane frightened her in a way that was completely unfamiliar to her.

Monday afternoon, curiosity got the best of her, so Carrie contacted Elizabeth Brandon at the gallery.

"Carrie, darling, it's good to hear from you."

Carrie drew in a deep breath. "Why didn't you tell me about Shane Reynolds?"

"But, darling, I did."

"All this time he's been buying my paintings."

"I already mentioned that."

"I know, but you claimed lots of customers ask for my work."

"You're becoming appreciated."

"But Shane Reynolds is different."

"How's that?" The soft lilt of Elizabeth's voice indicated that she was enjoying their conversation.

"He's the kind of man women follow around, drooling."

Elizabeth gave a tiny laugh. "A customer's physical attributes have little to do with his appreciation of the arts."

"That's not what I meant." The problem was, Carrie didn't actually know what she *had* meant.

"Listen, darling, I'm glad you phoned. I was about to contact you. The president of Little & Little called this morning, hoping I could get in touch with you about doing his portrait."

Smiling, Carrie decided she was wasting so much time worrying about Shane Reynolds that she was neglecting her business. In fact, if she didn't get another commission soon she would go crazy. Today even the seascape she was painting had the shades of Shane Reynolds's eyes in it. "I'm interested."

"I thought you might be. He wants you to come to his home for the initial interview. Have you got a pen?"

"Yes." Carrie pulled out a piece of paper. "Go ahead."

Elizabeth gave her an address in the Nob Hill area. "Can you make it soon?"

"Whenever he likes."

"Is tomorrow evening convenient?"

There wasn't any reason why she couldn't make it. It wasn't like she had a busy social calendar. Tomorrow would be like any other night of the week. She would microwave a frozen dinner and immerse herself in a good book. "Sure, I can make it."

"Wonderful. I'll send over the usual contract."

The following evening, at the appointed time, Carrie pulled up across from the address Elizabeth had given her. She tucked her sketch pad under her arm and swung her purse strap over her shoulder as she looked both ways before crossing the street.

The bell chimed once, and she prepared a ready smile. These early interviews could be the most important. The smile died, however, when Shane Reynolds opened the door.

A grin slashed his handsome features. "I hoped you would be on time."

Three

"You?" Carrie cried, managing to keep her anger at a low simmer. Shane had tricked her and used Elizabeth in his schemes. She was so furious she could hardly speak.

"Good to see you, too." His smile was warm enough to melt a glacial ice cap as he casually leaned against the door jamb and crossed his arms.

She refused to be trapped in his sensuous web and fumed at the amused curl of his mouth. "You think you're clever, don't you?"

"I try to be." To tell the truth, he wasn't all that pleased with the underhanded methods he'd used to get Carrie to his home. Once again he'd spent a sleepless night wondering why her reactions to him were so cold. After their meeting on the beach, she'd represented a challenge. Now it was more than that. She was a spirited, intriguing woman, and those wide green eyes spitting fire at him melted his determination to forget her.

Stepping inside the house, Carrie discovered a wide

entryway tiled in opulent marble. A winding staircase veered off to the left, and to her immediate right double doors opened into a large, old-fashioned parlor. At any other time she would have appreciated the character and personality of the house, but in the present circumstances, she couldn't see beyond Shane's deception.

"I suppose I owe you another apology," he began, but she quickly cut him off.

"Do you always go to such drastic measures when a woman refuses you?" Her voice was hard and flat. She pressed the sketch book so tightly against her chest that her fingers lost feeling. "I don't appreciate this."

"I didn't imagine you would. But I wanted to talk to you."

"We talked yesterday." Carrie couldn't take her eyes off him. His sports jacket was unbuttoned, held open by a hand thrust in his pocket. Her pounding pulse told her that she was flattered that he'd gone to all this trouble to see her again, but her head insisted the only reason was that so few women turned Shane Reynolds down, his oversize ego was on the line.

"We may have talked. But I didn't get to say all the things I wanted to," he countered. Although he struck a casual pose, she was aware that he was every bit as on edge as she was.

"If I sit down and listen, will you promise to leave me alone?"

He mulled over her words. "I don't know if I can verbalize everything."

"Then the deal's off." She spun sharply and marched

out the door. No footsteps sounded behind her as she crossed the street to her car. Her emotions were in an upheaval. She was running like a frightened child from the things she wanted most in life. She *was* scared. The attraction she felt toward Shane was so strong, she had to fight against it with every breath. Things would be so much easier if he hadn't bought the painting of Camille. She might have been able to rationalize the situation then.

A turn of the ignition key resulted in a grinding sound. She stared at the gauges in disbelief, hoping they could tell her something. Her minivan might be old, but it had always been faithful. Again she tried to start the engine. This time the grinding sound was lower and sicker.

Tossing a curious glance out her side window, she noted Shane standing on his front porch, watching her. He was smiling as though he had the world by the tail. She returned his taunting grin, thinking he was the most infuriating man she'd ever known.

She climbed out of the car and walked around the front to open the hood, chancing a look in Shane's direction. He'd come down the steps and was standing under a lovely maple tree on the other side of the street.

She felt her hateful freckles flashing like neon lights, she was so flustered. Not knowing what to do, she touched a couple of gadgets as though she were a faith healer. Then, feeling like a complete idiot, she closed the hood, climbed in the front seat again and turned the key.

Nothing.

"Did I ever tell you I'm a whiz with mechanical things?" Shane called, enjoying this unexpected turn of events.

"No," she grumbled under her breath. The least he could do was offer to help, but he didn't volunteer, and she refused to ask.

"I'm quite good," he continued. "From the time I was a child, there wasn't anything I couldn't take apart and put back together again. Including a car engine."

"How interesting," she returned sarcastically, getting out of the car again.

"I'm certain we could come up with a small compromise." He advanced a step.

"Exactly what kind of compromise?" She glared at him, her hands on her hips.

"Dinner in exchange for the magical touch of these mechanically tuned fingers." He held up his right hand and flexed his fingers.

"I was thinking more along the lines of contacting Triple A." She held her shoulders stiff.

"Carrie, Carrie, Carrie," he said mockingly. "Am I such an ogre? Is the thought of dinner with me so unappealing?"

She longed to shout that any meal shared with him would be divine. It wasn't him she didn't trust but herself. It would be far too easy to fall for this man.

"If you want my word that I won't touch you," he added, "then you have it." But he gave it grudgingly.

"That's not it," she murmured miserably.

"Then what *is* it?"

She hunched her shoulders, and tears brimmed in the murky depths of her eyes. "What—what do you want with someone like me? I'm not the least bit attractive and you're...well, you're one of the beautiful people of this world. I'm so ordinary."

Shane's smiling expression was gone. Vanished. He couldn't believe what he was hearing. Not attractive. Good heavens, where had she gotten that impression? She was magnificent. Spirited. Talented. Intelligent. He crossed the street in giant strides and paused to stand in front of her. His brow creased in thick lines as his frown deepened. "Not attractive? Who told you that? You're perfectly wonderful, and I defy anyone to say otherwise."

"Oh stop!" she cried, and wiped the moisture from her face, more furious with herself than with him. Tears were the last thing she'd expected. She would have believed him, if he hadn't bought Camille's portrait.

He began to lightly trace her face, starting at the base of her throat, stroking the triangle formed by the hollow there. The thick pad of his thumb sensuously brushed her collarbone, the feel of his finger slightly abrasive against her soft, clean skin. Carrie swallowed convulsively as the muscles in her throat contracted. She couldn't breathe properly. His touch was warm and gentle, reminding her of velvet. His words were just as smooth, and she knew she couldn't trust either one.

"I don't know you," she told him, her voice choked to a low, husky level. Her senses were whirling.

"And I feel like I've known you all my life."

"What do you want from me?"

"Time. When you get to know me better, you'll realize I don't give up easily. If I want something, I simply go after it."

"And for now you want me. But why?" Her knees shook under the intensity of his gaze. She fought off the sensation of weakness.

His hands cupping her shoulders, he tried to figure out how to put his feelings into words. When he looked at her paintings, he lost sight of the artwork, caught instead by the artist. "I'll never hurt you, Carrie. I promise you that."

Somehow she believed that he wouldn't intentionally hurt her. But already he had her senses spinning. He could easily pull her into his orbit, and then she would be lost. "If I have dinner with you, then will you help me with my car?"

"I'd help you even if you don't stay," he said with a roguish grin. "But I'd like it if you would."

"I…I am a little hungry."

The smile that lit up his eyes came all the way from his heart. "I was hoping you'd agree." He reached for her hand, curling his fingers around hers. "I'm an excellent cook."

Her guard slipped. It was so much easier to give in and smile at him than to struggle against the pull of her heart. "You cook, too, huh? I doubt that there's much you don't do."

He laughed, and the vibrant sound echoed around her. "You do have a lot to learn about me, Carrie Lockett." He led her back inside the house and into the plush dining room. The table was set with long, tapered candles at each end, and a floral centerpiece dominated the middle.

"Do you eat like this all the time?" She had assumed he was wealthy, but he didn't seem the type who would bother with formality at mealtime every night.

He looked almost boyish when his amused gaze met hers. "I wanted to impress you."

"You succeeded."

"Good."

But that wasn't the only thing he'd succeeded in doing. Against every inner battle she'd waged, Carrie lost. He held out the shieldback chair for her, and once she was seated, he proceeded to bring out their meal.

As he'd claimed, Shane was an excellent gourmet cook. With her defenses down, she chatted easily with him throughout the meal, telling him about art school, and how she'd met Elizabeth and come to work with her.

"Ask me anything you want," he told her over dessert, pleased with how well their meal had gone. "As far as you're concerned, my life is an open book."

Carrie took him at his word. "How old are you?"

He frowned slightly and touched the neatly trimmed hair, briefly worried that his premature gray disturbed her. "Younger than I appear—thirty-three."

"I think your hair makes you look distinguished." She didn't add "devilishly handsome" to the list. His ego was big enough already.

He smiled crookedly. "It's a family trait. My father

was completely gray by age thirty. By the time I was in high school I already had a few gray strands. I beat dad by two years."

Carrie found it amazing that he would be self-conscious of a trait that made him look so dignified and attractive.

"What about your tan? You didn't get that here." Not in San Francisco in June. She was sure of that.

"I recently took a business trip to Tahiti."

"It's dirty work, but someone has to do it. Right?" she teased.

"Right. Now, is there anything else that curious mind of yours wants to know?"

No need hedging around the subject. She longed to ask it, and she suspected he was waiting. "Have you ever been married?"

"No."

"Why not?"

"A variety of reasons."

She lowered her gaze to her strawberry torte. "Don't try to tell me there haven't been women."

"A few." He touched the corner of his mouth with his napkin. "During my college days I was too busy with my studies to be involved in a relationship. Later it was my career."

"And now?"

"And now," he repeated, looking directly at her, "it's time."

He said it so softly that she felt like a popcorn ball had stuck in her throat. "Oh."

"Okay," he murmured. "My turn."

Her eyes met his. "What do you mean?"

"It's my turn to ask the questions."

"All right." But she wasn't eager.

"Married?"

"No." She said it with a small laugh.

"Why is that question so funny?"

She couldn't very well tell him that she could hardly be a married woman and feel the things she did sitting across the table from him. "No reason."

"How long have you been painting?"

She grinned, warming to the subject of her art. "Almost from the time I could remember. As a little girl I gave the letters of the alphabet faces and personalities. It took me the first three years of grade school to learn to write without adding ears and mouths to each letter. Numbers were even more difficult."

"Numbers?" He frowned. "Why those?"

"It's hard to explain."

"Try me."

Somehow she believed that he would understand where others had failed, including her own father. "To me, each number has a color and a feeling. The number one is white and pure and lonely. Two is pink and healthy. Seven is red and vibrant. Nine is black and foreboding."

"Why?"

She shrugged one delicate shoulder. "I don't know. I've always thought of them that way. I gave up trying to figure it out." For that matter, so had her teachers.

"What about family?"

"I have one sister. What about you?" she asked, quickly steering the subject away from Camille.

"Three married sisters, and a passel of nieces and nephews." His gaze shone with a curious light, and it was impossible to look away.

Gazing at Shane, his eyes warm and electric, Carrie yearned to pick up her pen and pad. He intrigued her. He would make an excellent model; the planes and grooves of his face were just short of craggy, and yet he was incredibly good looking. She longed to capture him on canvas with exactly the look he was giving her at that moment. Every facet of his features suggested strength of character and an elusive inner spirit.

"I'd like to paint you," she announced, unable to tear her gaze from his. "I don't know if you were serious when you contacted Elizabeth."

"I *was* serious." But only because having Carrie paint him would give him an excuse to be with her.

"Then you should know what you're letting yourself in for. I require ten sittings of a half-hour to an hour each."

"Fine. When can we start?"

Shane might have readily agreed to her stipulations, but she realized that sitting still was contrary to this man's personality. He was a doer, a go-getter, a human bulldozer. It wouldn't be easy for him to sit quietly for any length of time. He would be a challenge, but already she felt that a painting of Shane Reynolds could well be her best work. "I'd like to make a few preliminary sketches tonight."

"Fine."

As it turned out, Shane worked on her car while she sat on the grass and tried to capture his likeness. "You're not making this easy," she complained. He was leaning over the engine of her outdated minivan, so the only clear view she had of him was from the rear. Quickly she penciled that. Laughing, she flipped the page and drew him in oily coveralls and a heavy beard.

"What's so amusing?" His voice echoed from under the hood.

"Nothing," she replied absently as her hands flew deftly over the page. "But I don't think I dare show you what I'm drawing."

"Instead of picking on me," he instructed, "draw yourself."

She did, depicting herself as a giraffe with long, wobbly legs and knobby knees. Thick, sooty lashes framed round eyes, and her hair fell in an unruly mass of tight curls around her face. Her freckles became the giraffe's spots. "Here, for your collection," she said and tore off the sheet, handing it to him.

Amused, he wiped his hands clean with a clean rag before taking the page. But the smile in his eyes quickly disappeared as he viewed her self-image. "You see yourself like this?"

"Of course." Her own good humor vanished. The eyes that had been so warm and gentle hardened as he glared at her, intimidating her with an anger barely held in check.

"You can't argue with the hair," she added hurriedly. To prove her point, she webbed her fingers through the glorious length, holding it out from her head. "The freckles are also beyond debate. You can't overlook them. And the knees, well, you've only seen me in a dress once, so…"

She didn't finish as Shane crumpled the portrait in a tight ball, destroying it. "Don't poke fun at yourself, Carrie. There's no reason."

"It…was only a little joke."

"At your own expense. I don't like it."

"Well tough toast, buddy." She didn't like the emotions he was bringing out in her. She wasn't Camille, and she'd been compared to her sister all her life—always coming in a poor second. Camille was the beauty and *she*… Well, she had her art.

His eyes seemed to burn straight through her. Carrie shuffled her feet uneasily. "The car's fixed?"

"You shouldn't have any problem with it now." Already he regretted his heated response to her sketch.

"I hate to eat and run, but I'd better think about heading home."

He didn't argue, and she awkwardly moved to the driver's side of the minivan. "Thank you for your help. I truly appreciate it. And the dinner was excellent. You're right about being a good cook. No wonder you never married." Realizing how sexist that sounded, she gulped and added, "That's not to say that you'd marry someone just because she was a good cook. You're not that kind of man." Wanting to make a hasty retreat, she opened the door and slid inside. "Nor would you marry a woman because she had money," she babbled on, furious with herself for not stopping. "Since you're wealthy yourself and all. What I mean…" She felt her freckles flash on like fluorescent light bulbs. "You just aren't the type of man to do that sort of thing."

Resisting the urge to laugh, Shane closed her door, his hands resting on the roof of the van. "You seem to have marriage on your mind. Is this a proposal?"

Carrie nearly swallowed her tongue. "Good grief no. It's just that…" Before she said anything more to regret, she busied herself with her keys, wanting only to escape further humiliation.

"Carrie." He said her name so softly that she jerked her head around.

He slid a finger under her chin and closed her gaping mouth. Her sensitive nerve endings vibrated with the contact. Slowly, he bent his head toward hers, his warm breath stirring the wispy hairs at her temple. Tripping wildly, her heart pounded against her ribs as she realized he was going to kiss her.

With unhurried ease, Shane claimed her mouth, his lips playing softly over hers, tasting, caressing, nibbling. When he'd finished and straightened, she gazed at him wide-eyed. Speaking, breathing—even blinking—was impossible.

"I'm serious about the portrait," he murmured, stepping away from the minivan.

Mutely, Carrie nodded, feeling lost and utterly confused. Fumbling with her key, she started the car and prepared to shift into Drive.

"Carrie?"

She turned to him.

"You're not a giraffe. You're a graceful, delicate swan who thinks of herself as an ugly duckling."

It was all she could manage just to pull away from the curb. The heat from her blush descended all the way down her neck. Like a fool, she'd babbled on, trying to cover one faux pas but instead creating another and another, until she'd made a complete fool of herself.

By the time she arrived at the beach house, she was convinced she could never face Shane Reynolds again.

"Where were you the other night?" Camille asked, her lithe body folded over in the white wicker chair while Carrie painted.

Carrie did her utmost to concentrate on her current project, a still life. "With a client. How did your dinner date go with Bob?" She preferred to stay away from the subject of Shane. Her sister was perceptive enough to recognize that Carrie's feelings toward him weren't ordinary. From past experience, Carrie knew better than to discuss any male friends with her sibling. More times than she cared to count, Camille had stolen away her boyfriends. The amazing part was that Camille hadn't even been trying. Men naturally preferred her to Carrie. Who wouldn't? Camille was beautiful.

If Camille did happen to learn about Shane, it could well

be that her twin would find him as appealing as she did. Few men were strong enough to resist Camille's charms.

"Bob fancies himself in love with me." Camille's dark head dipped as she ran a nail file down the length of her long nail.

"That's not unusual."

"No, I do seem to collect admirers, don't I?"

She said it with such a complete lack of interest that Carrie had to fight to hide a smile.

"I don't know, though," Camille continued, paying an inordinate amount of attention to her nail.

"Know what?"

"About Bob."

"What's there to know? Either you love him or you don't." Almost immediately Carrie realized how uncaring that sounded. Camille had come to her with a dilemma, and she was being curt. "I didn't mean that the way it sounded."

"That's all right. Bob is my problem."

"But I'm your sister."

Camille offered her a weak smile. "There are lots of other fish in the sea. What I think I need is a break from Bob so I can do a little exploring."

"Maybe that's what we both need, to explore." But Carrie wasn't silly enough to let her sister know about Shane.

"You always could love better than me," Camille admitted with a half frown that only slightly marred her stunning good looks. "And yet the men always flocked to me, even though I'm the cold fish."

"Camille, you aren't." Her sister might have a few

faults—who didn't? But Camille also possessed a wonderful capacity to love. She just hadn't found the right man yet.

Camille arched two perfectly shaped brows as she gave the matter some consideration. "You'll laugh if I tell you that I think I may be half in love with Bob."

"I wouldn't laugh. In fact, I think it's wonderful."

"Is it?"

"I think so."

"He's got his faults."

"Camille," Carrie said, and laughed aloud. "Everyone does."

Camille hesitated and concentrated on her fingernail. "I suppose. Now tell me about your new client. You're hiding something from me."

Returning her attention to the canvas, Carrie did her best to disguise her feelings. "What's there to tell? He wants his portrait done, that's all."

"Come on, Carrie." Camille laughed, sounding like a kitten purring. "You're holding out on me."

"There's a sketch of him over there if you're interested." She pointed to the pad on the tabletop.

Camille reached for the drawing Carrie had done of Shane as a bearded man in coveralls. "He doesn't look like he can afford to have you paint his portrait."

"You're probably right," she hedged.

With her head cocked to one side, Camille continued to study the drawing. "He does have an interesting face, though."

"If you like that type."

"I think I could get used to him. Did he give you the

name of the garage where he works? My car's been acting up lately. I might have him look at it."

Carrie pinched her lips together in an effort to disguise her anxiety. For her to show the least amount of interest in Shane would be to invite Camille's curiosity. "He didn't say." Taking a gamble, she added, "But I have his address if you want it."

Tucking her nail file inside her purse, Camille shook her head. "Another time, perhaps."

The tension between Carrie's shoulder blades relaxed. "Whatever you say."

"I've got to go. Bob's meeting me later, and I want to look good."

Camille couldn't do anything more to improve her already flawless appearance. It was difficult to polish perfection.

As soon as Camille was gone, Carrie reached for the phone. She'd delayed calling Shane all afternoon. Every time she thought of the things she'd said, the embarrassment went all the way to her bones.

"Hello." His greeting was brusque.

"This is Carrie Lockett. Is this a bad time?"

"Carrie." Her name was delivered with a rush of pleasure.

In her mind's eye, she could picture him relaxing and leaning back to smile into the receiver. Her own pulse reacted madly, and she pulled herself up straight. "I'm calling to set a schedule for your sittings. I'd like to begin tomorrow afternoon, if possible." She felt the need to elaborate. "The first few sittings can be done anywhere. I can come to your house or your office, whichever you choose. Later it would be more convenient if you could come here."

"Either is fine. Let me check my schedule."

In the background, she could hear him flipping pages. "How does four o'clock tomorrow sound?"

"That'll be fine."

"Would you mind coming to my office?"

"Give me the address, and I'll be happy to."

"My, my don't we sound formal. Has the car given you any more trouble?"

"No…but I haven't been out today."

"The next time you're at the service station, have the attendant check the carburetor."

"All right." She hesitated, not wanting the conversation to end. "I want you to know how much I appreciate your fixing it."

"And I'm grateful that you stayed and shared dinner with me," he added softly. "I'd be willing to do a complete engine overhaul if it meant you'd come again. Maybe tonight?" The warmth in his tone was disturbing. But then, everything about Shane Reynolds disturbed her.

"No thanks, perhaps another time."

"I'll hold you to that."

"I'm taking a class tonight," she said, then wondered why she felt compelled to explain.

"I'm pleased to know it isn't because you're seeing another man—or are you?"

"No." She didn't feel like admitting that he was the only man she'd dated in a month. Her "dates" were more getting together with friends than the result of any romantic interest.

"Good. What I know won't set me to wondering."

Carrie found it highly amusing that someone as handsome as Shane would feel threatened by anyone she'd dated.

"I'll see you at four tomorrow," she told him.

"I'm looking forward to it."

Unfortunately, so was she. Far, far more than she should.

Wednesday afternoon, Carrie entered Shane's building at a few minutes to four. She'd dressed in a blue linen jumpsuit, and tied her hair at the base of her neck with a silk scarf. She'd spent a good portion of the early afternoon preparing for this meeting, but not in the way that she usually readied herself for a sitting. Instead, she sorted through her closets, and spent extra time on her hair and makeup, all the while berating herself for the time and trouble she was taking.

"I'm Carrie Lockett," she told the receptionist. "I have a four o'clock appointment with Mr. Reynolds."

The attractive woman in her early twenties smiled at Carrie. "Mr. Reynolds mentioned you'd be coming. If you take a seat, he'll be with you in a moment." She punched a button on the phone line and spoke into her headset. "Ms. Lockett is here for her appointment."

Carrie took a seat and chose a magazine, since she knew she would probably have to wait a few minutes. After idly flipping through the crisp pages, she had just settled on an article when the door opened and Shane appeared. "I'm sorry to keep you waiting."

Slowly she stood. "I've only been here a couple of

minutes." They gazed at each other in a way that felt far too meaningful for what was supposed to be a business meeting of sorts.

"Come in, won't you?"

She would have willingly walked over hot coals to get to him. *You've got it bad, girl,* she mocked herself. "Thank you." She hoped her voice sounded cool and professional but knew she'd failed miserably.

"That'll be all for today, Carol," Shane told his secretary.

Carrie stepped inside his office and stopped cold. Camille's portrait hung on the wall opposite his desk in bold splendor, her dark-haired beauty dominating the room. Shane had told her the portrait would hang in his office, but she'd forgotten. Abruptly she looked away, fighting the tightness in her heart. Every day Shane sat in this room and stared at the compelling beauty of her sister. Each time he picked up the phone his gaze would rest naturally on Camille. As much as Carrie had tried to forget it, the fact remained that Shane found Camille beautiful. And if he stared at the creamy smooth perfection of her sister long enough, he couldn't help notice the flaws that stood out like giant fault lines in Carrie.

He motioned for her to take a seat. "Elizabeth sent over the contract," he said, holding out the paper to her.

"I hope you haven't signed it," she said in a low, tight voice. "Because I don't think this is going to work. I've given the matter some thought and decided that I wouldn't be the best one for this job. I'm sorry, Shane. Really sorry." She turned and fled from his office.

Four

"Carrie—" Shane raced after her, ignoring the startled look of his receptionist, who was gathering her things. He didn't know what was troubling Carrie, but he wasn't about to let her run away from him a second time. He caught up with her outside the elevator. "What is the matter with you all of a sudden?"

"Nothing." She swallowed down another lie. "Really. I…just realized that I'm overextended timewise and… doing another portrait now would be too much for me." She couldn't tell him that it was impossible for her to work with him, knowing that he spent his days staring at Camille's perfect features. She would undoubtedly be placed in the position of having to respond to his curiosity about the woman in the portrait. No one could look at Camille and not want to know her.

"I've got a contract, an agreement made in good faith," he reminded her, placing his hand on her shoulder in an effort to get her to face him. "We've agreed on the terms, and I expect you to hold up your end of the bargain."

"Shane...I can't."

Curious bystanders were beginning to gather around them, and Carrie was feeling more miserable by the minute.

"Let's get out of here," he mumbled, reaching for her limp hand. Instead of waiting for the elevator, he led her toward the stairwell. They hadn't gone more than a few steps when he turned to face her. "What is it with you? You have got to be the most unreasonable woman I've ever known. You're hot, then cold. First the portrait's on, then it's off. You can't seem to make up your mind about anything."

"I'm sorry."

"Don't tell me that again."

"All right." From the way she behaved around him, Carrie considered it a wonder that he wanted anything to do with her. "If we mutually agree to tear up the contract—"

"No." His voice was both hard and flat. "I hired you to do my portrait." He wouldn't let her slip through his fingers that easily.

"But surely you understand that I can't."

"Why not?" he shot right back.

"Because..."

"Carrie, come on." He paused and pushed his fingers through his well-groomed hair. "Let's get out of here. It's obvious we need to talk."

While they marched down the stairs, her mind frantically sought a feasible explanation and quickly came back blank. Nothing would satisfy Shane except the truth, and she wasn't willing to reveal that.

Once outside, he escorted her across the busy intersection into a nearby hotel. Carrie was grateful for the semi-darkness that shrouded the room as he led her to a table in the cocktail lounge. Her face felt hot with angry embarrassment. She was angry with herself and embarrassed that Shane wouldn't accept her feeble excuses.

They were no sooner seated than the waitress approached. Absently Shane ordered two glasses of wine, then paid when they arrived.

"All right, I'm listening," he coaxed. "Why do you want out of the contract?"

The smile that curved her lips felt as brittle as scorched parchment. Twirling the stem of the wineglass between her palms helped occupy her hands. "It isn't that I don't want to do your portrait."

"You could have fooled me," he muttered sarcastically.

"I think I'd do a good job."

"I *know* you would."

His confidence in her abilities produced a spark of genuine pleasure. "I...like you, Shane."

"I haven't made any secret about the way I feel about you. But you're like a giant puzzle to me...."

"And some of the pieces are missing," she finished for him.

He chuckled and relaxed, leaning back in his chair.

His smile was slightly off center—and devastating. "Exactly."

Carrie took a sip of her wine and felt the coiled tension drain from her arms and legs. She'd been looking forward to this meeting all day. Seeing Camille's portrait hanging in Shane's office had nearly ruined everything.

"Is there anything else you wanted to say?" he inquired, studying her.

"Yes." She paused and cleared her throat. She was anxious, yet aware of a tingling excitement deep inside her. It happened every time she was around Shane. He was the most special man she'd ever known. But she was afraid that once Camille learned about him, it would be all over. Since he found Camille's portrait so intriguing, she doubted that he would find the real woman any less so.

"Can we start again?" she asked, her voice slightly strained.

"I think we'd better." He stood and glanced around the room. His large hands folded over the back of the chair as he nodded in her direction. "I hope I haven't kept you waiting." He spoke as though he'd only just arrived.

Carrie chuckled and glanced at her wristwatch, playing his game. "Only a few minutes."

"I see you've ordered the wine." He sat and reached for his glass, tasting it. "My favorite. How did you know?"

"Lucky guess."

She resembled a frightened fawn, and Shane couldn't understand it. "Now, about the portrait," he said conversationally.

She stiffened. She couldn't help herself. "Which portrait?"

He didn't understand why there would be a question. "The one you've agreed to paint of me."

Visibly, she relaxed. "Ah, yes, that one."

"Shall we do the first sitting today?"

"Today?" She had everything with her. There wasn't any reason not to start with the preliminary sketches. "If you like."

"Of course." He stood and placed a generous tip on the table. "Are you ready?"

It took a minute for her to realize that he wanted to return to his office. "You mean now?" She groped for a plausible reason not to go back there. Her mind was befuddled. Her wits deserted her. "Today?"

"Yes." His arched brows formed an inquisitive frown. "Is that a problem?"

"Well, actually, I'm in a bit of a rush. I was thinking that since we're here...and your office is over there..." She pointed in the general direction of the street. "It seems a waste of time to travel all the way over there when we're..."

"Here."

"Right."

"Do you have something against my office?"

"Your office?" She swallowed uncomfortably. "Don't be silly. I've only been there once." As she spoke she reached for her sketchbook. "What could I possibly have against your office?"

"I don't even want to try guessing the answer to that one," he grumbled, downing the last of his wine.

Taking her thick-leaded pencil from her purse, Carrie angled the pad of paper in front of her and began sketching his bold features. Her fingers worked quickly, transmitting the image from her eye to the sheet. As soon as she completed one angle, she flipped the page and started on another, seeking the best possible way to catch the man and his personality.

She worked intently, unaware of the curious stares cast in their direction.

"When do I get to look?"

"Soon." The one word was clipped, a mark of her intense concentration.

"Do you want me to hold my head a certain way?"

"What I want is for you to keep your mouth closed."

He snapped it shut, but she noted the way his lips quivered as he struggled to hold back a lopsided grin.

Finally, when she couldn't stand it another minute, she rested the pad against the edge of the round table. "All right, what's so blasted amusing?"

"You."

"Me? Why?"

"Explaining would be impossible. But I'll have you know that I'm revealing my strength of character here."

"How's that?"

"I doubt that few men would demonstrate so much restraint."

Restraint. The man was speaking in riddles. "How's that?"

"Kissing you seems to be my natural inclination."

Shock paralyzed her. Her hand sagged against the paper, and the pencil slipped from her fingers and dropped unceremoniously to the floor. Quickly she retrieved it, her cheeks flaming with hot color.

Smiling boldly, Shane captured her gaze. "You heard me right."

"But the room's full of people."

"It's dark in here," he countered, giving her a grin best described as Cheshire-cat smug. "As I was saying, I'm showing a lot of self-restraint."

"Should I tell you how grateful I am?"

"It would help."

She finished the last sketch and handed the pad to him. "Then thank you, Mr. Reynolds."

His eyes studied the likeness she'd drawn of him. "Nice."

"Is there one you prefer more than the others?"

"No. You decide." He wasn't especially interested in her doing his portrait. It was all a ruse, an excuse to get to know her better and learn what he could about this complicated woman.

"I will, then."

"How about dinner?"

His invitation cut into her thoughts. She was trying to decide the best angle to capture the force of his personality.

"Pardon?"

"You know—dinner—the meal that's eaten at the end of the day, usually after a long afternoon at the office. And most often after the time when a man has had a chance to relax with a glass of fine wine."

"Oh, you mean *dinner.*"

"Right." He gave her an odd look. "How about it?"

"Yes, I usually eat that meal."

He chuckled. "Since it seems to be that time of day, and we've already relaxed with a glass of excellent wine, how about sharing dinner?"

He offered the invitation with such charm that Carrie doubted if she could have refused him. He had to be the most patient man in the world. Anyone else would have considered her a prime candidate for the loony bin.

"What kind of dinner?" The shop that employed Camille wasn't more than a mile from Shane's office, and if they chose a restaurant close by, there was the possibility that they would run into Camille. Although they didn't look the least bit alike, the way the two of them shared thoughts was sometimes uncanny. Only last month they'd celebrated their father's birthday and discovered that they'd each purchased him the identical golf shirt and birthday card. At other times, Carrie would be thinking about Camille and go to call her, only to have Camille ring first, claiming Carrie had been on her mind.

"What kind of dinner?" Shane repeated the question with a perplexed look that was becoming all too familiar. "I was considering food."

"A popular choice. However, I was thinking more

along ethnic lines. You know…Italian, Mexican, Chinese."

"You decide."

She didn't hesitate. "Chinese." Camille had never been especially fond of Chinese food. She leaned more toward a variety of expensive seafood dishes. For that matter, Carrie was fond of those herself.

"Fine," Shane said, though he didn't seem enthusiastic.

"You don't seem thrilled with my choice." Which didn't seem fair, given that he was the one who'd suggested that she choose.

He shrugged. "I was in Chinatown for lunch today."

"It doesn't matter to me," she lied. "You decide." Her fingers trembled slightly as she sipped the last of her wine.

"Do you like seafood?"

She released an inward groan. She should have known he would suggest that. "Seafood?" Her voice echoed his.

He shot her a brief, mocking glance. "Yes. You know, fish, lobster, crab. That sort of thing. I've heard Billy's on the Wharf is excellent."

"I suppose that's fine." She dropped her gaze to the table, not wanting him to know how distressed she was. Camille had often raved about the food at Billy's.

"Mexican?" he offered next.

Instantly she brightened. "Great choice." Camille usually said Mexican food was too fattening.

He mumbled something under his breath and shook

his head. Then he stood up and said, "Let's get out of here before you change your mind."

She found it amazing that he still wanted to have dinner with her after going through all that. She reached for her pad and purse. "I'm not going to change my mind."

A smile twitched at the corners of his mouth. "I won't believe it until I see it."

Shane held the door open for her, and they stepped outside into the bright sunshine. Side by side they walked along the crowded sidewalk. Rush hour traffic filled the streets. His hand came up to rest on her back just above her waist. Its guiding pressure was light, but enough for her to be aware of the contact and be unnerved by it. But then, everything about this man seemed to affect her.

They were halfway down the block when she caught a glimpse of a teal-blue convertible that resembled the model Camille drove. Rather than take a chance of being seen with Shane, she made a sharp right hand turn and headed into the nearest store.

She had disappeared before Shane realized it. She was there one minute and gone the next. Stunned, he did a complete three hundred and sixty degree turn. He was utterly perplexed.

"Carrie?" Shane whirled around again, attempting to locate her.

The car passed without incident. Carrie was so busy hiding that she didn't notice if it was Camille's car or not. Quickly she moved back outside. "Sorry, I…saw something on sale that I've been wanting." She flicked her wrist toward the black leather bedroom outfit, complete with handcuffs and chains, displayed prominently in the window. Then her shocked eyes went from the display window to the name of the establishment, which made it abundantly clear as to their specialty.

Sucking in a horrified breath, she instantly turned fifteen shades of red. "Then, of course, I realized that I was in the wrong store. It was…some…other store."

"Naturally."

They caught a taxi at the next corner, and Shane gave the man the name of a restaurant not far from Billy's on Fisherman's Wharf. After what had happened earlier, she wasn't about to try to get him to choose another place, even though this restaurant was too close for comfort to the one Camille frequented.

Their meal was delicious. Or it would have been if Carrie had taken more than a token taste. Her appetite had vanished with the toll of her minor subterfuge.

After dinner they took a short stroll, stopping in a few shops along the way. The whole time Carrie was conscious that it would be just her luck to run into Camille. They caught a taxi at the waterfront, and Shane escorted Carrie back to her minivan.

"Thank you for dinner." She stood with her back to the driver's door. Her hands gripped the handle from behind.

"You're very welcome." Shadows darkened his face. The streetlight illuminated the area, creating a soft romantic atmosphere.

Carrie wished the lights were dimmer. She wanted

Shane to kiss her and doubted that he would in such a
well-lit spot.

She could feel him watching her as she spoke. "I
had a nice time."

"Good. Maybe we can do it again soon."

She shrugged in an effort to disguise how pleased
she was that he asked. "Sure. There are lots of good
restaurants in Daly City."

"Daly City! What's the matter with downtown?" The
things she said were so ridiculous they should be doc-
umented.

"Nothing."

His throaty chuckle did little to ease her discomfort. For the entire evening, she'd made one outrageous
statement after another. This wasn't going to work. As
badly as she wanted to be with Shane, trying to keep
Camille a secret was far too complicated. She wasn't
talented enough to pull off another night like this one.

His hand rested on the slope of her shoulder as his
gaze caressed her. "Carrie, I want you to answer a question."

Danger alarms rang in her ears. Her instincts told her
to avoid this at any cost, but she couldn't. Nor would
she continue to lie. "A question? Sure."

"Not a difficult one." His hand slid from the curve
of her shoulder up to her neck in a gentle caress. "Are
you married?"

She relaxed and boldly smiled up at him while gently shaking her head. "No."

"You're sure?"

"Positive."

The only thing that could justify her behavior was if she had a husband or jealous boyfriend. His mind was afloat with questions. "Have you ever been married?"

"Never." So he assumed she was hiding from a man. She was so relieved she almost forgot herself and kissed him.

His hand molded itself to the gentle incline of her neck, his long fingers sliding into the silky length of her hair. "I want you to know how pleased I am to know that."

"At the moment, I'm rather pleased about it myself." But not for the reasons he assumed.

"I want to kiss you."

"I know." She wanted it, too.

His mouth made an unhurried descent to her waiting lips. It seemed a lifetime before his lips covered hers, his touch firm and blessedly warm. The moment their mouths met, her tension of anticipation eased away, and she responded by raising her arms and wrapping them around his strong neck.

The pressure of the kiss ended, but he didn't raise his mouth more than a hair's breadth. "I've wanted to do that from the moment I saw you this afternoon."

"You did?" All she could remember was him staring at the portrait of Camille.

He kissed her again. "After the wild goose chase you've led me on, you can't doubt it." His hands moved up and down her spine, arching her closer to his male length. "I'll see you soon?"

"Dinner?"

"If you like, but I was thinking more about the portrait."

She couldn't believe how quickly her memory had deserted her the minute she was in his arms. "Naturally. I think I'd prefer it if we met at your house...or you can come to mine." Though the latter was dangerous, on the off chance Camille showed up, which she often did. "Your place, I think."

"Fine."

"Friday?"

She blinked, trying to remember what day this was. "Okay."

He kissed her again, and the pressure at the back of her neck lifted her on her tiptoes. Her hands explored his jaw and the column of his throat, her fingers finally settling on his shoulders.

"Friday, then," he said as he breathed into her hair. Reluctantly, he broke contact. "Will you be all right driving back out to your place?"

"Of course."

"I could follow you, if you'd like."

And probably not plan to leave until morning, judging by the way he was looking at her. "I'll be fine," she insisted. "Thanks anyway."

His hand covered his eyes. Blurting out the wrong thing must be contagious. "I didn't mean that the way it sounded. It's just that I usually escort my dates home. It doesn't feel right to let go of you here."

For once Carrie felt in control. She received immense

pleasure at the look of consternation that tightened his face. "Are you saying you don't find me attractive?"

"You've got to know otherwise." Keeping his mouth shut seemed to be the best thing. He reached for her again, but she easily sidestepped his arms.

"You get an A for effort." Unable to resist, she tucked a strand of silver hair behind his ear and lightly pressed her lips over his. "I'll see you Friday. Seven?"

"Fine." He opened her door for her and stepped back as she climbed inside.

She offered him a tremulous smile. Her mouth still held the throbbing heat of his kisses.

The drive home was completed almost mechanically. Briefly, she wondered if Camille had seen her with Shane and what her sister would say if she had. Carrie knew she wouldn't be able to hide him forever. Perhaps if she subtly approached the subject of Shane, it might work.

It wasn't until the following Thursday that Carrie had the opportunity to do exactly that. Camille stopped at the beach house to repay the loan, tucking the fifty dollar bill under the salt shaker on the kitchen table.

Carrie washed her hands and made busy work in the kitchen, trying to come up with a tactful way of addressing the delicate subject.

She didn't get the chance before Camille brought it up on her own. "I thought I saw you the other day."

"Oh?" Carrie froze.

"You didn't happen to have dinner near Fisherman's Wharf this week, did you?"

Pretending to be distracted by slicing a lemon for the tall glasses of iced tea she'd prepared, Carrie shook her head. "I can't say it wasn't me." She hoped the double negative would confuse her twin into dropping the subject.

No such luck. "Were you alone?" Camille pressed.

"I went with a friend."

"Male or female?"

"Honestly, Camille, what is this? The Inquisition?"

"I'm just trying to keep tabs on you. You're my only sister, for heaven's sake."

"What were you doing there?" The best way to handle this, Carrie felt, was to raise a few questions of her own.

"Bob and I went to Billy's."

Carrie delivered the ice-filled glasses to the table. "The last time you were here, you said something about being half in love with Bob. Have you come to any conclusions since then?" Oh dear, she was going to make a mess of this.

"So you *were* with a man!" Camille cried with obvious delight. "I knew it. And obviously one you're wild about. All right, Carrie, give."

"You answer me first."

"You mean about falling for Bob? I wish I knew. I like being with him. He's fun. My whole life wouldn't depend on seeing him again, but then I think how much I'd miss him. As you can tell, I'm a little bit confused."

"Do you think about him?" Carrie's thoughts had been dominated by Shane almost from the moment she'd taken that peek at him in the gallery.

Camille shook her perfectly styled soft brunette curls. "I wish it were that easy. Whole days go by when I don't think about him. Well, he isn't completely out of mind. I don't know how to explain it." She studied her sister. "Are you in love?"

Carrie snickered. She couldn't help it. "With whom? It isn't like I've got scores of admirers just waiting for me to fall into their arms. Who would be interested in me when you're around?"

"It's not like I try to steal your male friends away. Half the time I don't even date them."

Camille had stated the problem in a nutshell. She wasn't attracted to them, but they sure were attracted to her. Shane would be, too, once he met her.

"Come on Carrie, tell me about him."

"There's no one," she insisted, taking a long swallow of her iced tea.

Camille cocked her head to one side as though viewing her sister for the first time. "You know I'd confide in you."

Carrie turned around. There had been plenty of times over the years when she'd resented her twin. Camille had it all, and for everyone to see. Few cared that Carrie had a sharp brain and a God-given artistic ability. Men in particular didn't see past the exterior.

The phone rang, and Carrie stared at it as if it were a burglar alarm blaring out of control.

"Aren't you going to answer it?" Camille asked.

"Yes." She made a show of drying her hands before reaching for the receiver. "Hello."

Her worst fears were realized the instant Shane spoke.

"Hello, Carrie."

She didn't dare say his name. "Hello," she said stiffly, holding her back rigid.

He hesitated, apparently sensitive to the reserved tone of her voice. "Am I catching you at a bad time?"

Ever since their evening together, she'd been hoping to hear from him. "Sort of," she admitted with some reluctance.

"Shall I call back a little later?"

"I could phone you." Her eyes looked everywhere except at Camille.

"I'm at the office. Do you have that number?" he asked.

"Yes. I'll call you there." She would find some way to get rid of her sister. For once she was going to hold on to a man, and she didn't care what tactics she was forced to use. Shane was the best thing that had happened to her in years.

"I suppose that was your handsome mechanic," Camille said when Carrie hung up.

"My what?" Carrie was genuinely baffled until she remembered how Camille had assumed that Shane worked on cars.

"Remember, you showed me your drawing of him the other day? You aren't going to be able to keep me from meeting him much longer," Camille insisted. "Don't you think I know what you're doing? You've never been able to keep anything from me for long. Good grief, every time you lie, your freckles become fluorescent."

Carrie's hand flew to her nose. "That's not true." Even as she spoke, she knew it was.

"And right now your nose alone could light up the entire Golden Gate Bridge."

"Oh, stop it, Camille. There is no one special in my life at the moment."

"And the Pope isn't Catholic."

"Camille…"

"All right, all right. I'll meet him sooner or later. You won't be able to hide him from me forever."

The words were like an unwelcome bell tolling in Carrie's mind.

"No doubt you're dying for me to leave so you can phone your mysterious 'friend.' Well, I won't delay you any longer." Camille deposited her empty glass in the sink. "I just wish you were a little more open about him."

"Why?" Carrie asked with a trace of bitterness. "So you can steal him away from me?"

"So there *is* someone." The delicate laugh that followed produced a shiver that ran up and down Carrie's backbone. "I don't think you have anything to worry about. Our tastes in men have never meshed."

That was true. Silently, Carrie watched as Camille waved and sauntered out the door. As far as men were concerned, beauty outdid talent and brains any day of the week. And Carrie was still afraid to believe that Shane might be the exception.

Playing it safe, she waited an extra ten minutes after Camille left before anxiously reaching for the phone.

Carrie fussed all day Friday, more nervous about this one sitting than a hundred others. This was Shane she was going to meet. Shane, the man who had withstood her re-buffs, her craziness and her complete lack of self-confidence, and liked her anyway. As she dabbed expensive French perfume behind her ears and at the pulse points of her wrists, she visualized how calm and collected she would be when they met. An eager smile curved the edges of her mouth. Shane wouldn't know her. Every time they'd been together, her behavior had been highly questionable. The man was a priceless wonder to have stuck things out with her. This evening she would shock the socks right off him with her calm, cool behavior. Tonight she had nothing to hide and no secrets to keep. She was there to sketch him, and he had insisted she stay for dinner afterward.

Grabbing a bottle of an excellent California Chardonnay, Carrie was on her way. She'd looked forward to this night. Everything was going to be perfect.

The drive went smoothly, and she was right on time when she pulled up in front of his elegant home.

Shane answered the door with a welcoming smile and rewarded her taste in wine with a light kiss across her surprised mouth.

"I thought we'd work in here tonight, if you don't mind." He led the way into the library.

"Sure," Carrie agreed, following him. It wasn't until she was inside the room that she noticed the portrait.

He had moved it. No longer was Camille's image hanging from the walls of his office. Shane had brought it home.

Five

Shane watched the expression of shock work its way across Carrie's pale features. She stood in front of the portrait and studied it as though seeing it for the first time and finding herself astonished. He wished he could read her thoughts. It was obvious to him now that the painting distressed her, yet he couldn't imagine why.

"You brought it here," she said in a tone that was so low he had to strain to hear her. "Why?"

"Is there a reason why I shouldn't have?" He moved around the desk and claimed the chair, hoping that his actions seemed nonchalant.

Carrie's attention drifted from Camille's flirtatious smile back to Shane. Taking his cue, she sat in a comfortable leather chair and set her briefcase on the Oriental carpet.

"She's lovely," Shane said, his gaze resting on the painting.

Carrie ignored him as she took out the supplies she would be using for this session.

"Don't you agree?" he pressed.

Her stomach bunched into a painful knot as she answered him with an abrupt shake of her head. The tingling numbness that had attacked her throat soon spread to her arms and legs, leaving them feeling useless.

"There aren't many women that lovely," he went on.

She clenched her jaw so tightly her molars ached. From the beginning she'd known how difficult it would be to stand in Camille's shadow. She'd so desperately wanted Shane to be different that she'd purposely ignored all the signs.

Holding her head high and proud, she boldly met his gaze. "She's probably one of the loveliest women you'll ever meet."

"I take it you know her personally?"

Her fingers curled around the chair arm, her long nails denting the soft leather. "Yes, I know her."

His eyes surveyed the portrait with what she could only describe as tenderness. "She's fantastic."

"Yes." Feeling a frantic need to be done with this assignment as quickly as possible, she began the preliminary sketch.

"She's—"

"Don't talk," Carrie barked. Her hands flew over the page, slightly softening the blunt lines of his craggy features as she worked.

Silent now, Shane relaxed against the back of the chair, crossing his legs and planting his hands on top of his bent knee. His gaze drifted from the portrait to Carrie, then back again. Slowly an amused grin appeared. Carrie had thought to fool him, but he had figured it out. She'd done an excellent job on the portrait, but he'd seen through the guise. *No Competition* had to be a portrait of the artist.

Viewing it now, he understood why the portrait intimidated her, and he wished he could change that. He was an architect, and his profession had taught him long ago that the outside was only a facade. Often alluring and appealing to the eye, but useless as anything more than a front. It was the inside that mattered. Carrie Lockett was a woman of grit. He realized that old-fashioned word didn't fit the image of this modern woman, but it was how he thought of her. In his mind's eye, Shane envisioned Carrie as she might have lived a hundred years ago. She was the pioneer type. One who would set out to tame a wild land. A woman of substance who could settle the farmlands and build the heart of a new country.

Had she lived in those times, she probably wouldn't have been given the opportunity to paint as she did now. Her artistic talent would have been utilized in different ways. Perhaps in a craft, such as quilting. His thoughts drifted to his own grandmother and mother, and he wished that they were alive so they could meet Carrie. Both of them would have loved her.

Fifteen minutes passed without a word being spoken. Carrie's concentration centered on her work. She'd captured Shane's likeness perfectly yet she'd failed to capture the way she saw him. A photographer would do as well and cost far less. Furious that she cared so much, she viciously jerked the huge sheet off the pad and wadded it into a tight ball.

"Carrie…"

Rising, she angrily met his gaze. "Do you want to meet her?"

"Who?"

"Who else?" She waved her hand at the portrait, determined to get this over with as quickly and painlessly as possible. Once he met Camille, he could have the woman he really wanted. Camille claimed that their tastes in men didn't mesh. This time her sister was dead wrong. Shane was definitely Camille's type. Handsome, secure, talented. Everything her sister wanted and a whole lot more. Of course, Camille wouldn't recognize his gentleness, his intelligence or his quick wit. But none of that mattered now. Shane wanted Camille and had from the very first. The adoring looks he'd been giving the portrait from the minute Carrie had entered the library proved as much. Shane would be enthralled to meet her twin.

"Meet her?" Once again she'd managed to perplex him. "What are you talking about?"

Rarely had a man been more obtuse. "The woman in the portrait will be at my house tomorrow evening at seven. Be there."

A long moment passed before Shane responded. "If you insist."

The soft sound of his chuckle infuriated her, and she glared at him with a lifetime of resentment burning in her green eyes. "It's what you want, isn't it? What you've wanted from the beginning? The artist was only the means of meeting the model. Fine. I just wish you had been up-front with me from the beginning."

Before he could move around the desk, she'd picked up her supplies and was marching out the den and toward the front door. "Carrie, would you just stop and listen to me?"

"No. Just be there."

He chuckled again. "I wouldn't miss it for the world."

"I didn't think you would."

He followed her down the front steps. "Do you want to schedule the next session now?"

"No."

"But I want you to continue the portrait."

She hesitated. "I doubt you'll feel that way after tomorrow."

"Don't count on it, Carrie."

Holding the handle of her briefcase as though it were a lifeline to sanity, she sadly shook her head. "We can wait until tomorrow night and discuss it then."

She had that hurt look about her again, and Shane yearned to reach out and hold her, but from experience he knew she wouldn't let him, not when she was in this mood. Some day she would come to trust him enough, but until then he had to learn to be patient.

"I'm not going to change my mind about the portrait or about you," he told her.

"Time will tell." One look at Camille, and Shane would willingly forget her *and* the portrait he'd hired her to paint. As she had a hundred times in the past,

Carrie would drift into the background while Camille took the stage. Only this time it would hurt more than it ever had before.

Shane escorted Carrie to her parked car. He patted the hood and absently ran his hand over the faded paint of her outdated minivan. He lingered while she climbed inside and inserted the key into the ignition.

"Have you had a mechanic look at it yet?" he asked.

"No. The man at the gas station told me to bring it in next week." She shifted into Reverse and waited for him to step back.

He did so grudgingly. He didn't want her to go but couldn't think of an excuse for her to stay. It wasn't until she pulled onto the street that he remembered their dinner warming in the oven.

Carrie's heart was so heavy that she felt as though a ton of bricks were pressing against her body, her mind and her soul. She shouldn't blame Camille for her beauty, but this time she did. And even though the last person she wanted to speak to at the minute was Camille, she knew she had to call her sister and be done with it as quickly as possible.

Once back at the beach house, Carrie didn't feel the comfort and welcome she usually did. Shadows lurked in the corners. Even the ocean below looked gray and depressing.

She didn't bother to turn on the lights and fumbled around in the dark, dropping her equipment as she came through the front door. She curled up on the sofa, wrapping her arms around her knees and tucking her chin into her collarbone.

There was no help for this. It had to be done. Gathering her resolve, she moved into the kitchen and lifted the phone. She hesitated an instant before punching out the number that was as familiar as her own.

"Hello." Camille's soft voice was fuzzy, as though she'd been sleeping.

"Camille, it's Carrie. Is this a bad time?"

A short, surprised silence followed. Carrie seldom contacted her sister. Camille was the one who came to her with a multitude of problems and questions. Carrie was the mother, Camille the child. This time, though, their roles were reversed. Camille would solve the problem that was burning through Carrie like a slow fire.

"Carrie, what are you doing phoning me? Is anything wrong?"

"No...not really."

"You don't sound right."

Carrie didn't doubt that. She felt terrible—on the verge of being physically ill. "I know," she said and her voice dropped almost to a whisper. "Can you stop by tomorrow night, say around seven?"

"Why?"

Carrie backed against the kitchen counter and lifted the heavy hair off her forehead as her eyes dropped closed. "There's someone I want you to meet. Someone who wants to meet you."

"I don't suppose it's a man?" Camille was joking,

seeming to enjoy this and noting none of the pain that had crept into Carrie's voice.

"Yes, a man, a special one I know you'll like."

"So you've decided to unveil your mechanic friend." The statement was followed by a low, knowing laugh.

"He isn't a mechanic. Shane's an architect. He's the man in the sketches you saw."

Camille hesitated. "He did have an interesting face."

"Yes." That was all Carrie would admit.

"Aren't you afraid I'll try to steal him away?"

Carrie bit unmercifully into her bottom lip. That wouldn't be necessary. Shane had never been hers in the first place. Their whole relationship had been built around the woman in the portrait. And that was Camille.

"I wouldn't, you know," her twin added, more serious now.

"He's yours if you want him," Carrie said with as little emotion as possible. "He's interested in you already."

"That's amazing, since I've never met him."

Carrie felt she might as well let the bomb drop now as tomorrow night. "He's the one who bought your painting."

"Really." A small excited sound came over the wire. "How extraordinary. And now he wants to meet me? I'm flattered."

"I knew you would be." A muscle leaped in her tightly clenched jaw as she uttered the statement in a faintly sarcastic tone.

"He must be wealthy, if he could afford one of your paintings."

"I thought money didn't interest you?" Jealousy seethed through her veins. She'd fought the battle so often and conquered it so readily that the ferocity with which it raged now shocked her. "I'm sorry to cut this short, but we'll have time to talk tomorrow night."

"You can count on it." Camille sounded like a schoolgirl who'd been promised a trip to the circus. She hesitated for an instant. "You're sure you don't mind? You know, if Shane and I go out? You seemed quite taken with him the other day."

"Mind?" Carrie forced a laugh. "Why should I mind?" Why indeed? she repeated as she severed the phone connection. Why indeed?

The following day Carrie refused to answer her cell phone. There wasn't a single person she felt like talking to, and anyone important would leave a message. By lunchtime she counted six calls. Playing back her voice mail, she discovered that Shane had phoned four times. The first time he told her that he was sorry to miss her and that he would check back with her later. The second call revealed a hint of impatience. Again he claimed he would catch her later. On the third call, he said that he knew she was purposely ignoring his calls, and that if he didn't have to attend an important meeting he would drive out and confront her. The last call was to apologize for his anger on the third call and tell her that he looked forward to seeing her that evening, when they would get this mess straightened out once and for all.

Carrie listened to each message with an increasing sense of impatience. She didn't know why Shane thought there was a mess. For the first time since she'd learned he'd bought *No Competition*, everything was crystal clear.

At six she showered and dressed, choosing her best linen pants and a pale silk blouse. No doubt Camille would arrive resembling a fashion queen. Carrie had no desire to further emphasize the contrast between them by trying to compete.

Using oyster shell combs, she pulled her thick hair away from her oval face and applied a fresh layer of makeup. The doorbell chimed just as she'd finished spreading lipstick across her bottom lip. She smoothed out the color on her way to the front door. Knowing Camille, she would be so eager to meet the man who had purchased her painting that she'd probably decided to arrive early.

She forced herself to appear welcoming as she pulled open the door.

"Hi," Shane said. "I know I'm early, but I couldn't wait any longer."

The shock of seeing him momentarily robbed her of her ability to talk.

"Did you get my phone messages?" He came into the cottage and paced the area in front of her sofa.

She clasped her hands together and shook her head. "I got them."

"But you didn't bother to return my calls."

Personally, she couldn't see any reason she should have. Seeing him again was difficult enough. "No."

"This has gone on long enough."

"What has?" He was clearly angry, but it seemed to be pointed inward, as though he was furious with himself.

"This whole business with the portrait."

She squared her shoulders. "I couldn't agree with you more."

"I know." He reached out and gently laid his hands on the ivory slope of her shoulders.

"What do you know?" Now she was the one in the dark.

"About the painting."

"Would you kindly stop talking in riddles?"

"I admit to being fooled in the beginning. The coloring was tricky, and the changes in the features were subtle."

She stared at him in wide-eyed expectation. "What are you saying?"

"I'm on to you," he said with a small laugh. "*No Competition* is a self-portrait."

Carrie was too stunned to respond.

"You took all the beauty stored inside that warm, loving heart of yours and painted it on the outside. Only—" He paused to position his thumb against her trembling chin. "Only you did yourself an injustice. Your beauty far surpasses the loveliness of the woman in the painting. Your brand of attractiveness is much more captivating than any surface beauty."

"Shane…" Shimmering tears filled her eyes. She couldn't believe what he was saying. No one had ever thought she was attractive. And certainly never lovely. Not when compared to Camille.

"If you recall, I didn't buy the painting that first day. To tell the truth, I was somehow…disappointed in it."

"But—"

The pressure of his finger against her chin stopped her. "The portrait was too perfect, almost disturbingly so, until I realized what you'd done. Then I remembered how I'd followed you to Fisherman's Wharf that day and witnessed for myself the real Carrie Lockett. And that was when I realized what you'd done and knew I had to buy your portrait. But the truth is, I don't need anything more than you, Carrie. Exactly as you are this moment."

"Oh, Shane." She blinked in an effort to restrain the ever-ready flow of emotion. "Don't say things like that to me. I'm not used to it. I don't know how to react."

"I was drawn to you the first time I saw you, and your appeal grows stronger every time we meet."

She stared at him in disbelief mingled with awe, unable to tell him how much his words meant to her flagging self-esteem.

"I don't need the beautiful woman in the portrait," he told her gently. "Not when the real flesh-and-blood woman is right here."

"You mean that, don't you?"

"With everything that's in me."

The realization that Camille—the real woman in the portrait—was about to descend on them at any second vaulted Carrie into action. "In that case, I'll let you take me to dinner."

"I was hoping you'd say that." He didn't seem to hear the urgency in her voice and walked around the coffee table to take a seat on the sofa.

Not wanting to reveal her reason for why it was important that they leave right away, Carrie reached for a light jacket and draped it over her shoulders.

"Shall we go to Billy's?" she asked, edging toward the front door.

"How about a glass of wine first?"

"I took my last bottle to you the other night." Panic-stricken, she searched her mind for an excuse to leave. "I really am starved." She made a show of glancing at her wristwatch. "In fact, I think I forgot to eat lunch."

"Then let's take care of that right now." With the agility of a true sportsman, Shane got to his feet.

She sighed in relief. Now all they had to do was get away before Camille arrived. Later she would come up with some wild excuse to give her twin. No doubt Camille would be furious, and with just cause. But Carrie was confident she could come up with some plausible explanation later.

Shane helped her into his BMW, then walked around the front of the car. She smiled at him shyly as he joined her and snapped his seat belt into place.

"You look good enough to kiss."

Quickly, she looked out the side window. She desperately wanted him to kiss her—but not now. And not here, with Camille within moments of discovering them.

"Carrie…" He touched the side of her face.

Feigning enthusiasm, she patted her abdomen. "My stomach is about to go on strike for lack of nourishment."

"Are you saying you'd rather eat than make love?" He frowned slightly.

"Feed me and you'll see how grateful I can be." She was flirting outrageously, and she knew it.

"Is that a promise?"

"We'll see."

Shane chuckled as he started the car and pulled onto the road. They weren't more than a hundred yards from the beach house when Camille's convertible came into view. Pretending to have found a piece of fuzz on her pant leg, Carrie took extreme care in removing it, lowering her head. She prayed that her sister hadn't seen her.

By the time they reached the San Francisco waterfront, Carrie's mood had become buoyant. When Shane parked the car, he paused and his eyes smiled into hers. Even as he grinned, a slow frown formed.

"What's wrong?"

"Wrong?" He shook his head, clearing his thoughts. "Nothing's wrong. I was just thinking that I've never seen you glow like this. Your whole face has lit up. You're lovely."

Her fluttering lashes concealed her reaction. "No one has ever called me lovely before."

"I can't believe that."

"It's true."

He shifted in his seat, turning sideways. "You are, you know. Gorgeous."

"Oh, Shane, I wish I knew how to react when men pay me compliments." Her heart felt ready to burst. He'd given her a priceless gift for which she would always be grateful.

"You could kiss me," he suggested, only half-joking.

"Here?" Lights shone all around them, and the sound of moving traffic drifted from the crowded street.

Sensing her shyness, he lifted a lock of her hair and let the silky smoothness slide through his fingers. "There isn't anything I don't like about you," he admitted softly, his voice low and filled with wonder. "I like the way your smile lights up your whole face." He traced the corner of her eyes with his fingertip. His mouth followed his hand, gently kissing each side of her face. "Your eyes are so expressive. No one could ever doubt when you're angry." With a tenderness she wouldn't have associated with a man, Shane leaned forward and brushed his lips over hers. He paused, then kissed her a second time and then a third. With each kiss, her mouth welcomed his, parting a little more as the kiss gained in intensity.

He paused then, his mouth hovering a mere inch above hers. "Feel good?"

For a heartbeat she didn't move, didn't blink, didn't even breathe. Answering him with words was impossible, so she gently nodded. Each kiss had wrapped her in a blanket of warmth and security. She felt cherished and appreciated. Feminine and attractive. Seductress and seducer all in one.

"Oh, my sweet Carrie." His breath felt hot against her flushed cheeks. "All I wanted was to hold you, but kissing you leaves me yearning for more." He moved his mouth to her throat, where his lips caressed her warm flesh.

She heard him draw a deep breath, as though he needed to regain control of his emotions, then he continued, "This isn't the best place to be thinking what I'm thinking. Let's go have dinner."

Her hand against the back of his neck stopped him. "I'm not hungry."

"Minutes ago you were famished."

"That was before." She tangled her fingers in his thick hair. "I...like it when you kiss me."

"I like it, too. That's the problem. And if we don't stop now, it'll be a lot more than a few innocent kisses."

The stark reality of their vulnerability to the world hit her as a truck passed, blaring its horn. The unexpected blast of sound brought her up short. She blinked and broke free, pressing her hands over her face. She couldn't believe they'd been kissing in broad daylight, with half the city looking on.

Noting her look of astonishment, Shane swallowed his growing need to laugh. Carrie never ceased to surprise him. She was a businesswoman who supported herself with her art and at the same time possessed a paradoxically sophisticated innocence.

"Are you ready now?" He was looking in the direction of the seafood restaurant they'd agreed on.

"I think so."

"Good." He got out of the car and came around for her. "By the way..." he hedged, instinctively knowing how dull his invitation would be. "There's an award banquet coming up at the end of next week. Would you be interested in attending with me?" He tried to make light of it, but it was the high point of his career so far to receive the Frank Lloyd Wright Award. Wonderful for him, but deadly dull for anyone else.

"As a matter of fact, I read about the award you'll be receiving."

He looked almost boyish. "Then you'll go?"

"I'd consider it an honor."

"My great-aunt will be there, as well. You won't mind meeting her, will you?"

How could she? Already she was falling in love with Shane. It would be only right to sit with his family when he was presented with such a prestigious award. "I'll look forward to it."

"She's anxious to see you again."

His casual announcement shocked Carrie. *Again?*

"You made quite an impression on my Aunt Ashley."

Instantly the picture of the astute older woman from Elizabeth Brandon's cocktail party flitted into Carrie's memory. "Ashley Wallingford is your aunt?"

"Does that bother you?"

"No. I'm just surprised." She lightly shook her head.

"I must have gone so long without food that my brain lacks the proper nutrients to think straight."

"Then I don't think we should delay any longer." Shane slipped his arm around her trim waist and led her toward Camille's favorite seafood restaurant.

"Where were you?" Camille demanded for the tenth time in as many minutes.

Carrie continued painting, doing her best to ignore her sister's anger. "Out to dinner. I'm sorry, Camille, really sorry."

"I thought you said he wanted to meet me?"

"He does—someday."

"Then why…?"

"It was a mistake. I've apologized, so can we please drop it."

Camille didn't look pleased. "I waited forty-five minutes for you." She crossed and uncrossed her arms, unable to disguise her indignation. "God only knows what could have happened to you. I had visions…" She left the rest unsaid.

Carrie felt terribly guilty. She set the brush aside and dropped her hand. "I realize it was a stupid thing to do."

"Where'd you go?" Camille asked.

"Billy's."

"Billy's! You know how I love the food there." Her voice was low and accusing, as though it should have been her and not Carrie who went. "I wouldn't see this mechanic…architect again, if I were you," she warned.

"Why not?"

"He sounds fickle to me. You don't need that."

Carrie felt obliged to defend Shane. "He isn't, not really. He thought... He did want to meet you, but..."

"But?"

"But he decided that it was really me he was interested in."

"How nice," Camille grumbled.

"You have Bob."

"You can have him," Camille tossed back flippantly.

"Who? Bob or Shane?"

"Don't be silly. Bob's mine. I could care less about your friend who doesn't seem to be able to make up his mind. He sounds like bad news to me."

A secret smile touched the edges of Carrie's mouth. If Camille only knew, her song would be a whole lot different.

Six

Carrie went out with Shane three nights in a row. Each time they got together she breathed in happiness and confidence and exhaled skepticism and uncertainty. Eventually the time would come when he would have to meet Camille, but she decided that there was no need to rush it. Nor did it matter that he believed she was the woman in the portrait.

Their first night out, he took her fishing in San Francisco Bay. Although neither one of them got a single bite, it didn't matter. The evening following the fishing expedition, they attended a concert in Golden Gate Park. Lying on a carpet of lush green grass, her head nestled in his lap, they listened to the sounds of Mozart. The next night they ate pizza on the beach and talked until well past midnight. Shane held and kissed her with a gentleness that never failed to stir her.

Between dates, Carrie painted his portrait. She'd been right to believe this one painting would be a challenge beyond any other. She captured his likeness as she saw him: proud, intelligent, virile, vigorous and overwhelmingly masculine. With every stroke of her brush she revealed her growing respect and love. Loving him had been inevitable. She'd known that from the first moment she'd peeked at him at the Dove Gallery the afternoon she'd delivered *No Competition*.

Camille complained about Carrie's absence early Thursday afternoon. "You're never home anymore. I hardly ever get to see you." Her bottom lip pushed out into a clever pout. It amazed Carrie how nothing seemed to mar her sister's good looks. Not even a frown.

"You're seeing me now," Carrie announced as she delivered a small plate of Oreo cookies and two glasses of iced tea to the coffee table. She sat back and reached for a cookie.

"It's not the same."

"What do you mean?" Camille often came to Carrie with problems, but as far as Carrie could remember, she'd always been there for her sister. "Is something wrong between you and Bob?"

"What could be wrong? Everything's dandy."

Carrie realized that her sister was doing a poor job of acting. Camille's words were meant to disarm her, but they failed. Carrie had watched her sister's relationship with Bob with interest. Her sister really did seem to be falling in love. For the first time in her life, Camille was on unsteady footing, unsure of herself. Carrie could almost witness the small war going on inside her twin.

"I don't know about you," Carrie admitted on the tail end of a drawn-out yawn, "but I'm exhausted." The tiredness wasn't faked. Staying out with Shane until all hours of the morning was beginning to demand its toll.

A long pause followed, and Carrie could feel her sister reassessing her. "I think Bob may want to cool things a bit," she admitted without looking at Carrie. "Naturally that choice is his. Either way is fine with me. There are plenty of other fish in the sea."

It sounded to Carrie as if Camille cared very much and was struggling valiantly to disguise her emotions. "What makes you think that?"

Carrie appeared distracted, fiddling with the long spoon in her glass of iced tea.

"He hasn't said anything really, but a woman senses these things."

"He must have said *something*." Idly Carrie reached for another cookie. Her bare foot was braced against the edge of the sofa.

"Not…really," Camille said, still not admitting anything.

"But you're convinced he wants to cool the relationship?" Carrie asked. She was well aware that Camille was leaving out all the necessary details. Even so, she had to admit that this latest development didn't sound good.

Camille paused to take a sip of tea. Carrie noted that her twin hadn't nibbled on a single cookie. Oreos had long been their favorite. Camille ignoring the treat was a sure sign of her distress. "He's still crazy about me, you know."

They all were. "I don't doubt it."

As though reading her sister's mind, Camille leaned forward and reached for an Oreo, holding it in front of her open mouth. "But maybe it's time I started going out with other men."

"Are you sure this is what you want?" She remembered how willing Camille had been to meet Shane and rethought her earlier opinion that Camille was falling in love at last. If she was truly in love with Bob, it wouldn't have mattered how many men showed an interest in her. Giving herself a hard mental shake, Carrie decided that she couldn't let herself be drawn too deeply into her sister's love life when keeping track of her own demanded so much energy.

Camille bit into the Oreo. "By the way, when am I going to meet this new...friend of yours?"

"Shane?" Carrie swallowed, immediately reluctant to reveal anything about him.

"If that's his name."

Camille stared straight through her. "You still answered my question."

"I...don't know when you'll meet." Her tone was raised and slightly defensive. "Soon."

"You're not hiding him from me, are you?"

"Don't be silly." Carrie lowered her foot to the carpet and brushed off imaginary cookie crumbs from her lap. "You're not making any sense. I've always introduced you to my male friends." *And lived to regret it,* her mind tossed back.

"This one seems important."

Carrie shrugged. "Maybe. I'm like you when it

comes to Bob. Shane's all right." Talk about an understatement! But she didn't dare let her sister know how involved her heart was. Some days Carrie felt that her feelings for Shane must glow from every part of her. Even Elizabeth had commented how *healthy* she looked lately. But, thankfully, Camille was so wrapped up in her topsy-turvy relationship with Bob that she failed to notice.

"Well, you certainly seem to be seeing a lot of him."

"I'm doing his portrait." That made everything sound so much more innocent.

"But you're together far more than necessary."

Carrie got to her feet and lifted her glass from the tray. "Why all the interest?"

"No reason."

"Then let's drop it, okay?"

Camille gave her an odd look. "Okay."

Her sister lingered around the beach house for another twenty minutes, asking questions occasionally. Camille had never been any good at disguising her curiosity. Carrie knew the time was soon approaching when she would be forced to introduce her twin to Shane. Dreading the thought, she quickly forced it to the back of her mind.

When Camille decided to leave, Carrie walked her out to her convertible. She felt wretched. Since their mother's death, she'd been the strong twin. Lately she'd been behaving like a fool. Love must do that to people, she decided. To her way of thinking, it was imperative to keep Camille away from Shane for as long as possible. Unreasonable? Probably. Selfish? All right, she admitted it. Scared? Darn right.

Camille pulled onto the highway, and as Carrie watched her sister leave, her discontent grew. Their conversation repeated itself in her troubled mind. She'd made her relationship with Shane sound as boring as possible. Yet, in reality, she thought about him constantly. Not an hour passed that she didn't recall his quiet strength and his lazy, warm smile. She remembered the laughter they shared and how even small disagreements often became witty exchanges. They seemed to challenge each other's thoughts.

She loved his fathomless eyes which seemed to be able to look straight through her and know what she was thinking even before she voiced the thought.

Slowing, she moved back into the house. Just thinking about Shane made her giddy with love. Somewhere, somehow, a long time ago, she had done something right to deserve a man like Shane Reynolds. Now if she could only hold on to him once he met Camille.

On the night of the award banquet honoring Shane, Carrie smoothed a thick curl of auburn hair away from her face. Her eyeliner smeared, and she groaned, reaching for a tissue, wiping it away to start once more. Again a thick curl of hair hung over her left eye. Irritably, she brushed it aside to guide the tip of the eyeliner wand across the bottom of her lid. A sense of panic filled her as she glanced at her gold watch for the tenth time in as many minutes. Oh no, this was the most important night of Shane's life, and she was a half hour behind schedule.

Frantically waving her hand in front of her eye in an effort to dry her makeup, Carrie hobbled into her bedroom with one high heel on and the other lost somewhere under her bed…she hoped. Quickly she sorted through her closet for the lovely green dress she'd worn to Elizabeth's party. Shane had already seen her in it, but that couldn't be helped. The dress was the most flattering thing she owned, and she desperately wanted to make him proud tonight.

Of all the afternoons for Camille to show up unexpectedly, it would have to be this one all-important day. At three-thirty her twin had descended on her doorstep, eyes red and puffy from tears. Sniffling, Camille had announced that she and Bob had broken up and it was for the best and she really didn't care anyway. With that she'd promptly burst into huge sobs.

Carrie had no choice but to comfort her distraught sister. Camille needed her, and Carrie couldn't kick her out the door just because she had an important date. Still, she'd been running late ever since her twin had left.

Carefully laying the silk dress across the top of the bed, she prepared to slip it over her head. The dress was halfway down her torso when it stuck. No amount of maneuvering would get it to proceed farther. Blindly walking around the room and hopping up and down didn't seem to help. It took her several costly moments to realize that the rollers in her hair were causing the hang-up.

Muttering grimly, she pulled off the dress, in the process turning it inside out. Trotting back into the bathroom, she ripped the hot rollers from her hair. By chance she happened to catch her reflection in the bathroom mirror and noticed that not only had the eyeliner on her left eye smeared—again—her right eye was bare. The job had only been half completed.

The sound of the doorbell shot through her like an electrical current. "Please, don't let that be Shane," she pleaded heavenward, reaching for her old faded blue robe.

Naturally, it was him.

He stepped into the house looking so strikingly handsome in his tuxedo that just seeing him robbed her lungs of oxygen. She felt ready to burst with pride just looking at him. He was dashing. Stalwart. Devastating. She couldn't come up with another word to describe him. He was a man people would expect to see with a beautiful woman. A Camille. Not a Carrie.

Dragging air into her constricting lungs, she froze, springy curls hanging around her head.

Shane's stunned gaze collided with hers before dropping to the hastily donned terry cloth robe, left gaping open in the middle, revealing a peach colored teddy. His gaze rose to her stringy curls and quickly shot down to her feet. One foot was bare and the other was wearing a high-heeled sandal.

"Is it that time already?" she asked, her voice shaking as she strove for a light air.

"What happened?"

She tightened the sash of the robe. "I'm running a bit late."

"I can see that."

Tears of frustration burned for release at the backs of her eyes, but she refused to vent them. She'd wanted everything to be so perfect for Shane tonight.

"Listen, Shane, maybe it would be best if you went without me." She kept her hands at her sides, hoping to appear lukewarm about the whole banquet. "As you can see, I'm a long way from being ready."

He didn't so much as pause to consider her suggestion. "I want you there."

"Look at me!" she cried, holding out her arms. She was a mess, and all out of magic wands. Her fairy godmother had recently retired. She was Cinderella long after midnight, when the magic had worn off.

A crooked grin lifted one side of his sensuous mouth. "I will admit that I'd prefer it if you wore a dress, but that's up to you."

"Don't joke," she said. "This is too serious." She sniffled loudly. "There's no way I can go now. Would you please be serious?"

"I've never been more so in my life." He pointed toward her bedroom. "Go do what's necessary, and I'll phone Aunt Ashley and tell her we're running a few minutes behind schedule."

"Shane! It's going to take me six months to get everything in order."

"Take as long as you want." He pulled out his cell phone and claimed the sofa, sitting indolently and crossing his long legs. He propped both elbows against the back, looking as though he had all the time in the world. "I'm not in any hurry. As it is, these dinners are always stuffy affairs."

"But you're the guest of honor!"

"It's fashionable to be late."

"Oh, stop." She sank onto the sofa beside him. "I can't go."

Up until this point, Shane had found the whole proceeding humorous. But the tears shimmering in Carrie's soft eyes clearly revealed how upset she was.

"Honey, look at me." His hand captured her chin and turned her face to him.

She resisted at first, not wanting him to see the tears that refused to be held at bay.

Lovingly, his finger traced the elegant curve of her jawline. "The reason this night is so important is because you can share it with me. I couldn't care less what you wear."

"I refuse to embarrass you."

"You could never do that." The distress written in her eyes tore at his heart. Over the past few weeks he'd witnessed a myriad of emotions in her expressive eyes. She'd teased him, riled him. She'd given him an impudent sideways glance and stolen his heart several times over. He was so hopelessly in love with her that he didn't think his life would ever be the same without her now. He loved her wit and her intelligence, and the way she could spar with him over one issue before turning around and agreeing with him, and then stubbornly defy him over another. But this time he was determined to win. She was going to this awards banquet with him if he had to drag her every step of the way.

"Shane, don't make me. Please."

Gently his hand smoothed away the tumbling curls from her forehead. "I want you with me."

"But…"

"Please." He said the word so tenderly that Carrie had no option.

Numbly she nodded and stood. She brushed the tears from her eyes. "I'll do the best I can."

Demanding that her frantic heart be still, Carrie worked with forced patience. Her eyeliner slid on smoothly and dried without smearing. With the hot rollers out of her hair, the dress glided over her head and whispered against her creamy skin. She wished she had more of a tan, wished her freckles would fade away, wished she was a ravishing beauty who would make him proud. A puzzled smile touched her lips as she reached for the brush to see what she could do with her hair. Shane should have a beautiful woman on his arm tonight. With everything that was in her, she wanted to be that woman. But could she?

Thirty minutes later, she tentatively stepped into the living room. Shane was idly leafing through a woman's magazine.

"I think we can go now," she murmured, feeling a little like a fish out of water. For better or worse, she'd done everything she could.

Shane deposited the magazine on the coffee table and glanced up. What he saw caused the breath to jam in his throat. Surprise exploded through his entire body. It wasn't the red-haired innocent who was more comfortable in faded jeans than a dress who stood before him but a provocatively beautiful woman. He couldn't take his eyes from her. The transformation was little short of amazing. Her thick, luxuriant hair spilled over her shoulders. The silk clung to her slender hips and swayed gracefully as she walked toward him.

"Shane?"

"Good heavens, you're lovely." He'd forgotten. The night of Elizabeth Brandon's party, he'd been struck by how beautiful she was. But that night he'd seen her from across the room. Now she stood directly in front of him, and he felt as though he'd been hit with a hand grenade.

"Will I do?"

He could only nod.

"Well, don't you think we should be leaving? We're already thirty minutes late."

"Right." He fumbled in the silk-lined pocket of his trousers for the car keys. "I phoned Aunt Ashley. To save time, she insisted on taking a taxi and meeting us there."

"Remind me to thank her." Carrie shared a warm smile with him.

"I will." He offered her his elbow and turned to her.

It took everything within him not to bend down and kiss her sweet mouth. What a surprise she was. A marvel. Just knowing her had enriched his life. Now all he needed to do was find some way to keep her at his side for a lifetime.

"Mrs. Wallingford?" Carrie's apologetic eyes met the older woman's. "I hope you'll forgive me for this delay. It was inexcusable."

The low conversational hum of the party surrounded them. Shane had gone for drinks after seeing Carrie and his great-aunt seated at the round, linen-covered table closest to the dais.

"Call me Ashley, my dear, and no apology is necessary. I've had days like that myself."

Carrie's gaze followed Shane as he progressed across the crowded room. He didn't seem to be able to go more than a foot or two before he was stopped and congratulated.

Good-naturedly, Shane paused to talk with his colleagues, but his own gaze kept drifting back to Carrie and his aunt. He could hardly take his eyes from her, half afraid someone would walk away with her. She was breathtaking in that dress. A siren the gods had sent to tempt him. Well, it had worked. He'd never wanted a woman more than he did Carrie. It astonished him that he'd only known her a month.

"You're in love with my nephew, aren't you?" Ashley Wallingford asked bluntly.

Carrie's gaze jerked away from Shane, and she was

aware that her heart must be boldly shining from her eyes. "Pardon?"

Ashley chuckled. "It's obvious."

Carrie twisted the gold link handle of her purse around her index finger. "I'd hoped it wasn't."

"I don't think Shane has guessed," the older woman reassured her. "He tells me you've been painting his portrait."

"Yes." Her eyes fell to the beaded purse resting in her lap. "He's an excellent subject."

"I can well imagine. The boy possesses a great deal of character. For a while there I didn't see much hope for him, though."

Carrie studied Shane's great-aunt, not sure she could believe what she was hearing. "Shane?"

"All he seemed to do was study. There wasn't any fun in his life." The older woman chuckled softly. "He took everything so seriously. Responsibility weighed heavily on him. He's the only boy, you realize. After his father died, Shane did what he could to hold the family together. His mother was a frail little thing."

From conversations with him, Carrie knew that Shane's father had died the year Shane was a high school junior. His mother had followed a year later. His whole world had been ripped out from under him within the space of two years.

"He came to live with me after that."

"He thinks the world of you." Carrie told her with pride.

Ashley Wallingford lightly shook her head. "It seems

unfair that a boy should be faced with such unhappiness. His sisters are all married now." Abruptly changing the subject, she continued, "There was a girl he loved, you know."

Carrie didn't. "He…hasn't mentioned anyone."

"She was a pretty thing. They met in college. To be honest, I thought they'd marry. But whatever happened, he didn't tell me. He didn't date for a long time afterward. For a while I assumed he'd given up on women. Until now. It's time." The older woman's keen eyes assessed Carrie. "Her name was similar to your own. Connie, Candy…no, Camille. Her name was Camille."

Carrie thought her heart would pound right out of her chest. Could it have been her sister? Camille left a slew of battered hearts in her wake wherever she went. It was possible that Shane could be one. But…that didn't make sense. He wouldn't have purchased the portrait if it were Camille, would he?

"Carrie?" Ashley Wallingford placed her hand over Carrie's. "You're looking pale. Was I wrong to have said something?"

"No, of course not," she assured the kind woman hurriedly. "It would be highly unlikely that Shane could reach this age without ever falling in love. I can't be jealous of anyone who helped make him the man he is."

"You're very wise."

"Not really." Only wise enough to know that she couldn't look for problems in the past when the future already held so many.

"Here we are," Shane said as he set down a round of drinks. "This place is a madhouse."

"I noticed," Carrie said with a small laugh.

"Everything should be starting any minute." He took the chair between his aunt and Carrie, and reached for Carrie's hand. "I told you we'd arrive in plenty of time."

"The entire room sighed with relief the minute you walked in the door."

"You're exaggerating," he said.

"I'm very proud of you, Shane. Proud to know you, and even prouder to be with you tonight." Emotion made Carrie's voice husky. "When I think back to all the things I said to you when we first met..."

"You mean like, 'get lost'? You certainly kept me running to keep up with you. Literally."

Carrie felt her heart swell with laughter. "You're speaking as though the chase is over."

Shane tossed back his head and laughed heartily.

A tall, distinguished-looking man approached the podium, and the room grew quiet.

From its poor beginning, the evening took a turn for the better. The dinner was probably one of the best catered meals Carrie had ever eaten.

Following dinner, the award was presented and Shane rose to give his acceptance speech. Carrie barely heard a word of what he said. Instead her eyes scanned the huge audience that filled the ballroom. She saw for herself the admiration and respect on the faces of his peers. Even his aunt looked as proud as a peacock, her ample bosom seemingly puffed up as though to announce to the world that this man was her nephew. Poignant tears of happiness welled in the older woman's eyes. Carrie pretended not to notice as Ashley pressed a delicate linen handkerchief to the corner of her sharp blue eyes.

As he spoke, a series of cameras flashed and several television crews jockeyed for position in the already cramped room.

After the banquet, he was delayed by several people from the news media who stopped to ask him questions.

The entire time, he kept his arm securely around Carrie's shoulders. His great-aunt, meanwhile, found an old friend and the two of them stood head to head, deep in conversation.

Once the interviews were over, Shane insisted they have a nightcap in the cocktail lounge off the hotel lobby. A small three-piece band played music from the forties. The dance floor was crowded, and it was apparent that this was a popular night club spot.

"Shall we?" Shane questioned his aunt and Carrie.

"You know I've always been an admirer of Glen Miller," Ashley murmured.

"Carrie?"

"I'm game." The whole evening had been even more wonderful than she'd dared hope. As it was, she was far too keyed up to go home and sleep.

Shane found them a table and ordered their drinks when the cocktail waitress approached.

"Aunt Ashley, would you excuse us a moment?"

"Of course."

He slid back his chair and reached for Carrie's hand. "I never could resist the opportunity to dance."

Carrie hesitated only slightly. Admittedly, she wasn't exactly light on her feet. Dancing was another in a long list of items that Camille accomplished so much more proficiently than she did. "I hope you don't mind if I step on your toes."

"I don't."

"Brave soul," she said under her breath as she got to her feet.

"It wasn't my soul you warned me about," he returned, leading her onto the dance floor.

The music was a slow, sensuous ballad, and he reached for her, holding her lightly against him. She wound her arms around his neck, lifting her head to smile into his warm eyes.

"What was it you and my aunt were discussing so intently earlier?"

"She was letting me in on a few family secrets."

"Uh-oh. And just which of my many indiscretions did she tell you about?"

She bit the bullet and asked, "Does the name Camille mean anything to you?"

The laughter quickly faded from his eyes. "She was a long time ago. I was a kid."

"Should I be worried about her?"

"No way. I think every guy has to lose his heart once before he learns what it is to be a man."

"My only concern would be if she's still carrying it around with her."

"No." His laugh was dry. "She tossed it back at me."

She smoothed the silver strands of hair along the side of his ear. Her heart filled with tenderness for the man who had given his love so completely, only to lose it all. "Should I admit how pleased I am to know that?"

"I don't know, should you?" His hands pressed against the small of her back, bringing her intimately closer to him. His lips nuzzled her neck, pressing tiny kisses to the delicate slope of her throat.

Carrie melted against him, aware with every fiber of her being that she loved this man. His arms around her gave her the most secure feeling she'd ever known. Camille might flit from one relationship to another, but she herself was utterly content with one man—this man.

"Shane?" she murmured a moment later.

"Hmm?"

"The music's stopped." The other couples on the dance floor were gradually returning to their tables.

"No, it hasn't," he countered. "I can still hear it loud and clear." He reached for her hand and pressed it over his heart. "Listen to what being near you does to me."

"Oh, Shane." She pressed her forehead to his shoulder, loving him all the more. "I hear wonderful music too."

"You do?" His eyes drifted open to stare into hers.

"I have from the moment you told me my freckles were beautiful."

"Everything about you is exceptional. Freckles." He paused to kiss her nose. "Eyes." His lips brushed over the corner of her eye. "But your sweet mouth takes the prize."

Artfully, Carrie managed to avoid his searching lips. She didn't know how to take him in this mood. He was serious, and yet she could feel the laughter rumbling in his chest. She became painfully conscious that they were the only couple left on the floor. "Shane...people are looking at us."

"Let them look." His grip around her waist tightened.

"Your aunt..."

"Right," he murmured, dropping his arms, and led her back to the table.

She was just about to sit when an all-too-familiar voice spoke from behind her. "Carrie, imagine seeing you here."

Dread settled like a lead balloon in the pit of Carrie's stomach. Slowly, she turned to face her twin.

Seven

"Hello, Camille." Carrie felt as though her fragile world had suddenly been stricken by global disaster. The feeling was strangely melancholy. Pensive and sad. Her numb mind refused to function properly, to question what her sister was doing here dancing when only hours before she'd been weeping uncontrollably. It took several painful seconds for her to remember how quickly Camille always rebounded from a broken heart. Bob was apparently forgotten, and once again Camille was on the prowl.

"So this is the man you've been keeping all to yourself." Smiling demurely, Camille moved forward, placing her hand on the rounded curve of her satin-clad hip as she studied Shane. She started with his handsome silver head, her eye roving downward with obvious interest. "Now I understand why." Fleetingly, her gaze returned to Carrie. "Aren't you going to introduce us?"

"Yes…of course." She couldn't look at Shane, couldn't bear to see the admiration in his gaze as he recognized the face in the portrait. "Camille, this is Shane Reynolds and his great-aunt, Ashley Wallingford. Shane and Ashley, my twin sister, Camille."

"How do you do, Camille." Shane's voice revealed little of his thoughts. "Would you care to join us?"

So polite, so formal. Carrie didn't know him like this.

"I'd love it."

Sure she would, Carrie thought. Why not? Camille had been without a man since early afternoon and there was little doubt in Carrie's mind that Shane appeared overwhelmingly attractive. He was just what the doctor ordered for a slightly wounded heart. Carrie had thought he'd looked devastating only hours before. She'd watched with a heart full of pride as he accepted a prestigious award. Later, feeling blissfully content, she'd danced in his arms. Now she was being forced to stand by and watch her sister steal him away.

Like the gentleman he was, he pulled out Carrie's chair, but before she could reclaim her seat, Camille took it. The action was so typical of her twin's behavior that Carrie had to swallow down an angry cry.

Without hesitating, Shane pulled an empty chair from another table and placed it next to his own. Carrie sat, her fists balled in her lap. She could feel Ashley studying her and did her utmost to appear poised.

"You must be the man who bought my portrait," Camille began, her voice animated. "I was thrilled to hear that you liked it so much."

"Yes, I did buy it." Shane placed his arm along the back of Carrie's chair, but she received little comfort from the action. Camille had only started to pour on the charm. Once she gained momentum, no man could resist her. Carrie didn't dare believe Shane would be the exception.

Leaning closer to him, Camille murmured, "I don't suppose Carrie's told you much about me."

"No, I can't say that she has."

Carrie refused to look in his direction.

"Carrie, dear," Ashley Wallingford whispered close to her ear. "Are you feeling all right?"

"I'm fine." Even her voice sounded strained and low. "Will you excuse me a moment?" she asked, rising. This could be the most important battle of her life, and she wanted to check her war paint.

"Naturally." Camille answered for the entire group. "That will give me a chance to talk to these wonderful people."

The words were enough to give Carrie second thoughts, but she couldn't very well sit down again and suddenly announce she wasn't going.

Refusing to run like a frightened rabbit, she crossed the room with her head held high, her steps measured and sure. She located the powder room without a problem and released a pent-up sigh the instant the door closed behind her. Her thoughts were in turmoil. She should have told Shane the truth about the portrait long before now. She admitted that much. But if he cared half as much about her as she hoped, it shouldn't matter. At least that was what she told herself while she repaired the damage to her makeup. Her reflection showed wide, apprehensive eyes and a mouth set with flint-hard resolve. For the first time in her life she was in love, and she would move heaven and earth not to lose Shane. Even if it meant fighting her own twin sister.

As Carrie approached the table, she noted that Ashley Wallingford was there alone. Carrie's heart plummeted with defeat as her troubled gaze scanned the dance floor. The self-confidence she'd worked so hard to instill in the powder room vanished when she saw Camille's arms draped around Shane's neck. They were making only a pretense of dancing.

As much as possible, she tried to ignore them, reclaiming her chair next to Shane's great-aunt.

"Do you feel better?" Ashley inquired.

"I did until a minute ago." Involuntarily, her gaze darted back to the dance floor.

"I wouldn't have guessed you two were twins."

"Not many do," Carrie admitted. "Believe me, our appearance isn't the only difference."

"I can see that."

The music ended, and Camille returned to the small table, her face flushed and happy. She was laughing at something Shane had said, but she sobered as she joined the other two women.

"I like your friend, Carrie," she admitted boldly, smiling up at Shane. "You should have introduced us weeks ago. Isn't that right, Shane?"

His response barely penetrated through the wave of pain that assaulted Carrie. Clearly he was already Camille's, and in record time. Her twin had once bragged that most men succumbed in less than a week, but this…! She had never seen Camille work so fast. She was out to capture Shane in one evening.

"I've always adored men with silver hair," Camille continued, sharing a secret smile with Shane.

"It's a family trait," Ashley Wallingford stated blandly. "All the Reynolds men gray prematurely."

"How interesting." Camille barely glanced in the older woman's direction as she spoke. "I still can't get over sweet Carrie dating such a handsome man."

"Thank you," Shane returned politely. "And I'd say that beauty runs in the family."

Camille's incredulous gaze flew to Carrie in disbelief. "Yes, yes, it does, although almost everyone believes I received more than my fair share in that department. But Carrie's so talented that no one seems to notice her…little flaws."

Carrie was stunned. She'd never seen Camille be so cruel before.

Shane was angry. Angry with this clinging twin of Carrie's who possessed all the sensitivity of a corn husk, and angry with Carrie. He loved her and had for weeks. It was a shock to learn she hadn't been completely honest with him, and a disappointment, as well. He wouldn't have believed she was capable of such deception. He wanted to shake her and in the same breath reassure her. He did neither.

"But then, you've seen lots of me already," Camille continued undaunted. "After all, you did buy my portrait."

"He thought it was me." Carrie realized the instant she opened her mouth that she never should have spoken.

"You've got to be kidding." Camille's features were frozen with disbelief. "Why, that's absurd. We look nothing alike."

"We *are* twins."

"But not *identical* twins," Camille countered.

"There are similarities," Shane inserted. "But now that I see the two of you together, I realize how wrong I was to have made the comparison. Carrie's nothing like the portrait."

Carrie paled, and a rock settled where her heart had once been. With virtually no effort, Camille had managed to wrap Shane around her little finger. She had hoped for better from him. But she wasn't about to give up. This was only round one, and she hadn't even put on her gloves yet. She loved this man, and she intended to fight for him. She'd allowed her sister to snatch other men from her grasp when she hadn't even been trying. This time Camille was going for broke, but Carrie wasn't going to sit back and watch, because in the past, no one had mattered as much as Shane.

"It's been a long tiring evening. It's time we got you home, Aunt Ashley," Shane said, pushing back his chair.

"I do feel a bit drained," the older woman responded. "But it's been most enjoyable. All of it."

Carrie stood, too. Her evening bag was clenched so tightly in her hand that her fingers had grown numb.

"Yes, it has been great," she agreed. "Most of the time," she added under her breath.

If Camille could dish it out, she should learn to take it as well. Although from the look that Shane was giving her, Carrie realized she would have done well to keep her mouth shut. Too late she remembered the protective reaction Camille often evoked in men.

"I know you'll want to get in touch with me," Camille said, and smiled boldly up at Shane. "I'm sure Carrie will be happy to give you my number. Of course, you don't actually need to ask. I'm in the book."

"It was nice to meet you."

"A pleasure," Ashley Wallingford murmured.

Wordlessly, the three of them left the hotel. The valet brought Shane's vehicle around, and soon they were driving through the well-lit city streets. The silence inside the car was thicker than any fog San Francisco had ever seen. Shane drove to his aunt's home in Nob Hill first. He refused an invitation for them to go inside for another nightcap. Carrie couldn't have agreed more, though she enjoyed his Aunt Ashley and knew that this perceptive lady was well aware of Camille's game. Carrie only hoped that Shane was just as intuitive.

Shane saw his aunt safely to her door and returned a couple of minutes later.

"Well?" he said once he'd climbed back inside the car.

"Well what?"

"Aren't you going to explain?"

"About the portrait? No." She couldn't see confusing

the issue at this late date. Everything seemed obvious. "However, if you're seeking an apology, you have it. I should have been honest about the painting. In light of what's happened this evening, my regrets have doubled."

He thought about her answer for a moment before asking, "You feel insecure next to your sister, don't you?"

"Insecure?" She tried to laugh off the truth. "Heavens, why should I?"

"You tell me."

He wouldn't be fooled easily, and she quickly abandoned her guise. "All right. I'm insecure. I have good reason. Camille's stolen away more men than I care to count. Most of them without even trying. I'd hoped..." She hesitated, unsure of the wisdom of revealing her feelings.

"You hoped what?"

"Simply that you'd show a lot more character than the others. Apparently I was wrong."

"Just what do you mean by that?"

"You're behaving like a besotted fool. Enthralled by her beauty. Drinking in her every word. Don't you think I already know that I'm a poor second next to Camille?" She was lashing out now, angry. "You told me I was lovely, and I was fool enough to believe you."

"You are."

"But Camille's perfect, and I noticed you certainly didn't waste any time enjoying her abundant charms. I would have thought that—"

She wasn't allowed to finish. "Just what on earth do you mean by that?" Every second of this conversation was irritating him more. He wasn't particularly fond of Carrie's twin sister, and he didn't like the sound of these accusations, either.

"I saw the way the two of you were dancing. Good heavens, you looked like you were glued together. It was disgusting."

"Was it so disgusting when I was dancing with you?"

"No," she answered honestly. "But then, you've known me longer than thirty seconds." The last thing she wanted was to argue with him, but her outrage grew and grew until she had no choice but to vent it. "Maybe you've always yearned for a Camille. That was the name of your first love, after all. Well, now you've found her again, in a way. Not exactly her, but another woman who should fit the bill nicely."

"Would you kindly shut up!"

"No. Perhaps you think I'm jealous. All right, I'll admit it. I am. But I thought so much more of you than this. If it's Camille you want, then fine. You're welcome to her. It's lucky you met her when you did. She's between men at the moment, and you'll suffice nicely. But when you've had your fun, don't come back to me. I never have appreciated Camille's rejects."

Shane's eyes narrowed to points of steel. He looked as though he didn't trust himself to speak. Instead, he started the car and pulled onto the street. His hand compressed around the steering wheel so hard that his knuckles turned white.

They didn't exchange another word during the thirty minute drive to the beach house. With every mile, her contrition mounted. She regretted each impulsive word. Only a few minutes before she'd been determined to fight for Shane, and now she was practically throwing him into Camille's arms.

He didn't shut off the engine when he reached her house. His hands remained on the steering wheel, and he stared straight ahead.

Carrie grasped the door handle, prepared to depart. Shane was angry, angrier than she'd ever known him to be. She'd been hurt by his thoughtless actions, and in her pain, she'd lashed out at him. She drew a tortured breath.

"Good night, Shane," she murmured in a small, distracted voice. "I'm very sorry that I ruined your special night. But I want you to know how proud I am of your accomplishments, and I'm so pleased you took me to the ceremony with you. I'll…I'll always remember that." Sick with defeat, the taste of failure and disillusionment coating her mouth, she slipped from the car and hurried into the cottage.

For ten minutes Shane didn't move. His instincts told him to drive away and not look back. He was tired and emotionally drained. But the sound of Carrie's tormented voice echoed around the interior of the car to haunt him. He couldn't leave her like this. He loved her. But she'd lied to him, deceived him. He needed time to sort out his reaction to that.

Angrily, he shifted the car into Reverse and roared

back onto the highway. They both needed space to bandage their injured pride.

Sitting inside the house, Carrie tensed when she heard Shane's car leave the driveway. For a few minutes she'd thought he might not go. But that hope died when he revved his engine and pulled away. She knew they both regretted their harsh words. If only he hadn't been so willing to dance with Camille—though what they'd been doing could hardly be termed dancing. Her anger mounted with the memory. Unable to contain it, she paced the narrow living room, more furious now than before.

If Shane wanted Camille, then she would let him go without a backward glance. She would wash her hands of him without remorse. Cast him aside and be grateful she'd learned what she had before she was completely in love with him.

It's too late, her heart taunted. *Far too late.*

Sleeping was impossible. Her mind spun out of control with questions demanding answers that she didn't have. The bedroom walls seemed to press in around her. An hour after going to bed, she abandoned the effort of even pretending she could sleep.

As she often did when her thoughts were too heavy to escape, she walked down to her private beach with a steaming mug of spiced tea.

Moonlight splashed against the sandy shore, its silver rays illuminating the night. There was a solace here that she could find nowhere else. For a long time she had thought the one great love of her life would be this beach. Now she knew how wrong she'd been. The only love of her life was Shane Reynolds, and she couldn't let herself just hand him over to Camille. If she wasn't careful, she was going to lose him. It might be too late already.

Sitting on the thick bed of sand, she pulled her legs up against her chest and wrapped her arms around her knees. The night was cloudless, the stars brilliant, like rare glittering jewels on a background of dark velvet.

"I thought I'd find you here."

Startled, she gasped at the sound of the unexpected intruder. The moonlight revealed Shane standing beside her. He'd discarded his tie, and the top three buttons of his starched tuxedo shirt were unfastened, revealing curling silver chest hair.

"Do you mind if I join you?"

"Please do." Her heart was singing, and she had trouble finding her voice.

He lowered himself to the sand next to her. "You couldn't sleep?" He made the statement a question.

"No. You either?"

"I didn't try. I parked a couple of miles down the road and stopped to think."

At least they were speaking to each other, even if their conversation was more like that of polite strangers.

"I tried," she admitted.

"I would have thought you'd paint."

"No." Slowly she shook her head. "Contrary to popular myth, art demands too much concentration. According to Camille, I work twelve-hour days but only make as much money as if I worked a nine-to-five job." She instantly regretted mentioning her twin's name. Shane's expression tightened, and she glimpsed a bit of his frustrated anger. Gathering her resolve, she gripped her arms more securely around her bent legs. "I honestly am sorry for not telling you about Camille."

"I wish you had, but having met your sister explains a great deal." His eyes captured hers, demanding that she return his gaze. "I suppose seeing her portrait in my office is why you bolted that day."

Her wry grin was lopsided. She nodded, all the more ashamed now. "Camille's always been the beauty in the family. You were right when you said—"

"I can't believe you." Hands buried deep in his pockets, he stood and paced the area in front of her, kicking up sand. "If you'd only told me."

"I know."

"All this time, I thought…"

"I said I was sorry." She felt worse than before he'd come. He had every reason to be angry. But he didn't understand what having a twin sister like Camille had meant in her life. However, now, when he was upset with her deception, wasn't the time to enlighten him. Given time, he would see the truth.

She tried again, wanting to set things right between them. "I didn't mean the things I said earlier."

"I know."

"I was…jealous when I saw you dancing with Camille." Carrie doubted he knew what it had cost her to admit that.

"She was the one who invited me to dance. A gentleman doesn't refuse a lady."

Somehow she had suspected that, but it seemed as if Shane could have found a way to extricate himself. He hadn't, and that seemed to prove that he wasn't as immune to Camille as he would like her to believe.

With her head drooping, she waited as the seconds ticked by. She yearned for Shane to take her in his arms and erase the hurts and anxieties of the evening. Finally she raised her eyes to him. "Shane," she whispered achingly, "would you please hold me?"

He reached down and brought her to her feet, then slipped an arm around her shoulders, catching the side of her chin with his index finger, lifting her mouth to receive his kiss.

Carrie twined her arms around his neck and pressed herself against him. She yearned to wipe the thought of Camille from his mind and replace it instead with the warmth of her love. With a smothered moan, she met his mouth in a hungry kiss, glorying in the feel of his lips over hers.

Her body molded to the hard contours of his chest. His hand pressed possessively against her back, sliding up and down her spine as he gathered her pliable form closer to his.

"Let's never fight again," she pleaded, breathlessly.

"Are you kidding? When we can make up like this?"

Without exactly knowing how it happened, she discovered that she was sitting on his lap, her arms draped around his neck. "I was hoping we could do this frequently without needing the incentive of an argument first."

"Agreed." His mouth brushed hers.

"Carrie," he whispered. "Don't you know that you're beautiful?"

Unbidden tears moistened the corners of her eyes. "I'm not." She wanted to believe him, but too many painful lessons over the years had proven otherwise. No one who saw her next to her twin could say she was beautiful. No one.

"Carrie." Camille slid into the opposite side of the booth where Carrie was waiting. "This is a surprise. It isn't every day that my sister calls and invites me to lunch."

Carrie's smile was forced. "We should do it more often."

"Especially if you're buying," Camille joked. She picked up the menu and scanned the contents, quickly making her choice. "I had a great time with Shane the other night."

"Oh?"

"He's so good-looking. Where'd you meet him?"

"He bought a painting."

"Of course," Camille giggled. "Mine."

With forced patience, Carrie set the menu aside. Her stomach was in turmoil, but she would order and make the pretense of eating. The time was long overdue for a heart-to-heart talk with her only sibling.

The waitress came and took their order. Not surprisingly, they both asked for the same thing: spinach salad with the dressing on the side. They were alike just as much as they were different, although they always seemed surprised when they discovered it.

The waitress left after filling their coffee cups.

"I always enjoy a good spinach salad," Carrie felt obligated to defend her choice.

"Me, too."

"It…seems that there's another thing we share."

"What's that?" Camille spread the linen napkin across her lap and glanced up expectantly.

"I'm going to be honest with you, Camille. I love Shane Reynolds."

Camille blinked but otherwise revealed none of her feelings. "Congratulations. Is he in love with you?"

"I think so."

"How nice."

"Camille, I didn't ask you to lunch to discuss the weather. I want to talk about Shane."

Her twin's look was only slightly smug. "I suppose you want to ask my advice."

"Yes." Carrie felt like shouting. "But first I want to give you some. For the first time in my life, I'm honestly in love. Please have the common courtesy to keep your hands off." So much for tact and subtlety. Any attempt at diplomacy was wiped out. All morning she had rehearsed what she wanted to say. Yet the minute Camille ordered the spinach salad, Carrie knew she was in trouble. They both liked the same things, and now apparently they also liked the same man. Already Carrie could see the long lonely years stretched out before her. The one romance of her life foiled by a spinach salad.

To make matters worse, she discovered that she was shaking from the inside out. She dared not reach for her coffee. The hot liquid would slosh over the edges of the cup.

"I can't help it if he's attracted to me," Camille countered.

"You practically threw yourself at him."

"Oh, honestly, Carrie, I wouldn't do that. He was your date."

"Do you notice the way you put that in past tense? The minute you appeared, anyone would have been hard pressed to say whose date he was. You were all over him on the dance floor."

Camille looked dumbfounded. "You're overreacting."

"No." Her hand closed around the fork as she dropped her gaze to the table top. "All right, maybe I am. But for the first time in my life, I'm head over heels in love, and I don't want to lose him."

"Carrie." Camille looked shocked. "Do you think I'm going to try to steal Shane away from you?"

"I don't know."

"I wouldn't. Honest. He's cute and everything, but if he's that important to you, then I'll forget him. He's history."

Carrie was so relieved that she felt like crying. "I'm sorry about you and Bob."

"Don't be. He was getting too serious." Quickly Camille changed the subject, lowering her eyes. "So you're in love. That's great."

"I think so. Shane hasn't said anything—yet. But I think he will. I mean...well, I feel that he loves me, too."

Camille laughed lightly. "It's such a surprise, you know."

"What is?"

"You falling in love first. I always thought it would be me." She raised her coffee cup and poised it in front of her mouth. "But this does create one problem."

"What's that?"

"Shane phoned me earlier and invited me to his house this evening. I suppose you'd prefer it if I didn't go now, wouldn't you?"

Eight

"Shane phoned you?" Carrie repeated numbly, trying to assimilate the news and its meaning.

"First thing this morning." Camille nodded for emphasis. "I was really surprised. Do you mind if I go?"

"He didn't say what it was about?"

"No."

Their salads arrived, and Camille smiled her appreciation to the young waitress who delivered their order. Then she reached for the dressing and ladled it over the top of the crisp spinach leaves topped with fried bacon and slivers of hard-boiled egg.

Carrie couldn't have taken a bite if her life depended on it. Her thoughts were in chaos. There could be no logical explanation for Shane contacting her sister. Especially knowing the way Carrie would react. If he'd been looking for a way to hurt her, then he'd gone straight for the jugular. He knew her feelings. That night on the beach, she'd bared her soul to him. She'd told him of her insecurities. He knew how she felt about

Camille's beauty. And his response was to contact her twin. She'd been fooled. Shane Reynolds wasn't the man she'd thought him to be.

"Well, what should I do?" Camille asked between bites. "I don't want to upset you, but on the other hand, I don't want to be rude to Shane, either."

"Go." At Camille's dubious glance, Carrie added, "I mean it. There are no commitments between Shane and me. If he wants to see you, then fine. Great. Terrific. Make the most of it. I would."

"Carrie." Camille said her sister's name softly. "I've seen you use that tone of voice before, and it usually means trouble."

"What tone of voice?" Pride demanded that she reach for her fork and plow into her spinach salad with the gusto of a starving woman. On the inside she was dying, but a smile lit up her face so no one would ever know. Not her sister, and definitely not Shane.

Camille chatted easily over their lunch, discussing her job and a pale blue summer dress she'd picked up on sale. She commented that she would probably wear the new dress when she went to Shane's that evening. She paused, her cheeks turning a light shade of pink when she realized she was distressing her sister. Quickly, she changed the subject.

The rest of their lunch passed in silence. Camille finally spoke after the waitress brought the bill to the table. "Maybe it isn't such a good idea for me to visit Shane, after all."

"I think you should. Otherwise, you'll always wonder," Carrie told her. It was the most honest thing she'd said since her sister had dropped her little bomb. Somehow she'd managed to finish her lunch, but the effort had been Herculean, and her stomach would ache afterward.

They parted outside the restaurant. On the drive back to the beach house, Carrie noted the thick clouds swollen with rain.

Once home, she moved directly into her studio and sat in front of the canvas that revealed Shane's serious eyes and strong facial features. She was proud of this portrait. She'd outdone herself. Her love had shone through every stroke of the brush as she'd painted the face of the man she cared so much for. Loved, yes. Trusted—she didn't know.

She checked her answering machine for messages before starting to work. The phone rang three times while she painted, but she didn't stop, preferring to work uninterrupted. She was close to being done with this portrait, and she felt it was imperative to finish it soon. Although it was her best work to date, she wished she'd never agreed to paint it. Having those lovingly familiar eyes follow her every time she moved was almost more than she could bear.

She worked straight through dinner and well into the evening, until the portrait was done. She was exhausted…mentally and physically. While she cleaned her brushes, she listened to her voice mail. "Carrie, it's Shane. I'm just calling to see if you're free for dinner tomorrow. If I don't hear back from you, I'll assume that we're on for seven. I'll pick you up."

She snorted. She wasn't about to call him. He could show up at seven, but she wouldn't be here. She could say one thing for him, he sure made the rounds—Camille tonight and her tomorrow. Between the two of them, his social calendar could be filled for the next six months.

The second message was from Camille. "Carrie, it's me. I've thought about it all afternoon. I'm not going to meet Shane. You love the guy. He's yours. I don't want to do anything to upset your hopes with him. You're my sister, and I'm not going to take him away."

The third message was Camille again. "Listen, don't be mad. Oh, this is Camille, you know I hate these stupid machines. I wish you'd answer the phone like everyone else. Anyway, I've changed my mind. I *am* going to meet Shane. I thought it over and well…there could be a very innocent motive behind this invitation."

"Sure," Carrie murmured under her breath.

"Anyway", Camille continued, "I'll call you first thing in the morning and let you know how everything went."

Yawning on her way into the bedroom, Carrie peeled her T-shirt over her head and reached for her Captain America pajamas. Heavens, she was tired. A glance at the clock radio on her nightstand told her it was 3:00 a.m. She stared at it in disbelief. She'd worked that long? Amazing. But the portrait was done, and that was what mattered. Her commitment to Shane was complete.

* * *

The phone rang early the next morning, disturbing her sleep, but Carrie was still exhausted and didn't bother to answer it.

She woke around ten. Bright sunshine crept into the bedroom, its golden light making further sleep impossible. Grumbling, she stumbled out of bed, yawning as she lazily walked into the kitchen.

Her dreams had been so delicious that she hated to get up and face the chill of reality. Her heart was heavy as she pressed the button on the answering machine.

"It's me. Sorry I'm calling so early, but I'm on my way to work and I wanted to tell you how everything went last night with Shane. You're right, Carrie, he really is a wonderful man. I think—"

Viciously, Carrie cut off the message mid-sentence. She didn't want to hear it. Not any of it.

Because she'd gotten off to a late start, the day was half gone by the time she showered and dressed. Lackadaisically, she scrambled a couple of eggs. She was about to pour those into the pan when a loud knock sounded against her front door.

For a moment she toyed with the idea of ignoring it and hoping whoever was there would simply go away. She wasn't in the mood to sign anyone's petition, nor did she feel up to entertaining company.

Another knock followed, and, groaning, she walked across the carpet intent on sending away whoever was there as quickly as possible.

"Yes," she said in her stiffest, most unfriendly voice.

The man standing in front of her was vaguely familiar. She was sure she'd met him before, but she couldn't remember when or where. He looked terrible. His clothes were badly wrinkled, and he was also in definite need of a shave.

"I'm sorry to bother you. I probably shouldn't have come." He buried his hands in his pockets and glanced at the sky. "You don't even remember who I am, do you?"

"No," she admitted honestly.

"Bob Langston. We met briefly a couple of months ago."

"Oh, sure," Carrie said, and relaxed. "You're Camille's Bob."

"Not anymore, I'm afraid."

"Would you like to come in for a cup of coffee?"

"If you're sure it's no problem."

"I wouldn't have asked you in otherwise." She unlatched the screen door and held it open for him. "In fact, I was just about to fix some breakfast." Bob looked as if he could use a decent meal as well, she thought.

"Please don't let me stop you."

"If you don't mind, we can talk as I cook."

"Sure."

He followed her into the kitchen and took a chair. She poured a cup of coffee and brought it to him. "Cream? Sugar?"

"No, this is fine. Thanks."

He looked so dejected and unhappy that she felt sorry for him. She had met him months ago, but his appearance was drastically altered from that first meeting. Well, she probably didn't resemble a beauty queen this morning herself. If he was looking for someone to commiserate with, she was certainly available.

Without asking, she added a couple of extra eggs to the bowl and whipped them with a fork until the mixture was frothy. "I suppose you want to talk about Camille."

His shoulders sagged as his large hands cupped the coffee cup. "She broke it off. I still can't believe it."

"Did she give you any reason?" She'd been so teary that day, that Carrie never had gotten the story straight.

"Tons, but none of them made sense."

A small smile lifted one side of Carrie's mouth. "I know what you mean."

"To make matters worse, she's already seeing another man. Some rich guy on Nob Hill. She went to his house last night."

"You…followed her?" If he was about to reveal the details of Camille's meeting with Shane, then Carrie didn't want to hear about it.

Bob was decent enough to look ashamed of his actions. "Yes. That has to rank right up there with the most unforgivably stupid things I've ever done."

Carrie couldn't recall much of Camille's explanation about why she and Bob had split. From what she did remember, she thought Camille had said that Bob was the one who had decided to call things off.

"Maybe you'd better start at the beginning." She added a slice of butter to the pan and heated it up, and, when it had melted, she poured in the eggs.

"There's not really much to tell. We'd been seeing quite a bit of each other. I was beginning to think that maybe we should think about getting married. We even talked about it a couple of times. Then, out of the blue, Camille says that she feels we need to see less of each other. I was furious. Good grief, I was carrying around a diamond ring in my pocket, looking for a romantic minute to slip it on her finger, and she says something crazy like that. I came unglued."

"That's funny, because it seems to me that she said *you* called it off."

"Me?" Bob's face was a study in incredulity. "That's insane. I *love* Camille. I have for months, but she took me on a wild-goose chase almost from day one."

"And last night, when you followed her, she was going to Shane Reynolds's house. Shane and I have been seeing a lot of each other."

"So it was all innocent." His relief was evident.

As best she could, Carrie swallowed down her pain. "I...I don't know."

"What do you mean?"

With her back to him, she stirred the eggs. "I did a portrait of Camille a while back, and Shane bought it."

"I wish I'd known about it. I would have loved to own it." His voice was thick with regret. "I still want to marry her, you know. I've waited a long time to settle down. I just never believed that the woman I love would walk away from me like this." He shook his head as though to clear his thoughts. "Sorry. Go on."

"There's not much to tell. Shane bought the painting. He says he did it because…well, he thought it was me." She felt a little crazy to even suggest something like that now, when the differences between the two sisters were so prominent.

"I can understand that," Bob murmured. "You *are* sisters. The coloring's a bit different, but you two resemble each other quite a bit. In subtle ways."

"Really?" Even though Shane had told her the same thing, she had trouble believing it.

"Sure."

"Anyway, I…I never corrected his impression. Then we happened to bump into Camille, and he learned the truth."

"So now you assume that he's more interested in *her?*"

"What else can I think? He invited her over."

"And she went? Knowing how you feel about Shane?" His brown eyes hardened.

Carrie nodded. "I told her I didn't mind."

"That sister of yours needs to be taught a lesson."

"As far as I'm concerned, it's Shane who should learn a thing or two." The room filled with an electric silence. She dished up the scrambled eggs and brought them to the table. But neither of them ate.

"Well, what are we going to do about it?" Bob asked.

"I don't know."

"Shane and Camille have no business being together."

"It could all be innocent," she felt obliged to say the words, although she could offer no plausible reason for why Shane would contact Camille. "Like us being together now." The instant the words left her mouth, an idea shot into her mind. "You know, I may be on to something here."

"What?" Bob leaned forward expectantly.

"We know *our* meeting is strictly innocent, but Shane and Camille don't."

"What's that got to do with anything?"

"They could see us together and wonder. In fact, it would probably do them both good."

"I couldn't agree with you more." Bob's eyes shone with a delighted twinkle. "I think I could come to like you as a sister-in-law," he said, reaching for his fork.

Breakfast took on more appeal for Carrie, as well. "Here's what I think we should do."

When Bob returned several hours later, he'd shaved, and his hair was neatly trimmed and combed back, revealing strong features. Carrie could understand why her sister had found him so attractive.

"You're sure Camille will be at Billy's?" Carrie asked.

"Positive." He chuckled under his breath. "You know, I'm almost looking forward to this."

"Me, too."

"Where to first?"

"Shane's. I want to deliver this portrait."

His gaze met hers. "I know the way."

He waited while she locked her front door. Then he

carefully secured Shane's portrait in the trunk of his car and helped her into the front seat.

During the drive into the city, they talked and joked like old friends. She found it easy to talk with him, and was furious with her sister for having led such a good man down a rocky road.

As Bob had claimed, he was well acquainted with the route to Shane's home on Nob Hill.

When he pulled up in front, he turned to her. "Do you want me to go with you?"

"No, I'd prefer to do this on my own."

"Okay, but if you need me, just say the word."

"Don't worry, I will."

Once again, he helped her with the large canvas. As soon as she was at the door, he returned to the car, leaning against the bumper.

Smiling, Carrie rang the bell and waited.

Shane appeared almost immediately. "Carrie, this is a surprise."

Her answer was a wry grin. "I only have a minute. I wanted to drop off your portrait."

"I would have picked it up myself if I'd known you were finished."

She noted the way his gaze darted past her to Bob. He picked up the canvas and studied it, his approval showing in his eyes. "This is marvelous."

"Thank you."

"Come in," he offered, "I didn't mean to keep you standing out here."

"I can't, thanks. I've got a dinner date."

"I thought *we* were going out tonight?" Again his eyes shot past her to Bob, waiting in the driveway. "I assumed—"

"I'm sorry, Shane, but I'd already made plans."

By the way his mouth compressed into an angry line, she could tell that he was striving to keep his temper. His eyes raked over her, then back past her to Bob.

"I felt we had an understanding, Carrie."

"To be honest, so did I," she said, for the first time revealing some of her own pain. "I…I've never felt closer to anyone than to you that night on the beach."

"What happened to change that?"

"That's more a question for you than me." To her horror, her voice cracked. "Really," she said and took a step backward, "I've got to be going."

"Carrie." Shane set the portrait aside and followed her onto the steps. "I don't understand."

"I don't know how you can say ...at. You're the one who's confused things. It's you who can't seem to make up your mind which twin interests you."

Shane was certain Carrie was referring to his meeting with Camille and was slightly annoyed. If she would stop playing the rejected lover, this would soon be resolved. "Carrie, I can explain, if you'd like to listen."

Backing away from him, she winced at the blaze of love and tenderness that shone from his handsome features. She tried to ignore it and concentrate on the anguish she'd suffered. "I heard that Camille was here the other night—at your invitation."

"I said I could explain that."

"I shared my deepest insecurities with you, and they meant nothing." She knew that dredging up everything now was unfair, but she couldn't help herself. Camille was so pretty that she couldn't blame Shane if he fell in love with her. But he didn't have to do it so soon.

"Everything you shared with me that night meant a great deal. I—"

"I imagine that once you met Camille, you were able to distinguish the differences between us more readily. She really is a beauty, isn't she? And you must admit, there's no competition between the two of us."

"Carrie, I'm trying hard to control my temper, but you're making this difficult." He realized that she was deeply hurt, and he blamed himself. He'd assumed— wrongly, it seemed—that Camille would have explained everything by now.

As she backed down the stairs, Carrie caught sight of Bob checking his wristwatch. "I don't have the time to talk now."

"I'll contact you later, then," Shane said in that calm, reasonable tone she wanted to hate. "When you've had a chance to think things through."

"Fine." For her part, she had expected to feel triumph and satisfaction for pulling off this minor charade for Shane's benefit. Turning away from him, she felt neither.

Ever the gentleman, Bob opened her car door for her and closed it once she was safely inside. She noted that Shane remained at the top of the steps even after they'd pulled out into traffic. Long after they were out of the sight of his house, she could still feel his eyes searing straight through her.

"Well, how did it go?" Bob asked, his voice keen with curiosity. "Did you bring him up short and surprise him?"

"I'm sure I did."

"Are you sorry we're doing this?"

"I don't know," she told him truthfully. "But I have the feeling it's going to work far better on Camille than Shane."

"I hope so," he grumbled, then stopped abruptly. "I didn't mean that the way it sounded. I'm anxious to get this settled with Camille. Thirty isn't that far away, and I'd like to start a family."

"That may frighten her," Carrie commented, recalling her own discussion with her sister on the subject of children.

"I'm not talking about a baseball team here. Just one child, maybe two. Camille wouldn't even have to work outside the home if she didn't want to. I make a good living."

By the time Bob had finished talking about his future with Camille, they'd pulled into the parking lot of Billy's restaurant. "You're sure you want to go through with this?" Carrie asked one last time.

"Positive. I don't want her to think I've been crying in my soup since she's been gone." He paused and chuckled, "Actually, I was weeping in my scrambled eggs, as I recall."

Billy's was divided into two distinct areas. The restaurant took up a good portion of the floor space and overlooked San Francisco Bay with its large fleet of fishing boats. The cocktail lounge engaged top-class entertainment and included a small dance floor.

"She hasn't wasted any time, has she?" Bob whispered close to Carrie's ear, and nodded toward a table directly across the room from them. Almost instantly, she spotted her twin sister.

Now that she'd had the last few days to analyze Camille's behavior, she realized that it wasn't like her sister to jump quite so freely from one relationship to another. Camille was carefree, but not to this extent. Carrie more easily understood her sister's behavior the night of the awards dinner. Camille's search for happiness had been almost desperate that evening, and Carrie herself had been trapped in a web of insecurities or else she would have noticed it earlier. If Camille danced with Shane and held him too tight, it must have been because she was pretending to be in Bob's arms. If her smile was overly bright, then it was to hide the pain of having lost Bob.

Tonight, Carrie noted that her twin was with another man, seeking to erase the hurt.

"Bob, will you excuse me a minute?"

"Sure," he murmured, and she wondered if he'd even heard her. He couldn't take his eyes from Camille. Those two were so much in love that she couldn't allow this charade to continue. Nor was she willing to cause her only sister any additional pain.

Without telling Bob what she was doing, she left

him standing by the reservation desk and wove her way through the tables.

"Hello, Camille," she said, reaching her sister's side. Camille's date stood and shook Carrie's hand, introducing himself. She didn't catch the name.

"This is my sister," Camille said stiffly in explanation.

"I'm pleased to meet you, Carrie. Would you care to join us?"

"Carrie appears to have her own date." Camille's voice dipped softly, but she couldn't disguise her surprise at seeing her sister with Bob.

"Could I talk to you a minute?" Carrie asked.

"Alone?" Camille's eyes met her date's.

"Why don't I go see what's keeping our drinks?" Mr. Nameless said, rising from his seat.

The moment the man was gone, Carrie took the empty chair. "How did it go with Shane last night?"

"Fine. What are you doing here with Bob?" Camille leaned forward slightly, then, straightening, folded her hands in her lap like a polite schoolgirl.

"He loves you."

Camille's short laugh bordered on hysterical. "You've got to be kidding. I tested him, and he failed. If he honestly loved me—"

"He had a diamond ring in his pocket the night you said you thought that you should cool things down a bit."

"A diamond?" Camille's gaze softened as it flew across the restaurant to Bob, who remained standing in the reception area. "He was going to ask me to marry him?" She jerked her head back to study Carrie as though searching for any signs of dishonesty. "Then why didn't he simply tell me so?"

"Pride. The same kind of pride that prevented me from listening to your telephone message this morning. But I want to know now. I need to know."

"Know what?"

"Why did Shane contact you?"

"Oh, he gave me the painting. He said that…you should probably ask him why." Ever so slightly, as though being pulled by a powerful magnet, Camille's eyes returned to Bob. "Are you sure Bob's telling you the truth?"

"I'm sure." Carrie felt like the world's biggest fool. Naturally Shane wouldn't want the portrait any longer. Not when he knew the painting was of Camille and not her. She'd forgotten that completely. But she didn't have time to deal with her own foolishness now. Camille's happiness was at stake. "Bob came to me today, completely miserable because he'd lost you. He loves you."

Carrie was convinced her sister hardly heard her. "I thought I'd cry when he agreed to my crazy scheme," Camille murmured. "Then he suggested we ought to make this cooling off period permanent, and I wanted to die. For weeks I'd been thinking about being a wife, and you know what?" She didn't wait for a response. "I know I'm going to like it. I've even given some thought to having children. I wouldn't mind being a mother if I could have Bob's babies."

"If you went to him, I think you two could solve this misunderstanding."

"Maybe?" The shield of pride was quickly erected.

"Maybe!" Carrie echoed. "Don't be a fool. The man you love is waiting on the other side of this room for you. If you've got so much pride that you can't go to him, then I think you deserve to lose him." Standing, she said, "I can't do anything more for either of you. In fact, I've got my own bridges to mend." She smiled gently at her sister. "It seems we've discovered love together. Let's not be stupid and throw away something so precious."

Camille's hand around her wrist stopped her. "You're going to Shane?"

"Yes, and not a minute too soon."

They exchanged encouraging looks. "Good luck."

"You too."

As Carrie sauntered past Bob, she winked and tilted her head toward Camille. "Everything's settled. I know you'll be a fantastic brother-in-law."

Instantly Bob's countenance brightened, and his eyes softened with love as his gaze locked with Camille's. Carrie didn't stay to watch the lovers' reunion.

A taxi was idling outside the restaurant, and she climbed in the back seat and gave the driver Shane's address. She only hoped that she wasn't too late and that he was still home.

The taxi ride seemed to take an eternity. All the way there, she rehearsed what she planned to say. There was always the humorous approach. She would tell him that dating Bob was all a joke—which it was, in a way. Then there was the "pretend nothing was wrong" angle. But she didn't know how successful that would be. Honesty would work best, but admitting what a fool she'd been wouldn't be easy.

The cab stopped in front of Shane's house. The light shining from his living room window was encouraging. At least he was home. She had visions of working up her courage and coming this far only to have the house empty.

She paid the driver, and the sound of the cab driving away echoed in her ears as she stood outside Shane's front door.

A full five minutes passed before she had courage enough to ring the doorbell. Another minute came and went until he finally appeared.

Finding Carrie standing there was a shock. All evening he'd been planning what he wanted to say to her. It was apparent that they had a terrible communication problem.

"Hello, Shane." Her smile was falsely cheerful.

He looked past her. "Are you alone this time?" His tone was gruffer than he'd intended.

"Yes. I guess I should apologize for that. I saw Camille, and she explained about the painting...well, you know."

"Yes, I do know."

"May I come in?" This was even worse than she'd imagined.

"If you'd like." He stepped aside and followed her into his home, indicating that she should go to the sitting room on her right.

She saw that he'd already hung the portrait she'd delivered that evening. Seeing it caught her by surprise. "It looks nice."

"I'll tell the artist." His features softened perceptibly.

"I want to apologize for my atrocious behavior earlier."

"I figured as much," he said, and rubbed his hand along the back of his neck. "You're needlessly insecure."

"You certainly didn't do anything to help me overcome that," she flung back, angry with him for making this so difficult. "One day I bare my soul, and the next thing I know you're dating my sister."

"Meeting her is a far cry from dating her."

"Not in my book. Surely you must have known she'd tell me. What would it have cost you to let me know your plans?" She knew she sounded like an unreasonable shrew, but she was embarrassed and angry. She'd expected that this meeting wouldn't be easy, but she hadn't thought he would make it *this* unpleasant.

"I expected you to trust me."

"From past experience with men, I find that difficult."

"What do I have to do to help you to trust me?" He threw the words at her like a challenge.

His raised voice caused her to grimace. "Well, trust is something special. It's not like we're engaged or anything."

"Engaged? You mean we have to be married before I'm entitled to your trust? Is that what you mean?"

"I…"

"This sounds a lot like a marriage proposal. Is that what you're suggesting?"

At the end of her patience, Carrie tossed her hands in the air. "I don't know. No. Yes."

"Fine, then."

Nine

"Fine what?" Carrie stared at him blankly.

"We'll get married."

She was astonished that she'd answered such an outrageous question so flippantly. Stunned that Shane treated the subject so lightly. And furious with them both.

"You don't seem very happy," he commented, his look dark and intense.

Her face was flushed, her eyes wide with shock. "When?" The feeble voice hardly sounded like her own. Still, he'd handed her an answer to her insecurities, and she jumped on it.

"Three months."

This isn't right, her conscience accused. Marriage was sacred. A blending of hearts and souls. A linking of two lives, intertwining personalities, goals, ambitions, destinies. Good heavens, this wasn't some silly game. It was their very lives they were treating so offhandedly. She should never have agreed…but yet she loved Shane. It shouldn't matter that she'd been the one to offhandedly approach the subject. He'd agreed of his own free will. He wanted this, too. Now wasn't the time to question his motives.

"Well?" he asked. "Does three months give you enough time?"

"Yes." Once again she replied in a low, shaking tone. She couldn't quite believe this was real. She felt as if she were intoxicated. Her head spun, and a queasy sensation attacked her stomach. "I'll be a good wife to you, Shane."

"What about children?"

"Children? I haven't given the subject much thought."

"Well, if we're going to be married it's something we need to discuss sooner or later."

"I agree."

"I know your art is important to you. I want you to realize that if we have children, you won't have to give up the things you love."

From his response, she realized that he thought she didn't want a family. "I love children and…I'll love having yours." The words stumbled over each other in her eagerness to assure him. "It's just that I'm having trouble accepting that all this is happening."

"Believe it."

"Do you feel we should start a family right away?"

Shane chuckled, bringing her into his arms. His look was faintly amused. "I think we'd better hold off until after the wedding, don't you?"

"All right." She hardly realized what she was agreeing to.

His arms tightened around her waist, bringing her even closer. "In case you didn't know it, I want you, Carrie Lockett. Desperately." His voice was as smooth as satin. Husky. Sexy. Romantic.

Carrie's eyes drifted closed. This was too good to be true. She was sure she would wake up any minute and discover it had all been a delicious dream. But when his warm mouth found hers, the sensations that flooded her were far too real to be imaginary. His touch left her dazed and uncoordinated. Shell-shocked. She was drunk with love!

"We should tell someone," he whispered against her neck, continuing to spread tiny, biting kisses down the slope of her throat.

"Who?"

"My great-aunt."

"And Elizabeth Brandon," Carrie suggested. After all, it was Elizabeth who was responsible for getting them together. "And Camille."

"Should I talk to your father?"

"Dad? Why?"

"Isn't that the way these things are usually done?"

"I…don't know." This wedding idea was becoming unexpectedly complicated. "I'm sure Dad would like to meet you."

"No doubt."

"He lives in Sacramento."

"Should we phone him?"

"He's probably already in bed. He goes to sleep early."

Shane growled close to her ear. "Don't mention the word bed to me. It's going to be difficult enough keeping my hands off you for the next three months."

"That long?" she murmured.

"All right, two months."

Suddenly Carrie worried about agreeing to such a long wait. Shane could change his mind. He could call everything off at the last minute. He could want out, and she wouldn't blame him.

"Could we hurry things along?" she murmured.

"Brilliant idea. When?"

"Two weeks!"

He chuckled. "What about tomorrow?"

For an instant she honestly considered it, until she realized he had to be teasing. "Two weeks."

"If you insist." He curved a hand around the back of her neck and leaned over to kiss her again. "You have the sweetest mouth."

"Thank you."

"You know what I think?" He spoke even as he kissed the corner of her lips.

"What?"

"If we're planning to go through with this in two weeks' time, we need to talk to our families soon."

"Right."

"I'm going to phone Aunt Ashley." The conversation was momentarily interrupted by a lengthy kiss.

"Now?" Carrie asked once she'd surfaced.

"Right now." He reached behind her for the phone on his desk, punching out the number as he continued kissing her.

She could hear the ringing as the call went through. When his aunt answered, he abruptly broke off the kiss, but he continued to hold Carrie in his arms, his eyes smiling into hers.

"It's Shane," he said into the receiver.

Faintly, Carrie could hear his aunt's voice coming over the wire. "Is something wrong?"

"Something's very right. Carrie and I are going to be married."

"That's wonderful news. When?"

Carrie grinned at the delight the older woman's voice revealed. "Soon. Two weeks, I think."

"Two weeks! Why, that's impossible," Ashley continued. "Your sisters will never forgive you if they aren't invited."

"Of course they're invited," Shane countered.

"But they can't drop everything on such short notice. Caroline's youngest is only a year old."

"Yes, yes, I know," Shane grumbled.

"Tell her we'll schedule the wedding later if it's more convenient," Carrie whispered in his ear, distracting him.

"Aunt Ash, hold on. Carrie's saying something." He covered the telephone receiver with his hand and kissed her on the bridge of her nose. "Have I told you that I love your freckles?"

She felt the heat seep into her cheeks and knew that those freckles would soon switch to their glowing stage.

"According to Aunt Ashley, two weeks is out of the question. We would offend half my family if we don't give them proper notice. It looks like we may be in for a longer wait than we'd originally planned."

"How long?"

"It might be best if we go back to what we first thought—three months."

"That'll be fine." If Shane called off the wedding between then and now, so be it.

He uncovered the mouthpiece and placed the receiver back against his ear. "How's three months?"

"Much better. Can I talk to Carrie?"

Shane handed her the phone. "My aunt wants to talk to you."

She accepted the phone and paused to clear her throat. "Hello."

"Carrie, dear," Ashley Wallingford said warmly. "This is fantastic news. Welcome to the family."

"Thank you. I'm very pleased." Shane was making coherent conversation nearly impossible. While she was speaking, he was kissing the side of her neck, his lips nibbling upward toward her earlobe. Delicious shivers shot up and down her spine. She thought her knees would give out from under her.

"I realize you and Shane have a lot to discuss. We can talk tomorrow. I just wanted you to know that I'm willing to help any way I can."

"Thank you. I'll remember that." Shane had located

the tiny pearl buttons to her blouse and begun unfastening them one by one.

"We'll talk soon, then."

"Soon," Carrie repeated.

"Good night, dear, and tell that rascal of a nephew of mine that I'm exceptionally pleased with his choice."

"I will."

The line disconnected. Carrie gasped for breath as they kissed again.

"I love you," she murmured, tightening her arms around his neck. "I love you so much." She couldn't get enough of him. Couldn't press herself close enough to satisfy the longings of her heart.

"I'd better take you home while I've still got the strength."

As they drove to the beach house, he hummed along with the music playing on the radio. His mood was glorious. Hers was weighted down, wondering if they were basing the most important decision of their lives on over-excited hormones.

Once they reached the cottage, Shane leaned over and kissed her lightly. He kept the car engine running while he walked her to the front door. When she asked him why, he explained, "That's my insurance." His kiss was reverent. "This way I won't be tempted to haul you into that house and cart you off to the bedroom."

He lowered his head, bringing his face inches from hers, and gave her a feather-light kiss. "Night, love."

"Night." He straightened and took a step back.

Long after he had left, she stood on the porch. Her mind was fuzzy. She didn't know what to do. They'd treated the idea of marriage so flippantly, so casually, as if to prove something to each other. This wasn't a healthy scenario.

She would sleep on it, she decided, holding back a yawn. In the morning everything would be clear and she would know what she should do.

Painting was impossible. All morning Carrie tried to occupy her mind with her art, but to no avail. At noon, she gave up the effort. As she cleaned her equipment, she sorted through her thoughts. She felt the need to talk to someone. She toyed with the idea of contacting Elizabeth Brandon, but decided against it. The one person who readily came to mind was Camille, but she wasn't entirely convinced she could trust her twin sister. Sad, but true. They were so different. Camille was water, shimmering and changing. Carrie was the earth, stable and secure. Together, they made mud.

Undecided, she changed from her faded jeans into a pale pink dress. If she was going to talk to anyone, it would have to be Camille. They might not be alike, but Camille always came to Carrie with her worries and anxieties, and now the roles were going to be reversed.

After a brief telephone conversation to verify when and where to meet, Carrie left the house, determined to tell her sister everything. She would start at the beginning, when Elizabeth Brandon mentioned Shane, and explain how attracted she'd been to him that first day.

She would be forthright, she decided. She would tell Camille how she'd fought the attraction, knowing that if Shane bought *No Competition* he would probably be drawn more to Camille than to her. But those problems had been solved, others had cropped up faster than she could handle. Now she was engaged to the man, yet she wasn't entirely convinced he loved her.

Camille was waiting for her in a seafood restaurant close to her office.

"Hi. You look awful."

Carrie took the chair across from her sister. Camille had decided to disperse with tact. "Thanks, I needed that."

Camille seemed genuinely contrite. "I didn't mean anything."

Carrie waved the apology aside with a flick of her wrist. "Don't worry about it. How did things go with Bob last night?"

Camille's happy smile said it all. "Wonderful. We've decided to get married." She held out her left hand so Carrie could admire the beautiful solitaire diamond.

"It's lovely. Congratulations."

"What about you and Shane?"

"We're engaged, too." She didn't need to be told that she revealed none of the happiness that was so obvious in her sister.

"Congratulations," Camille said, but her eyes narrowed and her perfectly shaped mouth thinned slightly.

Knowing her sister, Carrie recognized the expression as one of doubt. "What's wrong?" She decided to meet the question head on.

Camille shook her head. "You don't look pleased."

The waitress came. Carrie hadn't bothered to glance at the menu. There was no reason to. Her sister would probably order what she would have chosen anyway. Camille gave the waitress her selection of French onion soup and a fresh green salad, and Carrie seconded it.

"We've been doing that a lot lately. Have you noticed?"

Carrie nodded.

"I can't understand it," Camille continued. A tiny frown marred the smooth perfection of her face. "We fought like cats and dogs the whole time we were growing up. Sometimes you were so perfect that I thought I hated you."

"Hated *me?* For being *perfect?*" It was so close to her own feelings that Carrie was too stunned to respond. For years she'd felt totally lacking compared to Camille. Her sister was the angelic ideal. "*I* wasn't the gorgeous one." She revealed only a hint of the bitterness she'd held on to all these years.

Slowly Camille shook her head, her lovely dark curls brushing the tops of her shoulders. "I can't believe I'm hearing this. I had to play up what little beauty I had to make up for the fact that you were 'the gifted one.' And you were more than just smart. You had this incredible artistic talent. All my life, the only thing I had to compensate with was my face."

Carrie remained speechless for a full minute. "You were jealous because I did well in school?"

"Uncontrollably."

"But all my life I've envied you your beauty."

"Good looks are superficial. No one knows that better than me. I'm a beauty consultant, remember?"

A loud clap of thunder or a surging bolt of lightning couldn't have had more impact. Her gorgeous twin sister had been jealous of her! Carrie was floored.

"All these years, we've been competing against each other?"

From her startled look, this discovery had jarred Camille, as well. "It seems so."

"I can't believe this. Camille, you're warm, loving, generous and a lot of fun."

"I agree," her twin concurred with no lack of modesty. "But I didn't make the honor roll once."

"No, you were the homecoming queen when I had to scrounge the bottom of the barrel for a date." Carrie swallowed a laugh. Two days before the big dance, she'd been asked by the least popular boy in the entire school. Camille had been dating the quarterback of the football team.

"Didn't you go to the prom with Tom Schrieder?"

"Right. His athletic prowess was on the golf course as I recall." In other words, he wasn't a muscle-bound, popular quarterback.

They broke into simultaneous giggles. Carrie felt like crying and laughing at the same time. It was as if she'd been informed, out of the blue, that she had another twin sister. As if they'd been separated at birth and hadn't been given the opportunity to meet each other until now, as adults.

"I think you're wonderful, Carrie."

"I feel the same way about you."

"Then why are we always at odds with each other?"

Carrie shook her head with the wonder of it. They'd wasted a lot of years. "Not anymore," she vowed. "There'll be no competition between us. Agreed?"

"Agreed." Camille took a long drink of her iced tea. "Now that we're both engaged, what do you think of a double wedding?"

"And let you steal the show?" Carrie joked, but the humor was as artificial as her smile. Her lips trembled with the effort. Soon she was biting the corner of her mouth to control her unhappiness.

"Carrie, what is it?" Her sister took her hand and squeezed her fingers. "I don't think I've ever seen you cry."

"I do, you know. A lot lately."

"But why?"

"Shane."

"You're engaged. You love him, don't you?"

"Yes," she admitted forcefully. "I love him so much I could die from it."

"I don't believe you need to go to those lengths to prove it."

"Don't joke, Camille. This is serious."

"Sorry." She was instantly contrite. "Now tell me, what's wrong?"

Carrie bowed her head, her fingers shredding her paper napkin into a hundred infinitesimal strips. "I can't. It's too embarrassing."

"I'm your sister!"

It wasn't fair that their newfound understanding had to be tested so quickly. "We may be engaged, but I don't know if he loves me. In fact, I proposed first."

"So? Shane didn't argue, did he?" Camille didn't seem to notice anything out of the ordinary. "He couldn't have been opposed to the idea."

"I don't really think he is, but we'd be getting married for all the wrong reasons."

"You love him. What's wrong with that?"

Spilling out the story of her various insecurities wouldn't do either of them any good, so Carrie just kept quiet and refused to meet her sister's eyes.

"If you have doubts," Camille suggested softly, "then talk to Shane. He loves you."

Carrie thought it best to avoid the subject of Shane for the moment. "Have you and Bob set a date for your wedding?"

"He's seeing what he can do to arrange things quickly. I want you to be my maid of honor."

"I'd love that. And when I get married, you can return the favor." Although at the moment she wasn't sure of her future. "However, I don't doubt that you'll get more attention than the bride."

"You could always carry a small, tasteful watercolor instead of the traditional bridal bouquet," Camille teased. "Once people saw how talented you are, they wouldn't bother to look at me."

They both laughed, feeling free to tease each other for the first time.

From the restaurant, Camille returned to work and Carrie did some shopping, killing time, avoiding the inevitable confrontation with Shane.

She'd hoped to sort out her thoughts while the afternoon passed, but she didn't have any success.

Close to Shane's quitting time, she called his office from her cell phone as she stood on the sidewalk just outside his building. His secretary put her directly through.

"Carrie, love." Shane's greeting was happy, animated. "Where are you?"

"Downstairs."

"Great. Come up. Now that we're engaged, there are several people you should meet."

She hesitated, not knowing a gracious way to turn down the invitation. "Can I do it another time? I look a mess."

"If you like."

"Have you got a moment to talk?" She braced her hand against her forehead and closed her eyes.

"All the time in the world. Hang on and I'll be right down."

"No—no thanks. I want to talk now."

"Over the phone?"

"It'll be easier this way."

"Carrie, what's wrong?" His voice grew heavy and serious.

"Nothing…everything."

"Where are you? I'll be right there."

"No!" she cried. "Please don't do that. I'm not up to seeing you."

"Why not?"

"I told you, I look dreadful."

"Not possible," he said, his tone sincere.

"I must be crazy. I'm head over heels in love with you."

"There's nothing wrong with that, especially since I feel the same way about you."

"Oh, Shane, do you really?"

He didn't know what was going on in her mind, but he didn't want to leave any room for doubt. Not about this. "I adore you."

"That's going to make what I have to say all the more difficult."

He didn't like the sound of that. Not one bit. This woman was unlike anyone he'd ever known. He supposed that was part of what had drawn him to her so fiercely.

"I've been thinking about what happened last night."

"Or what didn't happen?" he teased lovingly. Half the night had been gone before he slept. Leaving her alone at her door had been unbelievably difficult. Now he wondered if he'd done the right thing.

"Shane, listen to me, because what I have to say is important."

"What is it, love?"

She didn't pause, blurting out the words in one giant breath before she lost her nerve. "I think it's best if we call off the wedding."

Ten

"What?" Shane exploded. "Where are you? I'm coming down right now, and we're going to talk about this."

"Shane, listen to me. I apologize. I really do, but I can't go through with it. Goodbye."

"Goodbye! What do you mean by that?"

His question was angrily hurled at her. Carrie heard it loud and clear as she clicked her cell shut. Her whole body was trembling, but she couldn't see how shouting at each other over the phone—or in person, for that matter—would do either of them any good. There didn't seem any point in explaining her reasoning. She couldn't, not when it remained unclear in her own mind. She needed time to think.

The five o'clock throng of people heading home clogged the sidewalk as Carrie walked away from Shane's office building. She made a sharp left, and wove her way in and out of the mass of homeward-bound humanity.

She paused at the busy intersection closest to his office to wait for the traffic signal to change. Shane had claimed to love her. That was a perk she hadn't anticipated, but then, any man who had put up with her craziness as he had these last weeks, must hold strong feelings for her.

The light changed, and she stepped off the curb. It was then that she heard someone shout her name. She glanced over her shoulder to see that Shane had somehow managed to catch up with her.

She moved back onto the sidewalk to wait for him. The last thing she wanted was a chase scene reminiscent of some melodramatic movie.

By the time he reached her, he was panting, his shoulders heaving with exertion.

His expression was stern. He was furious, angrier than he could remember being in his life. He couldn't understand this woman. While he regained his breath, he leaned against a lamppost and shook his head. "Come on," he grumbled. "Let's talk."

"I don't think—"

"For once, Carrie, don't argue with me. I'm not in the mood for it."

He didn't say a word as they trudged the short distance back to his building. The strained silence in the elevator was even worse, if that was possible.

The door to his office was wide open in testimony to the urgency of his rush to locate her.

"Sit," he demanded, pointing to a chair.

She did as he asked, but only because she didn't have the energy to defy him.

"All right, talk," he said once he was seated across from her. His desk was the only thing that separated them.

"What do you want me to say?"

"What made you come up with that lunatic decision about calling off the wedding?"

"Insulting me isn't going to help, Shane."

"All right, I apologize. I simply want to know what led to this most recent announcement." He wasn't going to let Carrie walk out. He loved her, needed her, and in the same instant he wanted to shout at the top of his lungs at her for the anxiety she'd caused him. When he was done with that, he wanted to hold her for an eternity. If she was mixed up, he was doubly so.

Meanwhile she just stared at the items on the top of his desk. Anything that prevented her from looking at him fascinated her.

"Just explain what happened between last night and this afternoon that caused you to change your mind."

"I...I don't know where to start."

"Might I suggest the beginning?" he offered somewhat flippantly.

She shot to her feet. "This is exactly what I mean. This...casualness. We were making the most important decision of our lives based on a stupid joke."

As he'd feared, he couldn't follow her reasoning. "What do you mean?"

"You...you asked me what you could do to help me to trust you, and I blurted out what seemed like a marriage proposal."

"Didn't you mean it?"

"I…I'm not sure. Yes. But that shouldn't matter."

"I agreed, didn't I?"

She was angry all over again. "That's the crux of the problem. It wasn't right."

"Why not?"

"Because you were treating the whole thing like some big joke and it isn't. Marriage is precious."

"I realize that." He was beginning to get the gist of her problem. "And I love you. I very seriously and not jokingly love you."

"Well, thank you very much. I love you back," she said as she got up and whirled around, presenting him with a clear view of her back as she strode over to look out the window at the city below. She folded her arms around her waist and swallowed down the hysteria that threatened to choke her. If the subject weren't so serious, she could almost have laughed at what was happening. They might love each other, but a sea of murky water still lay between them.

"Okay, now that we've got that matter cleared up, let's get married."

"No!"

He couldn't believe he'd heard her correctly. "*Now* what's the problem?"

"First you were being flippant. Now you're angry."

"I don't understand you."

"Are you sure you want to be married to a woman you don't understand?"

"Carrie, please…"

"Are you raising your voice at me?"

Shane snapped his mouth shut and clenched his teeth so tightly, his jaw ached. She was so serious that he was momentarily speechless. He forced himself to be calm, relaxing the tense muscles of his shoulders. Standing, he joined her at the huge window that overlooked the downtown area. But he had no time for the skyscrapers that brushed the edges of the heavens.

"I remember the first time I saw your art," he said, his sober tone rounding off the sharp edges of his anger. "It was a seascape. The sky was the pewter color of pre-dawn, and the sun was just breaking over the horizon, golden and filled with the promise of a new day. I stared at that painting for ten minutes. I couldn't take my eyes off it. Something about it touched me as no painting ever has."

Carrie knew exactly which seascape he was referring to. She'd worked on it for weeks, searching for the proper way to express her feelings. It had been a period of disillusionment in her life. Her father had moved to Sacramento. She and her sister had been drifting apart, and she had felt like a loner, a recluse. As an artist, she didn't work with others, and her contact with the outside world had seemed to be narrowing as she found fewer and fewer interests to share with family and friends.

"I knew then," he continued, "that the person who'd painted that seascape had reached deep within herself and triumphed over disenchantment." His smile was a bit crooked. "When I learned that the painting had already been sold, I was disappointed. That was when I asked Elizabeth to call me if something else came in by the same artist."

"I remember the painting," she murmured, not knowing what else to say.

"When Elizabeth contacted me to say there was another seascape of yours available, I told her to consider it sold without even seeing it."

"You did?"

His eyes were unnaturally bright as he nodded sharply. "I wasn't disappointed."

She bowed her head.

"I think I may even have started loving you way back then. A whole year before I followed you on Fisherman's Wharf."

"Shane…"

"No, let me finish. I couldn't understand why you were such a prickly thing. After buying all those paintings of yours, I suppose I felt you owed me something. After all, I thought I knew you so well. It was a shock to have you behave so differently from the way I expected. I don't think I fully understood you until I met Camille."

"We talked today…Camille and I. Really talked. I'm hoping a lot of our problems are over. We aren't competing against each other anymore. There'll be no competition between us again."

"I'm glad."

A short silence followed.

"I guess what I'm trying to say," Shane said, speaking first, "is that I've had an unfair advantage in this relationship. I love you, Carrie. I've loved you for months.

It's true that I've probably gone about everything the wrong way, but I was impatient. I rushed you when I shouldn't have. It isn't any wonder you're filled with questions. I nearly blew this whole thing."

"You didn't do anything wrong," she said softly. "I did."

Tenderly he brushed the hair from her temple, then paused, dropping his hand as though he didn't trust himself to touch her. "When you said yes to getting married, I thought, great, wonderful. It was what I'd hoped would happen all along."

"I was outraged with myself for treating the subject so lightly. Then I was furious with you for answering me."

"If you didn't honestly mean it, why didn't you say something at the time?"

Now it was her turn to swallow her pride. "I *did* mean it. I wanted to be your wife so badly that I was afraid if I didn't follow through with the marriage now, I might not get another chance."

"Oh, my sweet, confused Carrie."

"And then you started talking about children, and I wanted to have your babies so much I was willing to overlook just about anything. I think any children we have will be marvelous."

"Yet you were willing to walk away from all this happiness when it's here waiting for you?"

"I couldn't help it!" she cried. "What else was I to think? I couldn't really believe you loved me. All these weeks I've walked around in fear that once you met

Camille, I would be history. You did buy her portrait. And worse, every time you looked at her, it was like you were worshiping some love goddess."

"I thought the portrait was you."

"I know. But that only made things worse."

"How?" Once again, he had problems following her reasoning.

"Because it only made me feel more guilty about deceiving you." She recalled the relief mixed with guilt that she'd suffered during those frantic days before he found out about Camille.

He turned sideways then, fitting his hands on her shoulders. His long fingers closed over her upper arms. "I've made my own mistakes. Ones I want to undo right now. To simply say 'I love you' doesn't cover what I feel for you, Carrie Lockett. I love everything about you, from that turned-up freckled nose to that yard-wide streak of stubbornness."

The words washed over her like a cooling rain in the driest part of summer. "I think you must honestly love me to put up with me. And I do trust you—with all my heart."

"You think we should consider marriage, then?"

"Yes."

"But I'll do the asking this time." His hands dropped from her arms to circle her waist. His eyes grew warm and vital. "I've been waiting a lifetime for you, Carrie. Would you do me the very great honor of being my wife?"

She blinked back the tears that sprang readily to the surface and burned for release. Words were impossible.

"Well?" he prompted.

Her response was to nod wildly and sniffle.

"That better mean yes."

"It does. Now will you stop being such a gentleman and kiss me?"

Shane was only too happy to comply.

* * * * *

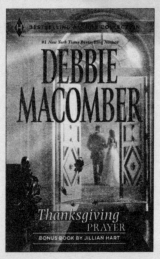

Spend some time in Cedar Cove with

#1 *NEW YORK TIMES* BESTSELLING AUTHOR

DEBBIE MACOMBER

Available wherever books are sold.

REQUEST YOUR
FREE BOOKS!

2 FREE NOVELS
FROM THE ROMANCE COLLECTION
PLUS 2 FREE GIFTS!

YES! Please send me 2 FREE novels from the Romance Collection and my 2 FREE gifts (gifts are worth about $10). After receiving them, if I don't wish to receive any more books, I can return the shipping statement marked "cancel." If I don't cancel, I will receive 4 brand-new novels every month and be billed just $5.99 per book in the U.S. or $6.49 per book in Canada. That's a saving of at least 25% off the cover price. It's quite a bargain! Shipping and handling is just 50¢ per book in the U.S. and 75¢ per book in Canada.* I understand that accepting the 2 free books and gifts places me under no obligation to buy anything. I can always return a shipment and cancel at any time. Even if I never buy another book, the two free books and gifts are mine to keep forever.

194/394 MDN FELQ

Name   (PLEASE PRINT)

Address   Apt. #

City   State/Prov.   Zip/Postal Code

Signature (if under 18, a parent or guardian must sign)

Mail to the **Reader Service:**
IN U.S.A.: P.O. Box 1867, Buffalo, NY 14240-1867
IN CANADA: P.O. Box 609, Fort Erie, Ontario L2A 5X3

Not valid for current subscribers to the Romance Collection
or the Romance/Suspense Collection.

Want to try two free books from another line?
Call 1-800-873-8635 or visit www.ReaderService.com.

* Terms and prices subject to change without notice. Prices do not include applicable taxes. Sales tax applicable in N.Y. Canadian residents will be charged applicable taxes. Offer not valid in Quebec. This offer is limited to one order per household. All orders subject to credit approval. Credit or debit balances in a customer's account(s) may be offset by any other outstanding balance owed by or to the customer. Please allow 4 to 6 weeks for delivery. Offer available while quantities last.

Your Privacy—The Reader Service is committed to protecting your privacy. Our Privacy Policy is available online at www.ReaderService.com or upon request from the Reader Service.

We make a portion of our mailing list available to reputable third parties that offer products we believe may interest you. If you prefer that we not exchange your name with third parties, or if you wish to clarify or modify your communication preferences, please visit us at www.ReaderService.com/consumerchoice or write to us at Reader Service Preference Service, P.O. Box 9062, Buffalo, NY 14269. Include your complete name and address.